Wife

Extraordinaire

BY KIKI SWINSON

KS Publications
www.kikiswinson.net

Don't Miss Out On These Other Titles:

Wife Extraordinaire

BY KIKI SWINSON

Trice

I was so fucking nervous about the arrangement my husband, Troy, had made with this guy named Leon Bunch. I would soon learn to take the bitter with the sweet. I mean, it wasn't like it was the end of the world. I was only going to swap lives with Leon's wife for a period of seven days. Leon and Troy had signed us up for the *Trading Wives* contest, which was similar to *Wife Swap* and the *Trading Spouse* reality shows on TV. The only difference with what we were doing versus the other two shows was that we wouldn't have a camera crew following us around.

But a crew of camera technicians came by and installed cameras throughout our house as well as Leon and his wife's house, so they could get footage to air our dirty laundry on TV on a later date. And to compensate us they added the incentive of ten thousand dollars at the end of the seventh day.

So when Troy brought this to me, I jumped on board because he was the only breadwinner around the house, and I knew that money would definitely take some strain off him. He was my rock. So much so, I'd do anything for him. However, the idea of living in someone else's house was another matter.

I was accustomed to a certain kind of living and the only thing I knew about the other couple was that Leon was a mechanic in the service department at a Nissan dealership in Chesapeake, while his wife, Charlene, was a stay at home mom with their five-year-old son. My life was somewhat similar to Charlene's life. She and I both were stay-at-home wives. The only difference with our employment status was that I volunteered my services to a non-profit organization twice a week and Charlene sat around and waited on an unemployment check every week.

Troy and I had a nice three-bedroom home in the Pine Crest neighborhood of Virginia Beach, while Leon and Charlene's townhouse sat in the Five Points section of Norfolk. When you think of the Five Points area of Norfolk, you thought of the ghetto, the 'hood. I knew I was going to spend a lot of my time inside the house.

"Trice, do you have all your things packed?" Troy asked me.

I had just zipped up the last compartment of my luggage when Troy appeared before me. I stood by the bed and looked directly at him. "Yeah, I think so," I finally said after I looked at him from head to toe.

I had to admit that my husband was one handsome catch. He was five eleven, with a nice build and light skin complexion, the pretty boy look, how I loved my men. He sort of reminded me of the actor, Michael Ealy, that played Chris Brown's older brother in the movie called *Takers,* opposite of rapper T.I and Idris Elba. We'd been together for more than seven years, so we were thick as thieves, which was why I went along with this whole set up. I felt as if this would be a good experience and I could probably take something from it. So after I assured Troy that all my things were packed, he helped me carry everything to the car.

"Are you nervous?" he asked me after he placed my luggage in the back of the trunk and closed it.

"Not really. But I do feel a little weird staying at one of your homeboy's house," I replied and then I sat down on the passenger seat and closed the door behind myself.

Troy climbed into the driver's seat and closed the car door. "Leon ain't just my homeboy, he's like a brother to me. Trust me, he's going to make sure you're all right."

Troy turned on the ignition, put his black F-150 in drive and then sped off. As he drove away from our house, I took one last look at it because I knew it would be seven days before I saw it again.

The ride to Norfolk didn't take long at all. Troy and I talked about the dos and don'ts the entire drive. And before I got out of the car, I laid down a few rules myself. Just like the TV show, I instructed him to make her sleep in the guest room. I also instructed him to make sure she walked around in presentable attire. And before he went to bed at night, he needed to call me. He promised me that he would take care of everything and that I had absolutely nothing to worry about.

"We're here." He pointed out as soon as we pulled up in front of a tan, vinyl siding duplex on Chesapeake Boulevard.

I looked at the building and then I looked back at my husband. "I sure hope the inside is much cleaner than the outside."

Troy cracked a smile. "They keep a decent clean house, so you'll be fine."

I gave him a nonchalant expression. "Yeah, they better," I commented, and then I leaned forward to kiss him on the lips.

After our lips parted ways, I turned back around so I could open the passenger side door to get out and saw that Charlene was walking towards the car. I had to admit that she was indeed an attractive woman. She looked to be a size twelve, which was one size bigger than I was but she was shaped appropriately. Her hair was short but it was cut nicely into a Chinese bob. I could instantly tell it was hair weave because it was too shiny and straight to be her own. Black people don't have that type of hair. So whatever Korean sold her that hair was dead wrong because it didn't go along with her complexion. She was too dark.

I had the perfect light skin complexion. Not to mention I had beautiful hazel colored eyes. So if she and I both stood side-by-side, all eyes would be on me. She had absolutely nothing on me and I'm convinced that my husband would see that too. If anything, she needed to be worried about her husband trying to mess around with me. I was a force to be reckoned with, so she'd better be careful.

She walked up to the car showing all her damn teeth. "How y'all doing?" she asked. I didn't say a word, but I smiled. Troy returned the greeting and then he introduced us. She extended her right hand and I shook it.

Her husband, Leon, came behind her. I looked over her shoulders to get a good look at him. He wasn't my type in the least bit, so Troy definitely didn't have to worry about me fucking around with him. Leon did however seem really cool. He smiled from ear-to-ear when he saw Troy. "What's good nigga?"

Tory reached over me to shake Leon's hands. After they shook, I eased out of the car so Charlene could put her things in the back seat.

"You ladies ready to see that the grass ain't greener on the other side?" Leon asked.

"I never said it was!" Charlene spat.

"Well, I'm just going on for the ride. I mean, I might just learn something from it," I replied.

Leon took my two pieces of luggage from my hands. I expressed my gratitude while Troy watched Charlene shove her bags into the back seat. I looked at him and shook my head because sometimes he could truly be lazy.

"You better take care of my wife!" Troy told Leon.

"Oh, she's in good hands. So, you better do the same thing," Leon replied.

Troy gave Leon a smirk. "Oh, don't worry, because when this is all over, she's going to come back home and tell you about all the shit I schooled her on."

Leon threw his hands up. "Yeah, whatever nigga! We shall see," he commented, and he and I watched as Troy pulled off in his black Ford F-150.

After Troy disappeared, Leon turned to me and asked me was I ready? I smiled at him and said, "I guess I am."

Once we were inside his duplex, I immediately noticed a strong smell of bleach and ammonia. He walked ahead of me, down a short hallway that lead to his kitchen and an open family room with a 52 inch flat screen TV. After I entered into the den area I sat my things down on the floor near the sofa. I took a seat and let my eyes wonder around the room.

"Where is your son?" I wondered aloud.

"My wife's parents just picked him up last night so he could spend the summer with them in Florida."

"Wow! Florida sounds nice. I know you're going to miss him."

Leon closed the mini blinds in front of windows in the den area. After he finished, he looked at me and asked me if I were ready for him to show me where I would sleep. "Sure. Why not," I said and stood to my feet.

He grabbed my bags from the floor and led the way. I followed him up a flight of stairs to the first room on the left. Before we entered, he looked back at me and informed me that we were about to enter into his son's bedroom and this was where I would be sleeping. "Oh, okay. That's fine," I assured him.

Leon smiled and pushed the door open. I walked into the room behind him. I immediately surveyed my surroundings and noticed how decorative this little boy's room was. The theme of the bedroom was World Wrestling Champions. He had professional wrestling figures on his dresser with matching curtains, comforters, sheets, pillows cases and a throw rug. It was really cute so it made me smile.

Leon sat my bags on top of his son's bed and told me if I needed anything to make sure I let him know. I assured him I would. And when he walked out of the bedroom, he closed the door behind him.

I took a seat on the twin size bed and reflected on my decision to go along with this plan of theirs. I also wondered in the back of my mind what my husband was doing and if he'd gotten home yet. My mind would not allow me to play the guessing game, so I grabbed my cell phone from my purse and dialed his number. He answered my call on the second ring. The music coming from the speakers of his truck was extremely loud, so I found myself yelling through the receiver.

"Why do you have the music playing so loud?" I screamed.

"Cause my song is on," he screamed back. "Baby, you know I like this new joint by Jay Z."

I sighed. "You know I'm beginning to miss you already."

"Damn Trice, we've only been apart for ten minutes."

"I know but the thought of us being away from each other for one whole week got me a little sad."

"Come on now, you a big girl. Everything is going to be all right. I mean, it ain't like we won't be able to speak to one another. So just call me every time you get lonely."

I sucked my teeth and sighed once more. "It's not the same though."

"I know. But seven days isn't long so as soon as you blink your eyes those days are gonna fly right by."

"Easy for you to say."

"Come on, Trice, you a soldier. And besides, look at this vacation away from each other as a $10,000 investment. Now, suck it up and call me back before you got to bed. Okay, baby."

"Yeah. All right," I replied nonchalantly and then I pressed the end button.

After I hung up, I got myself together and headed back downstairs. Leon was in the den area watching TV when I walked in. He was watching the news. He was not only watching the news, but engrossed in it. I had the chance to look at him from another angle. He wasn't as handsome as Troy but he had chiseled features. He was dark skinned with dark brown eyes. His hair was locked with shoulder length dreads, which was unattractive to me. Seeing long hair on men was not my cup of tea. But for some reason it looked okay on him, because he had natural curly hair at the scalp. His choice in attire was cool. I honestly liked how he coordinated his yellow Lacoste polo shirt with his ash washed True Religion jeans. Troy told me he was a mechanic but from the looks of his hands, it seemed impossible because this guy's hands looked well manicured.

"Hungry?" he asked me.

"Not really," I said and took a seat down on the sofa next to him.

Leon rubbed his stomach in a circular motion and said, "Well, I am. So I'm gonna order me a pizza with some hot wings."

Before I could utter a word, he stood up and grabbed his Blackberry from the end table next to the lamp. I took it that he had Papa John's pizza on speed dial because he only pressed one button from the touch pad of his phone and then I heard it ring. After he placed his order, he hung up and walked out of the room.

"Want something to drink?" he yelled.

"No. I'm fine."

"You sure? Because I got juice, bottle water and cold beer."

"Yes, I'm sure," I assured him.

Ten seconds later he reappeared with a cold and refreshing looking bottle of Corona in his hand. After he sat back down, he grabbed the remote and surfed through the channels until he came across the sitcom, *Two and a Half Men.*

"I love this show. Charlie Sheen and that little boy are funny as hell."

"Yeah, they are," I commented.

We both sat there and watched the show. It quickly became apparent that he was somewhat cool with a sense of humor. So I relaxed a little and prayed that these days would go by very quickly.

Wife Extraordinaire

BY KIKI SWINSON

Troy

Trice didn't know it but it was all my idea to swap Leon's wife for her. Leon owed me from a bet on last week's NBA finals game, so he either had to kick off two grand or relieve me of my wife for seven days. Don't get me wrong, I loved my wife. But Trice could be a difficult woman to live with at times. She nagged me about everything I did. I never did anything right if you ask her. She wanted everything around the house to be perfect. So if I left my clothes on the floor in the bathroom or left my dishes in the kitchen sink overnight, she blew up about it and I would hear about it for at least another twenty–four hours. Not to mention I had to damn near get on my knees to beg her to fuck me. I didn't get my dick sucked at all, so I made it my business not to ask. She had this phobia of putting my meat in her mouth. So when I asked her about the phobia, she wouldn't give me an explanation.

Over the past seven years, I could honestly say the first two years were good. But the last five had been a complete nightmare. My marriage was falling apart by the seams and she couldn't even see it. I wasn't happy anymore, which was why I opted for Leon to let his wife stay here. I mean, I needed to see if the grass was greener on the other side. Leon's wife didn't know he was about to file for a divorce. He was tired of her more than I was with Trice. So you see, this arrangement would hopefully be good for all parties. But I guess we would see.

"You and your wife have a nice house," Charlene expressed after I took her on a tour of the house.

I smiled as I escorted her back into the kitchen. "I picked out the house. But Trice decorated every room herself."

Charlene took a seat on the barstool in front of the island situated in the middle of the kitchen. After she sat down she made a comment about it. "Oh my God! I've always wanted a kitchen like this. I love the fact that you got the stove built in the island. I'm so used to seeing kitchens with the stove placed by the wall."

"Yeah, me too. But it was all Trice's idea. She's very particular about what she likes and how she wants things to look."

"I could tell when I first laid eyes on her."

"Want something to drink?"

"You got beer?"

I opened up the refrigerator and pulled out a bottle of wine. "Nope. But I got a bottle of Moscato."

Charlene smiled. "That's even better."

I popped the bottle open and poured us a glass of wine. But before we took the first sip, Charlene raised her glass in the air and suggested we make a toast. "To the future," she said.

"To the future," I repeated and then we clinked wineglasses.

We both put the glasses up to our lips simultaneously and allowed the flow of the wine to pour into our mouths. It was cold and sweet, harmony to my taste buds.

I could tell Charlene liked it too. Amazingly, it took her a matter of sixty seconds to swallow the entire glass. Immediately after she sat the glass down on the counter top of the island, she let out a loud and disgusting burp and smiled. "Wow! That was really good."

"Sounds like you've got indigestion."

She smiled bashfully and covered her mouth. "I guess you're right."

I picked up the bottle of Moscato and poured her another glass. "Take your time, sweetheart. There's a lot more where that came from," I told her.

She took another sip and then said, "I know. But it's so good."

I walked back over to the refrigerator and grabbed a block of cheddar cheese from it. Then I grabbed a pack of Ritz crackers from the bread container. "Got some cheese and crackers," I announced as I sat the items down in front of Charlene.

"Wow! I've never had cheese and crackers with wine before," she acknowledged.

"You've got to be kidding me, right?" I replied as I grabbed a cheese knife from the utensil drawer.

"Trust me, I'm dead serious. Me and my husband are ghetto as hell. When we sip on alcohol we got a bag of chips or a bowl of peanuts in our hands."

"That's not ghetto. Hell, I used to get it cracking the same way. My wife, Trice, got me on the wine with the cheese and cracker thing. She's a high maintenance type with an image. So when it's time to entertain her family and friends she pulls out the most expensive wine or champagne and then she'll prepare them a cheese, vegetable and fruit plate. And everyone loves it."

"So you're married to one of those high class types, huh?"

"Something like that," I commented as I began to cut up the cheese and make little bite size sandwiches.

"How long y'all been married?"

"Seven years," I told her and then I bit down on the cracker with the piece of cheese.

"How long were y'all together before you got married?" she asked and then she bit down into the cheese with the cracker.

"Three years."

"How old is she?"

"Trice is thirty-five. She got me by two years."

"Oh, so you're a young buck, huh?"

"How old are you?" I asked her.

"Twenty-seven." she replied bashfully.

"You're the young buck!" I commented jokingly.

Charlene burst into laughter. She must've found my comment to be amusing. So while she smiled, I got a chance to get a good look at her teeth. And I had to admit that they were beautiful. It was no secret she was a street chick, because of her mannerisms. But I could see that there was a softer part of her buried beneath her outer shell. I've heard a lot of stories from Leon about how lazy she was and how she didn't like cooking. He even shouted her out about how she nagged all the fucking time. But that was nothing new to me. All women nagged if they weren't getting their way. So I just told him to get used to it because he's going to get that from every woman he messes around with. It's just what women were born to do.

So while I was staring at her she broke my train of thought by asking me what was I staring at. Without hesitation, I told her the truth. She looked as if she was at a loss for words. Instead of making a comment she looked at me in a provocative way. Then she licked her lips in a manner in which she was inviting me to shove my tongue down her throat. Her actions completely caught me off guard. But I played it off and remained cool about it. I even went to the extent of acting as if what she did never happened.

I also changed the subject as I looked down at my watch. "Damn, time is flying. I gotta make a quick call," I lied. And as

I stepped away from the island I assured her I would be right back.

As soon as I walked out of the kitchen and into the hall-way, my urge to rip her panties off and fuck the shit out of her decreased a little. My dick was hard as a rock, but it slowly deflated as I got further away from her. But to make sure I got myself back on track, I rushed outside to the back patio to get some fresh air. I guessed I must've stayed gone too long be-cause I heard her calling my name.

When I reentered the house she was standing in the hall-way. "Do you mind if I take a shower?" she asked me.

"Nah, go ahead," I told her as I continued to walk towards her.

She stood there in a skimpy looking sundress. I was shocked Leon would let her leave the house with something like that on. I could literally see through the damn thing. She left nothing to the imagination. I could tell from five feet away how thick her thighs were and how tiny her waist. She was sexy as hell. She wasn't as pretty as Trice, but she was thicker. She was basically any man's dream sex toy. And if her fuck game was anything like her body, she'd have it going on.

"Where do you keep your towels?" she asked me and then she put her right hand on her hip.

"Upstairs in the hallway linen closet next to the bathroom."

She smiled at me and said, "Thanks." Immediately thereaf-ter she turned her back towards me and headed upstairs.

I couldn't help but watch her as she walked away. Her ass was so fat, my dick got hard all over again. If she would've stripped down and got butt naked right there in front of me, I know I would've jumped dead on her. And not feel a thing for her after I bust my nut. Shit, men do it all the time. So maybe before all this was over, I would have my chance. I just hope she wouldn't try to get attached to me, because Trice wouldn't be too happy about that. I was sure Leon wouldn't be happy about it either.

Meanwhile, while Charlene showered, I started cleaning up around the kitchen. As I was putting everything away, I heard her cell phone ring. I picked it up off the island where she had sat it and looked down at the caller ID. When I noticed it was Leon calling her, I rushed upstairs to hand her the phone. I knocked on the door when I approached the bathroom.

"It's open," she yelled.

So I cracked the door open just enough to stick my arm inside. "Leon is calling you," I told her.

"Tell 'em I'm in the shower and I'll call him back," she instructed me.

"Come on, Charlene, you know better than that! How do you think that's gon' look with me answering your phone? Nah, you tell him," I replied as I stretched my arm out further so she'd be able to grab her phone.

But before she could grab and answer it, the phone stopped ringing. So while I stood there with the phone in my hand I heard her turn off the shower and step out of the tub. I couldn't see what she was doing but I felt her vibration on the floor as she walked towards my arm. With her wet hands, she finally took her phone from me, then she opened up the bathroom door so I could get a full view of her body. I couldn't help it but my dick rose to its fullest peak. The jean shorts I had on didn't help to conceal my manhood at all.

When Charlene noticed it, she smiled and said, "Well, it didn't take you long to get aroused."

I placed my hands over the bulge in my shorts and smiled bashfully. "That's because I see something I like," I finally said as I looked at her from head to toe.

Indeed she was about ten pounds heavier than Trice but Charlene's body was tight. Her titties weren't perky but they didn't sag either. They had to be at least a 'C' cup because they looked as if they'd fit in the palm of my hands easily. Her tummy was flat as a board. It was hard to tell she had a child because I didn't see a stretch mark anywhere. And as my eyes moved down to her thighs, I noticed she had a gap between her thighs which I thought was sexy as hell. I love to see chicks with a fat butt and thick thighs and they got that gap between the upper parts of their thighs. It's a fucking turn on to me.

However, I did notice a few spots of cellulite in her hip areas. But it wasn't enough to talk about. In other words, definitely not a deal breaker. Other than that, she reminded me of one of those video vixens you'd see shaking their asses in one of those rap videos. So I was hoping she'd let me test the waters.

While her body was dripping with water, she placed her left hand on her hip and said, "Well, if you like it then why are you just standing there?"

I stood there with the dumbest looking expression on my face. Although she'd just invited me to come and test the water, I instantly got cold feet. I mean, I didn't know this chick for real. All I knew about her was that she was my homeboy's wife and in less than two hours, she had made my dick hard two times. So she could be trying to set me up. Cry rape if I bend her ass over and fuck the shit out of her. And I wasn't trying to have that. I didn't need that headache. With a rape charge came attorney's fees for a divorce, prison time and a big old sex offender label stuck on my forehead. And since I wasn't in the mood to acquire any of these things, I shook my head and took two steps backwards.

Charlene gave me a disappointing look. "Where you going? I thought you like what you saw?" she questioned me.

"I do. But I got too much to lose and I don't need the drama," I told her.

She took three steps towards me. "I promise, I won't cause no drama," she replied seductively as she pressed her naked body against mines and wrapped her arms around me. The feeling of her pussy pressed against my dick sent an electric shock through my groin that shot directly to my heart. I swear I immediately wanted to rip my own fucking clothes off but I played it cool. I didn't want to seem too eager. But my plans went straight out of the window, because as soon as she released her arms from around my neck, she turned her body completely around and pressed her fat ass against my dick.

And when I say my dick was pulsating, believe me, that's an understatement. I felt like a fucking teenager getting my first piece of pussy on prom night. My adrenaline was pumping like mad and all the worries of the consequences I could face went out the window. I wanted to fuck her! Point blank! And if she'd promise to keep her damn mouth closed, I'd give her the best piece of dick she would ever have in her life.

While a whole bunch of shit was going through my mind, she pressed her ass against my dick a tad bit harder. Then she grabbed my hands and placed them on her breasts. I took the lead and began to massage them while I grinded my dick on her soft fat ass. She loved what I was doing to her more than I was enjoying it, because she started talking really reckless.

She reminded me of a whore on a porno movie. "I want you to fuck me hard!" she began. "I want you to shove your dick deep in my pussy! And then I want you to fuck me in my ass!"

I was caught off guard by the cash smack shit she was talking, but I liked every damn word she uttered from her mouth. It's been a long time since I fucked around on my wife. But when I did fuck around, the chicks never talked to me like this and I had to admit, this shit turned me on.

Come to think about it, I believe if my wife would sometimes get gutter and hoodish like this, then our sex life would be much better. See, Trice liked the regular missionary position. Plus, she wasn't into sucking my dick, so my sex life was pretty much ordinary. Better yet, it sucked. Believe me, I probably would've left her a long time ago if I were only in the relationship for the sex. Thank God, she's smart and she could cook a damn good decent meal. If it wasn't for that, I would've bailed out on her a long time ago and got with someone like this butt naked chick bent over in front of me.

"Troy, please stop making me wait!" Charlene started whining. "I want to feel your big dick inside of me," she begged.

"I wanna push my dick inside of you too," I assured her as I grabbed a hold of her hips and pulled her closer to me as I grinded on her ass harder.

"Fuck me now!" she continued to beg. So I unzipped my jean shorts and pulled my dick out through the slit of my boxer shorts. My meat was hard as a rock and it had started dripping right before my eyes. I couldn't wait any longer so I grabbed her hips to cock up her ass so it would be easy for me to slide my dick inside of her pussy. So while I was trying to find her hole, it dawned on me that I needed a condom. I couldn't fuck her without protection. I wasn't trying to get this broad pregnant nor was I trying to catch something. Trice would fucking kill me if I brought her back with a case of herpes or worse waiting for her at home. So I stopped in my tracks and said, "Wait, I need a condom."

She sucked her teeth. "Well, hurry up and get one. Because I am so hot and my pussy is throbbing for you," she replied as she looked back at me.

I immediately became devastated because I didn't have any condoms. Trice and I had been together for over seven years and the last time I fucked around on her was about three years ago. So if I did have any condoms they would be expired by now, which meant I was up a creek without a paddle. What the hell was I going to do? My dick was rock hard and I had a butt naked, big booty chick in my grasp and I had the slightest idea how I was going to maneuver this situation.

I was fighting with the decisions of fucking her without a condom and risk getting something I couldn't get rid of or not fucking her at all since I didn't have a condom on hand. Damn, what was a man to do?

Charlene stood straight up and turned towards me. She wrapped her arms around my neck and began to kiss me on my lips. "Come on, Troy, whatcha gon' do? Let this good pussy go to waste?" she uttered between kisses.

She was making it really hard for me to turn her down. But I knew I had to stand for something. Because like I said, I had a lot to lose. So I couldn't let a piece of pussy ruin that for me. I had willpower. So that's what I intended to use.

"As bad as I wanna fuck you, Charlene, I can't go there baby girl," I finally told her and then I gently pushed her away from me.

It didn't take a rocket scientist to see she took what I said for a joke, because she forced herself back on me. But as soon as she grabbed me back into her arms, I pushed her back with a little more force. This time when I got her off me, I stepped backwards, turned around and left her standing where she stood. I thought she was going to run behind and pursue me more but she didn't. I was glad. If she had, I don't think I would've been able to resist her any longer. God knew what he was doing. I wasn't a religious type of cat, but I remember growing up and hearing my mama say that God wouldn't put more on me than I could bear. So I take those words every-where I go, whether it be a good situation or bad.

Wife Extraordinaire

BY KIKI SWINSON

Trice

"Whatcha doing?" I asked Troy the moment he answered the phone.

"Straightening up the kitchen. Why?" he asked me. I ignored his question because I had a few more question of my own.

"You sure you're in the kitchen? Because it doesn't sound like it."

"How is it supposed to sound?" he asked me.

Again, I ignored his question and asked him one of my own. "Where is Charlene?"

"She's upstairs. Why?"

"Because Leon just tried to call her, and she didn't answer her cell phone."

"That's because her phone is down here in the kitchen."

"What is she doing upstairs?" I wanted to know. Shit, the bitch could have been upstairs in my bedroom snooping around in my personal belongings and I couldn't have that.

"She asked me where the bathroom was so I believe she's up there taking a shit or something," he replied sarcastically.

I wasn't feeling his sarcasm, so I quickly put him in check. "Troy, please don't get cute right now because I am not in the damn mood. Now all I asked is what you were doing and then I asked you what she was doing, because her husband just tried to get in touch with her. So don't act like I'm doing something wrong."

"Look, Trice, I am not acting like anything. Right now I am trying to get the kitchen straight, because I know how you are about dishes being dirty overnight. So—"

I cut him off in mid sentence. "What dishes are you talking about? I cleaned up the kitchen before I left the house."

"Well, I pulled out some leftovers from the refrigerator and microwave it. So I had a few items that were dirty."

"Troy, you better not be lying to me," I said sternly. I could tell when he was lying to me. He had done it plenty of times in the past, especially when I suspected that he cheated on me with a corporate attorney named Lisa Alvarez. To this day he denies ever sleeping with her, but I saw the text messages. So the writing was on the wall, even though I didn't actually catch him in the act. And if he knew like I knew, he'd better not get caught out there again or it's bon voyage.

"Listen baby, I am not lying to you. So don't start getting paranoid on me. Believe me, I am not going to do anything that would jeopardize my marriage. I don't give a damn who it is or what that person got going on. You are my wife and I won't let no one come between that. You follow me?"

I hesitated for a bit and then I responded. "Yes, I follow you."

"All right. Well, let me get back to what I was doing. And I'll call you back before I go to bed."

I sighed heavily. "Okay," I replied.

"I love you," he told me.

"I love you too," I assured him.

Immediately after I hung up with Troy, I went back into the den area and joined Leon. He was once again engrossed in another episode of *Two and a Half Men*. He was laughing his butt off too. I took a seat beside him and forced myself to watch the show. I figured it would take my mind off my temporary living arrangements. But that idea went straight out the window, because as soon as a commercial came on, Leon turned his attention towards me.

"Did you get a chance to talk to Troy?" he asked me.

"Yeah, I just hung up with him."

"Did you get a chance to tell him I tried to call Charlene?"

"Yeah, I told him. And he said she was upstairs using our bathroom," I responded nonchalantly and then I turned my attention towards the TV.

"You all right?"

"Yeah, I'm fine," I assured him without looking at him.

"Well, you look like you're on the verge of crying."

"No, I'm not about to cry. I'm just a little frustrated is all."

"Care to talk about it?" he pressed the issue.

I shook my head and told him no. I also told him that it really wasn't important and I was just going through the motion. "I'll be fine by the morning," I continued.

Leon shrugged his shoulders and said, "Okay."

After the sitcom ended, I retired to Leon's son's bedroom. I laid in the dark for almost two hours waiting for Troy to call me. By the time ten o'clock rolled around, my Blackberry still had not rung. I was furious and took it upon myself to call him myself, since it seemed as if he was too preoccupied to call me himself. Unfortunately for me, when I called his cell, he did not answer his phone. I called twice and allowed it to ring five times each call. So I called the house phone and fortunately for him he managed to answer that line.

I ripped him a new asshole when he finally answered. "What the fuck is going on Troy?" I snapped.

"What do you mean?"

"I just tried to call your cell phone twice and you didn't answer it. So tell me what the hell you got going on that would prevent you from answering your damn phone?" I roared, because I was pissed. The only thing that raced through my mind was the possibility of him fucking around with Leon's wife. And the thought of him doing it in my house got me sick to my stomach. Not too mention, they could be fooling around in my bed.

"Can you calm down for a minute and let me explain?" he snapped back.

"I'm listening."

"First off, I wasn't doing shit to prevent me from answering my phone. I'm chilling in our bedroom watching TV while my phone is charging up. So stop calling me with all the unnecessary drama. You giving me a fucking headache!"

When Troy screamed at me the way he did, I knew he was serious. And I could tell he wasn't doing anything he wasn't supposed to be doing. In the past when I suspected that he was doing underhanded shit, he'd stutter when I would ask him certain questions and he would sometimes avoid my questions altogether. So I felt like he was on his best behavior.

After he snapped at me, I fell silent because I was at a loss for words. I really didn't know what to say because I was feeling really stupid. Thankfully enough, he broke the silence barrier and told me I had nothing to worry about. So after he assured me a couple more times that he wasn't thinking about Leon's wife, he gave me a kiss over the phone and told me good night. After I hung up the phone, I felt at ease and went straight to sleep.

The next morning I was awakened to some good smelling breakfast food. It smelled like Leon was cooking a pan of turkey bacon and some pancakes. I wasn't a breakfast type of girl, but the way he had that kitchen smelling, I had to go downstairs to see what was doing on. I got up, slipped on my robe, went into the bathroom to freshen up and then I headed downstairs. I had my hair wrapped up with a couple of bobby pins so I looked somewhat presentable.

"Good morning," I said as I entered into the kitchen.

Leon's back was facing me when I walked in so I startled him. He jumped just a tad bit and then turned around completely. "I am so sorry for startling you," I told him.

"You're cool," he replied and then he turned his attention back to the pan and the cooking utensil he had in his hand.

I took a seat in one of the chairs placed around the kitchen table. "Do I smell turkey bacon and pancakes?"

"You sure do. You hungry?"

"I normally don't eat breakfast but you got it smelling really good in here."

Leon stacked two pancakes on a plate and then he placed three slices of turkey bacon on top of the pancakes. "After you sink your teeth into this, you ain't gonna look at breakfast food in a negative manner ever again," he stated, and then he walked over and sat the plate directly in front of me.

"Yeah. Yeah. Yeah," I commented and then I smiled. It's really funny because even though Leon wasn't my type of man, he was very charismatic. The more I hung around him the more I noticed he was developing something I never thought he had—sex appeal. He stood before me shirtless so I was able to get a full view of his washboard abs, enormous pecs and biceps. It took everything within me not to comment on his body. I felt like it wouldn't be appropriate considering he was in fact my husband's friend.

The butter he placed on top of my pancakes melted instantly, so he took the liberty to assist me by pouring a hefty amount of syrup onto my plate. "Taste it and tell me if you like it or not," he encouraged me.

I grabbed the fork that was placed before me and cut into the pancakes. The syrup and butter soaked heavily into the pancakes and made them look desirably delicious. When I shoved the first bite of pancakes into my mouth, my taste buds went haywire. The pancakes damn near melted in my mouth.

Leon noticed how I was enjoying his work of art, so he made it his business to comment on it. "I told you it was good, didn't I?"

I smiled with a mouthful of food and gave him a nod.

He grabbed himself a plate of pancakes and a few strips of bacon. Then he took a seat at the table across from me. He tore into his food as if there was no tomorrow. I sat there and watched him eat every single morsel of food. His table etiquette was on zero but his cooking skills were charted at ten on the scale. It took me longer to finish my food. And when I was done, Leon kindly took my plate and started cleaning the kitchen. Meanwhile, he and I got into a heavy conversation while I continued to sit at the table.

"Talk to Troy this morning?" he asked as he paraded around the kitchen in his blue Nike basketball shorts and bedroom slippers.

"Yeah, I talked to him before he went off to work."

"I thought he was off today."

"He was but he got a call early this morning telling him he had to come in."

"That's crazy that they make him work damn near six days a week."

"I know. He hates it. But what can he do when there are bills to pay?"

"Yeah. True. But those crackers 'round there don't give niggas like me and Troy no slack. They're quick to call us to come in and work six days a week, but they bite their damn tongues when it's time to give out raises, which is why I bailed out on their asses and got me a job at the Nissan dealership in Chesapeake. Those people over there take care of their employees, which is why you see me walking around in my kitchen right now. I keep telling Troy to come over there with me but he won't listen to me."

"It's not like he doesn't want to come. It's just that he's been with Lexus for so long, he doesn't want to lose his seniority and his benefits."

"Excuse my French, Trice, but fuck them damn benefits they dishing out. That shit they trying to pass off to us is bogus as hell. Tell Troy to try to use his vacation time and see how much trouble they give him. Them motherfuckers over there ain't shit. All they want to do is work you too death and send you home with a pat on the back. But no way, I got tired of them pimping me. So I jetted on their asses and I am doing better than ever now."

"Well, I don't believe Troy is having the problem you had. Because it seems like every time he calls in sick they don't give him a hard time."

Leon walked towards me and then he stopped. He wanted me to give him my undivided attention and that's exactly what I did. "See, them crackers over there don't give a damn about sick leave. But they do care about that vacation time and the raises. So when Troy starts to ask for one of them, then trust me, they're going to give him some problems. Mark my words."

I sat there and listened to the words Leon uttered from his mouth. But I was more focused on his physique. I was completely mesmerized. I also couldn't help but noticed how big his dick was. It hung from his groin area like a horse penis. It easily rested on the middle of his thigh. I wanted to ask him had he ever measured it, but I knew that would be crass and dead wrong if those words came from my mouth. Not only would I be disrespecting Troy, I would be disrespecting myself as well. So I casually eased my attention away from his private area and drew my attention to his face. Besides, he was talking to me. So I did the right thing, the polite thing and focused on his face.

Once he got all the mayhem he experienced working for the Lexus dealership off his chest, he asked me about me and Troy's plans to spend our ten thousand dollars.

I thought for a brief moment and then I said, "Well, I really don't want anything. Troy and I talked about him putting the money in our savings as an emergency fund. But I'm sure he's going to go out and buy me something nice. That's just his character."

It felt good explaining what I thought or hoped we would do with the money. I redirected the question to him. "So what have you and your wife decided to do with the money y'all get?"

"Since I'm the breadwinner around here, I decided to pay off my truck. I only owe a little over eight grand. And then I'll probably use the rest on a set of new tires. If I got any left, I'll get Charlene's hair done."

I burst into laughter. "All she gets is a hair style from the money?"

"You damn right! She better be lucky if she gets that, especially when she gets her little unemployment checks and don't contribute any of it to the house fund. She's selfish as hell! All she thinks about is herself, which is why I was eager to get rid of her for the next seven days. And if you want to know the truth, I would've sent her ass off on a weeklong excursion even if those contest people weren't given up the ten grand. That's just how bad I needed a break from her."

"Well, if y'all relationship is that bad then, why are you two together?"

Leon thought for a second and then he said, "It's my son that's keeping me here with her, because if he wasn't in our lives then I would've left her years ago."

"What is it that you don't like about her?" I wanted to know.

"There are so many things I don't like about her. But the three things that stick out more to me is the fact that she's lazy, she doesn't like to cook and she's a nagger."

I burst into laughter once again. "Wow! Those are the three most important areas of a relationship."

"I know. That's why I said that if we didn't have my son then I would've been gone a long time ago."

"Have you two discussed the possibility of getting some marriage counseling?" I said.

"Who's gonna pay for it?" he shot back.

I threw my hands up as a defense shield. "What! Hold up! Don't shoot the messenger," I commented and then I cracked a smile.

Leon toned down his aggressive behavior and said, "I'm sorry, Trice. But if I gotta spend a coin to get someone to help me and Charlene to see eye-to-eye so we can stay together, then it's a moot issue for me, because it will never happen. I spent enough money to keep the household together. So to get me to spend money on something else is out of the question."

"Can you tell me what you like about her?" I asked him, in an effort to shift the conversation in a positive direction.

"Nope, I can't think of anything," he didn't hesitate to say. "Come on, Leon, there has to be something other than the fact that she's your son's mother."

He mulled over my question for a couple of seconds and then he broke his silence. "The sex is good. But that's about it."

I was appalled at his answer. But it also struck a cord with me because he'd just admitted that his wife was good in bed, which of course made me feel intimidated because this same woman was at my house entertaining my husband who was a sex addict. One of the problems Troy and I had in our relationship was that he had a huge appetite for sex, whereas I only wanted to have it once a week. Not to mention, I didn't like to give him head. So I believed if Charlene was given a chance, then she might be able to woo him over. And I couldn't have that because it would be a disaster.

The thought of how great she performed sexually got me sick to my stomach, so I immediately changed the subject. I got up from my chair and patted him on his shoulder. "Don't worry. It'll get better for you and her."

Leon chuckled at my statement. "Trust me, I ain't gonna hold my breath," he replied and then he looked down at his wrist watch. "Time to go do my morning run."

"You workout?"

"Yep. I run at least two to three miles five days a week. I gotta keep my body in shape."

I gave him a puzzling look. "You didn't strike me as a man who worked out."

"What kind of man did you think I was?"

"Well, I knew you had locks in your head and that you hung out at the sports bar with Troy. So I automatically assumed you were a blunt smoking hood cat who thought he was God's gift to women."

He smiled. "Really?"

"Yep."

"But I don't even smoke."

"I see that now."

"Wow! It's funny how people always make assumptions even when they only know a little about you."

"Very true," I agreed. "So where do you do your running?"

"I run around the track at Norfolk Academy. Why, you wanna go?"

"Sure. I would love to tag along. But wait, I don't think I packed anything I could workout in."

"Don't worry. I got a pair of gym shorts you could fit."

"All right. Well, let's do it," I replied as I waited for him to exit the kitchen so I could follow him to his bedroom to get the shorts he said I could borrow.

After he handed me the shorts, he told me to meet him downstairs by the front door when I had gotten dress. I told him okay and disappeared into his son's bedroom.

Wife Extraordinaire

BY KIKI SWINSON

Troy

When I woke up this morning I had a hard on that was out of this fucking world. And knowing that Charlene was in the next room didn't make my situation any easier. The thought of her grinding her ass up against my dick last night did something to me while I slept, because I couldn't get my mind off her. I just wished I could get a chance to taste her pussy without it backfiring on me. I mean, if I knew for sure that she would keep her mouth close and Trice wouldn't find out about it, I would jump at the opportunity. There's nothing like fucking new pussy. The excitement and the rush that came from blowing a chick's back out was indescribable. I would say the wetter her pussy was the more enjoyable the sex. Too bad I walked away from the perfect opportunity to find out how wet her coochie got, because if it was anything like I imagined, then I would've been in for a treat.

So while I reminisced about our little episode last night, my Blackberry rung. I looked at the caller ID and noticed it was

Trice calling me back. When I spoke with her earlier I told her I had to go in to work. I lied to her so she wouldn't be sweating me for most of the day by calling me all the time, wondering what Charlene and I were doing. Since she figured I was at work, I had to play the part. Unfortunately, there wasn't enough acoustics in my bedroom to give off the sound that I was in a garage, so I grabbed my phone and raced downstairs and out the front door.

"Hello," I finally said, panting as if I was out of breath.

"Why you breathing so hard?" she asked me.

"That's because you just called me while I was in the middle of carrying a shitload of car tires."

"What time are you getting off?"

"Probably around three. Why?"

"There's no particular reason. I just wanted to know."

"Well, what are you doing?"

"I just had breakfast and now I'm on my way out the door to take a morning run."

"Wait! When did you start running?"

"This morning. I figured it's time I start to get in shape."

"Who said you were out of shape?"

"Nobody. But what's wrong with building up my endurance?"

"Nothing at all."

"Exactly. So whatcha got planned after you get off work?"

"I don't have anything planned. Léon's wife did mention she wanted to go and rent a couple of movies from the Red Box. But other than that, I have no real plans."

"So y'all are going to chill out and watch a couple of movies together, huh?" Trice replied. She sounded like she didn't like the idea of Charlene and I chilling. But hey, we were only gonna watch a couple of movies..

"Look baby, I don't know why you're even sweating that. We're gonna only be sitting around in the den watching a movie and that's it. Nothing else. So, please don't stress yourself out about it."

"I'm not stressed out. But it amazes me that you can go out and rent movies for you two to watch but if I asked you to do the same thing, you'd make up every excuse in the world about how busy you are or that you're not in the mood."

"You know what? You're right. But guess what?

"What?"

"She and I got nothing else to do. But check it out, if you rather for me to take her out to dinner or take her to a movie then I'll do that."

"Troy, don't be a smart ass!" She snapped.

"I'm not being a smart ass! I'm just trying to get you to see that what I am doing is harmless." I replied and then I fell silent. I wanted to give her the opportunity to lay all the cards out on the table. But she didn't take the bait. She remained quiet so I came back at her. "Look Trice, I gotta go back to work. But in the mean time, don't stress yourself out. We only have six more days and then you're back at home. Not to mention, you'd be bringing home that ten thousand dollar check."

She sighed. "All right. Go back to work. But call me when you get off."

"I will." I assured her.

Wife Extraordinaire

BY KIKI SWINSON

Charlene

I slept like a baby last night even though I was in the bed alone. This was my second day at my husband's friend's house and at the end of the seventh day, Leon and I would be ten thousand dollars richer. My hands were itching as I thought about it. I swear I couldn't wait until we got that big check in our hands. It felt as if we're about to hit the damn lottery.

As I sat down on the bed in the guest room and thought about all the stuff I would get with the money, Troy knocked on the door. I was dressed appropriately in my blue satin pajama shorts with the shirt to match, but I felt as if I was overdressed and had to shed some clothing to see if I could entice Troy. So before I told him to come in, I took off my top and my bra and then I told him to enter. When he turned the doorknob to open the door, I acted as if I was trying to put on my bra. He caught another glimpse of my *C* cups. But he quickly stepped back out the door and covered his eyes with his hand.

"I'm sorry. I thought you were dressed," he said.

"It's okay. You can come in," I told him.

He pulled the door back but left a slight crack open so he'd be able to communicate with me. I couldn't see his face, but I could hear him pretty well.

"Nah, I'm cool. I was on my way out to go to the store and wanted to know if you wanted me to pick you up something while I was there?"

I thought for a second. "Yeah, pick up a pack of condoms," I replied.

He hesitated a minute. I knew I caught him off guard with my response. I laughed to myself and approached the bedroom door with my bra and shirt in hand. When I grabbed a hold of the doorknob, Troy let it go and stood there.

I smiled at him and took another step towards him. "So are you going to get me the condoms or not?"

He didn't respond. Instead, he looked back at both cameras that were installed on both ends of the hallway. "You're afraid that your wife is going to see me naked on tape, huh?"

"Yeah, so you need to get back inside of the room."

"Don't worry because I've already disconnected the wires in both cameras."

Troy became alarmed. "But why did you do that? The technicians told us not to tamper with the cameras or we'd forfeit the money."

"Stop sweating it. I can rig it back up."

"Well, do it. Because my wife would kill me if I lost that money."

I smiled at him and very casually began to put my bra and shirt back on as he turned to leave. It was a misleading smile. I started to tell him to go straight to hell. But I decided against it and closed the bedroom door. I mean, who did he think he was? I've never had a man turn me down in all the years I had been fucking. I was a bad bitch with some good pussy, a top contender when it came to sucking dick and I liked to get fucked in my ass.

So what was his fucking problem?

I mean, he had to be gay or something because this just didn't happen to me. Not only that, his fucking wife was an average chick who volunteered her time to homeless shelters and whatnots. I wasn't your typical ride or die chick. I was the type that would go harder and he needed to recognize that before it was too late.

And whether he knew it or not, I hated to be turned down. So I vowed I would get him before I left this house. I already had it in my mind that when I was done with him, he was gonna wished he'd fuck me the first night I walked through his front door. You could mark my words on that.

After he left the house, I pulled out my phone and called Leon, my husband. It was a nice Saturday morning, so I knew he'd either be out running or he'd be just getting back in the house and on his way to take a shower. But to my surprise, he didn't answer, which was kind of odd. Leon always carried his Blackberry everywhere he went, so why wasn't he answering my call now?

Pissed off by his actions, I hung up the phone and threw it on the bed. Then the thought of what he could be doing with Troy's wife quickly followed. She wasn't all that pretty to me but I knew she was Leon's type. He used to always tell me how I needed to act more like a lady than a hood chick. But I wasn't about to let him tell me how to live. Shit, he met me while I was living in the 'hood with my mama so what did he expect me to do? What? Act like I'm some upper class chick from Virginia Beach or something? Hell nah!

I was one of those chicks that would go out on the block and flip a couple of packages, or shake my ass at a strip club if I had to, so he needed to be grateful before I left his ass and got with a man who would appreciate me. And whether Troy believed it or not, he might just be that man.

While he was gone to the store, I rearranged the wires on both of the cameras in the hallway to make it look as if I fixed them. I knew he'd probably go behind me and check them. This was my shell game. I refused to reconnect them because I didn't want the cameras to catch any footage of me trying to seduce Troy. I also couldn't risk the people getting any footage of me going into their bedroom. So, while I had time, I snuck into their room and started rummaging through their things.

I could care less about Troy's things. Trice's things were what I was interested in. I wanted to see what type of perfume she wore and I wanted to see how tidy she kept her closet. When I looked at her cosmetics on her vanity, I quickly learned that she was a Prada and a Givenchy girl when it came to the smell goods. Additionally, when I looked in her closet, I could tell she had a shoe fetish out of this world. She didn't have all the name brand shoes like all the celebrities I saw on TV, but she had a big collection of Nine West, BeBe and Nicole Miller. Her shoe size was an eight. I was a nine, so trying on her shoes to see how they looked on my feet was out of the question.

After I looked through her shoes I looked at every shirt, skirt and dress she had hanging up in her closet. To my surprise, Troy had more clothes than Trice. His clothes took up the most space in the closet. Of course that was a complete turn on for me. The labels in his clothes were Ralph Lauren, Lacoste, True Religion and Rock & Republic. His cologne collection consisted of Unforgivable by Sean John, Ed Hardy, Gucci and Burberry. The one that stood out for me was the Burberry and I was gonna make sure I made him aware of that.

While I was going through Trice's panty drawers to see if she had any panties with holes in it or stains in the crouch area, I heard Troy unlocking the front door. Thoughts of him catching me looking at him and his wife's personal shit made my heart race, so I quietly closed her top drawer and slipped back out of their bedroom before he could step foot into the foyer of the house. He called my name right after he closed and locked the front door.

I stood at the top of the stairs and answered him. "Yes."

"I stopped by Denny's and got you and I some breakfast," I heard him yell from the kitchen.

"Okay, I'll be down there in a minute," I told him and then I raced back to his bedroom to see if I left anything out of place. I refused to leave any evidence that would let him know I had been in his room, much less going through his things. When I was done, I made my way downstairs to join him in the kitchen.

When I entered the kitchen he had my food laid out on the kitchen table with a tall glass of orange juice. I didn't know whether to thank him or pretend he wasn't in the room, since he chewed me up before he left the house. I wasn't expecting him to say anything to me about it, but he did. It shocked the hell out of me.

He stood with his back against the stove and gave me the sincerest look he could give me. "I'm sorry about earlier," he said.

I took a seat at the table. "It's okay. Don't worry about it," I assured him. I was really trying to smooth things over and make him think everything was cool between us. Then I was going to come back on him like a thief in the night. I had to admit I was jealous of the fact that Troy loved his wife. And the fact he resisted all this ass I had because he didn't want to cheat on her made me even more jealous.

I could use all my fingers and toes to count the number of times Leon had cheated on me. So to run into a man who didn't cheat made me a bit envious.

Why can't I have a man like Troy? Why did I have to have Leon as my fucking husband?

All the shit Troy said Trice did for him, I used to do. I used to iron all his clothes, did the laundry, and stayed in the kitchen, cooking my ass off. But as soon as Leon started cheating on me, I stopped it all. Cold turkey like a muthafucka. I wasn't about to be his fucking maid and slave, cooking his ass hot meals while he was out fucking different hoes. No way!

When I got my chance to fuck around on him, I did it. But what I hadn't done was fuck one of his homeboys. I knew that would upset his perfect little world. And before I leave this household, I was gonna have another secret to write down in my diary.

Once Troy was done with his apology, I dug into my food and he joined me. We ate and talked about my son. About how I knew I was going to miss him for the summer. Then we talked about the NBA playoffs. He got excited that I loved basketball because his wife didn't. That was one thing he and I had in common. He ate that idea up.

That was my cue to pour the syrup on thick. Before he even realized it, I had him eating out of my hands once again. I figured out very quickly that I couldn't be aggressive with him. I had to do some sneaky shit behind his back if I wanted to seduce him. So I put my thinking cap on and started coming up with a better plan.

Wife Extraordinaire

BY KIKI SWINSON

Leon

This was the first time I ever had someone tag along with me while I did my morning run. It was really nice to have such a sexy woman run side by side with me and go as hard as Trice did. She turned me on like a mutha-fucka. So when we got back to my house I thanked her for hanging out with me. She climbed up the stairs to get to the front door as if she was out of breath.

"You're welcome. But warn me the next time you want to run more than three miles. My legs aren't used to that much exercise at once," she told me as she stood by the front door and waited for me to open it.

"But don't you feel good?" I asked her.

She exhaled. "I guess."

I opened up the front door and let her go ahead of me. She was sweating bullets. But she looked good doing it. "I gotta jump in the shower right now," she insisted.

"Be my guest," I replied and watched her as she walked away from me. She headed upstairs so I got an eyeful. Seeing women working out was the sexiest thing in the world. If I could get my wife to work out with me, then our marriage would probably be twenty percent better.

After Trice disappeared into the bathroom, I headed to the bathroom in my bedroom so I could get out of my sweaty clothes as well.

My Blackberry rung as I began undressing. I knew it had to be Charlene, so I answered it without looking at the caller ID. "Hello."

"Where you been at?" she roared.

"I went running. Why?" I snapped back. I wasn't in the mood to argue with her. She always brought out the worst in me. With the good morning I was having with Trice, I definitely wasn't about to let her ruin it. She was a fucking drama queen. Hell, if I decided to hang up on her, I damn sure wouldn't have lost any sleep behind it.

"I tried to call you earlier but you didn't answer your phone. So I wanted to know where you been!" she continued. She seemed as if she was irritated. But I let what she said go in one ear and out the other.

"Look, Charlene, if you called me to fuss then I'm gonna hang up, because I'm not gonna let you give me a headache this morning."

"Leon, I know you ain't trying to show off in front of Troy's wife. Because you know I don't play that shit! I will hop in a cab and come right over there and blow up your spot. So you better change your fucking tone!"

I knew what she said was in fact true, because that's her way. That was how she rolled. She loved to draw attention to herself and make me look bad in the process. But I was not about to feed into her bullshit this morning. And before she said another word, I politely told her I would call her back after I got out of the shower and then I pressed the end button on my phone. I knew she would try to call me back, so I turned my phone off immediately after I hung up on her. We didn't have a house phone so I didn't have to worry about her calling it.

It didn't take me long to shit, shower and shave. I was in and out of the bathroom in thirty minutes flat. I heard Trice rummaging around in my son's bedroom when I walked into the hallway. I knocked on the door. "Wanna go hangout?" I yelled threw the door.

She opened up the door to answer me. "Sure. Where you wanna go?"

I was getting ready to ask her if she wanted to go see a movie but I was sidetracked by the smell of her perfume and the way she looked in her sundress. The dress wasn't all that glamorous but it had sex appeal. To see her hair combed back into a ponytail was also sexy. She had on a pair of diamond studded earrings and diamond encrusted pendant around her neck. She looked like the girl next door. And when she smiled, it took my breath away.

"Where you wanna go?" she asked me once again.

I had to be honest and let down my guard. "You got a brother speechless right now," I admitted.

She smiled at me again. But this time it was one of those bashful type smiles. "I wished my husband would talk to me like that," she told me.

"Wait, you telling me Troy doesn't tell you how beautiful you are?" I asked her.

She walked out of the bedroom and into the hall. "No. He doesn't."

I let her walk in front of me so I could get a better look at her. Her ass wasn't as fat as Charlene's but it was nice. The idea of spanking her ass while I bent her over gave me chills. I knew I was wrong for thinking about my homeboy's wife, but I couldn't stop being a man. I was sure Troy was looking at my wife the same way. And the only difference with the way I felt about my wife versus him was I could care less if he fucked Charlene. That's just how I rolled.

Chicks like my wife came a dime a dozen. But to have a woman like Troy's was like winning the lottery. The chances of getting a chick like Trice on your team were like one in a million. Since I knew it would be a long shot that I would ever hook up with someone like her, I figured nothing was wrong with me relishing in the moment while I had her.

"I know you probably hear this all the time, but if you were my wife I would be with you every chance I got. I mean, you are so pretty and down to earth. You're not flashy or arrogant. And I like the fact that you were willing to go running with me this morning. The thought of you taking care of your body is a huge thing for me."

She didn't respond to my comments but she did smile.

When we got downstairs I finally remembered to ask her if she wanted to go check out a movie.

"Yes, I would love to go to the movies," she replied cheerfully.

"Well, let's go then," I said and led her out of the house. I rushed towards the passenger side door of my white Dodge Magnum. As soon as she stepped to the curb, I opened the door for her and after she got in, I closed it.

She smiled the entire time. I knew I was winning brownie points with her. That was just the way I wanted it. She was a beautiful woman. And I was damn happy to have her in my company.

Wife Extraordinaire

BY KIKI SWINSON

Troy

Charlene stepped out of the TV room when she got Leon on the phone. She went into the kitchen to get some privacy but I still heard her fussing with Leon. They didn't talk long. A minute or two into their conversation, I heard her mumble underneath her breath about how he had hung up on her. She was very angry. Instead of coming back into the TV room with me, she left and went outside. I went and looked out the mini-blinds of my living room window and saw her pacing back and forth on the front lawn area with her arms folded. From where I was standing, she looked as if she was talking to herself. That was a bad sign. When women did that, niggas had to watch out. *A woman scorned is a treacherous woman who will pour sugar in your gas tank and then laugh in your face.* That's what my dad used to tell me. I thank God I wasn't on her shit list.

When I got tired of staring at her from the window, I exited the front room of the house and made my way back to the TV room. There was a Victoria Secret commercial on TV that reminded me of Trice, so that prompted me to call her. I knew my surrounding needed to sound like I was at work, so I turned the volume of the TV down. I hoped Charlene stayed outside while I was on the phone, because I didn't need her blowing my cover.

Come to find out, it really didn't matter because Trice didn't answer her phone. I called her three times back-to-back and each time it rung four times and went to voicemail. She didn't normally do this, so I called Leon's phone to get him to relay the message for her to answer her phone. Hell, his phone didn't ring at all. It went straight to voicemail. That was unusual for Leon's phone to be off. I had never called his phone and it went straight to voicemail. So my gut instinct told me something wasn't right with this picture. However, before I drew a conclusion, I tried calling her two more times. Again, it rung four times and then went to voicemail.

I had to admit that I wasn't happy about my wife not answering her phone. I couldn't say what she had going on that prevented her from answering her phone, but whatever it was it couldn't be that important.

Several minutes later, Charlene came back into the house. She walked straight back to where I was. She didn't make it a secret that she was upset. She slumped down on the sofa next to me and ranted like she was angry at the world.

"I swear, I can't wait until this week is over because after those people give me and him that check, I'm gonna get my half off the top and then I'm leaving his sorry ass!"

I started to probe into her business, because I knew Leon did something to upset her to the point she thought about divorcing him. My curiosity was killing me. I figured that whatever it was, maybe it had something to do with Trice. But strange things tend to happen and sometimes, you don't have to say a word.

"I hate to be the bearer of bad news but my husband might have fucked your wife," she said.

Her words were chilling and they went through my heart like a sharp knife. The thought of Trice letting another man make love to her made me sick to my stomach. Not only was this man a homeboy of mine, we grew up in the same neighborhood. So this was a crucial situation. I tried not to wrap my mind around the idea. Charlene was upset and pissed off, and worse, her ghetto ass wasn't making it any easier for me.

The thought of it was too painful to digest. "Look, Charlene, I know you're upset, but you can't be going around making assumptions like that, especially if you don't have any facts. You know you can get people killed like that."

She looked at me as if I said something wrong. "Look, I know my husband," she began. "And I know what that muthafucka is capable of doing. He has already cheated on me with a whole bunch of bitches. And believe me when I tell you that your wife is going to be next if he ain't already done her by now."

I knew I had to defend my wife's honor. She had never stepped out on me during our entire marriage. In spite of all the arguments we've had, I knew she wouldn't fuck around on me. I had always been the fuck up in our relationship and crept around with a couple of those chicken-head bitches in the streets. I was hating myself for inviting Leon and his hood rat wife, Charlene, to join in this endeavor.

"Charlene, I know my wife, and I know she wouldn't sleep with your husband. Now maybe Leon has screwed around on you with other chicks but me and him are like blood, so I would bet money that he wouldn't cross that line with Trice. I just know he wouldn't," I replied, trying to convince her.

It became obvious that what I said went through one ear and out the other, because she kept pressing the issue.

She turned completely around and faced me. As she poured her heart out to me, I began to feel sorry for her.

"I know Leon has probably told you that I nag him all the time and that I don't want to work or cook. But guess what? He

| 46 |

made me like that," she explained, on the verge of tears. "When me and him first got together, I did everything for him. He didn't have to lift a finger to do a thing. But after I started finding phone numbers and bitches started calling him all times of the night, I stopped cooking, I stopped cleaning up behind him and I stopped helping him pay the fucking bills.

"I felt like he didn't appreciate me. So why let him have his cake and eat it too? And what's crazy is after I found out about the first two chicks I forgave him and tried to put it behind us. But six months later he was back out in the street, fucking with another ho. And then after her, he picked up another one. I swear, after a while I couldn't keep up with him. It seemed like he was switching fuck partners every four to five months. But what broke me down was the fact he didn't have enough respect for me to hide it. If one of them called, he would talk to them right in my face."

Tears fell down her face. I didn't have any Kleenex around so I got up and left her in the TV room while I retrieved a few napkins from the kitchen. When I returned I handed her a handful of paper towels. She continued to pour her heart out to me and then she apologized to me for trying to seduce me the night before.

"I am so sorry for the way I acted last night and this morning. I only did it because I wanted to be in the arms of a man. I am a very lonely woman."

"You don't have to apologize. Everything is cool," I told her in an effort to down play what happened between us.

She wiped the tears from her eyes. "Well, I appreciate you saying that but I still had to get that off my chest."

I reached over and patted her on her back. "You good. So don't continue to sweat it."

"Can I ask you a personal question?" she asked me.

"It depends on the question," I replied hesitantly.

"Have you ever cheated on your wife?"

I took a deep breath as I contemplated on whether or not it would be in my best interest to divulge that type of information to her. She didn't know this, but I had already known about all the chicks Leon fucked with behind her back. But the thought of her feeling as if she could confide in me about the problems in her marriage got me to feeling a little vulnerable. Then I thought about me digging a hole for myself by letting the skeletons out of my closest kiss the vulnerable part of me goodbye. She seemed like she was cool and all, but I figured if I showed her the cards I had been dealt, then she wouldn't have any fighting power, especially if my shit hit the fan.

"I came close to doing it a few years back. But I walked away," I lied.

"What made you turn the woman down and walk away?" she probed.

"Because I wasn't trying to risk losing my wife," my lies continued.

Charlene began to sob uncontrollably. "Why couldn't Leon be more like you?"

I reached over with both arms and hugged her. "Not all men are the same," I replied.

While I embraced her, she placed her arms around me and held me tight. "Please don't let me go," she begged me.

I could feel her heart beating as the shoulder area of my shirt became saturated with her tears. She was really distraught. After holding her in my arms for more than five minutes, I began to really feel sorry for her. The fact she smelled really good started getting me aroused, so I released my hold on her and gradually pulled back from her. She released her hold on me as well, but I could tell that wasn't what she wanted to do. I realized if I would have held her for another hour than she would have been fine. However, it didn't slip past me that she had put me in another awkward situation. I played it off very casually.

"Do you think you're going to need some more napkins?" I asked her.

"No, I'm fine," she assured me. So I sat back on the sofa and occasionally rubbed her back. I wanted her to feel like I was there for her and that everything would be all right.

Wife Extraordinaire

BY KIKI SWINSON

Trice

Leon and I caught an early matinee at the Military Circle mall. We saw the movie *For Colored Girls*. I have to admit it was a damn good movie. But what really surprised me was the fact Leon wanted to see it more than me. After we walked out of the theater I noticed him pressing down on the power button of his Blackberry.

"You turning your phone off?" I asked him.

"Nah. I just turned it back on," he told me. "Charlene called me with a whole bunch of drama before we left the house."

Before I could make a comment, his phone began beeping. He looked down at it. "She sent me a text message," he said. Then he looked down at it closer.

"She probably wanted to tell you that she loved you," I commented.

He chuckled. "Nah, definitely didn't tell me that. She cursed my ass out! She said she's over my shit and that I can keep showing off around you if I wanted, because when she comes back home shit is going to change."

"When did you show off around me?" I asked him.

"I'm assuming she thought that when she and I talked earlier, that you were listening to our conversation."

"Why would she think that?"

Leon stuck his phone back into the holster attached to his belt. "I don't know. And I'm not gonna give it much more thought than that."

I cracked a smile. "As you wish," I replied.

He reached over and tried to tickle me in my left side. "You're being sarcastic?" he smiled.

I jumped before he could penetrate me with his hand. "And what if I was?" I replied.

He made a break towards me so I shot off into the opposite direction. We were literally running in the mall. We had run about thirty feet before I stopped in my tracks. It was kind of weird, but I wanted him to catch me. He grabbed me around my waist and pulled me into his arms. Now I can't tell you how this happened, but when he grabbed a hold of me, he somehow positioned me to step backwards, allowing my butt to press against his dick. It happened so quickly. So when I felt his stiff meat had become erect at the mere touch of my ass, a tingly feeling shot through my body. I couldn't believe it, but my pussy got soaked in a matter of seconds. I felt like a fucking high school girl again, allowing my high school crush grind on my booty.

But I snapped back into reality and realized I was in the arms of my husband's friend. A guy he grew up with, so I felt as if I was forbidden fruit. But then the strong urge inside of me surfaced and dared me to explore this new territory. *So should I give in to this emotion or not?* While I mulled over the situation, I eased my ass away from Leon's groin. I played it off with charm.

"Wanna get something to eat?" I asked him, hoping it would turn his attention away from what had just happened.

I noticed how he discreetly placed his right hand over the bulge in his pants. I acted as if I had not seen it because I was sure he was embarrassed enough.

"Yeah, sure. Where you wanna go?" he finally responded as he walked in the direction of the food court, which was in the middle of the mall.

"It really doesn't matter to me," I acknowledged as I walked alongside of him. When we approached the entryway of the food court, we looked at all the selections from where we stood and came to the decision that we were going to leave the mall and stop at an Applebee's restaurant.

A few minutes into the drive my cellular phone started ringing. I knew it was my husband, Troy, so I answered it after the first ring. "Hello."

"Whatcha doing?" he didn't hesitate to ask me.

"On my way to Applebee's with Leon," I told him.

"Y'all in the car?"

"Yeah. Why?"

"Just asking."

"Are you still at work?" I wanted to know.

"I just got off."

"I thought you were working until three."

"They let me off early."

"Well, what are you getting ready to get into?"

"I don't know. I'll probably go back to the house and throw some leftovers in the microwave. But other than that, I'm just gonna chill."

"How are you and Charlene getting along?"

"She's cool. You know me, I don't talk much. I miss the hell out of you though."

"Oh, that's so sweet!"

"Tell Leon I said what's up?"

I looked back at Leon while he was driving and told him what Troy said. "Tell him I said what's up?"

"Leon said what's up, baby."

"You keeping it tight for me?"

"Keeping what tight?" I asked him because I was taken ab-ack with that question. I had no idea what the hell he was talk-ing about.

"Nothing," he said, acting somewhat irritated. "Tell Leon Charlene was trying to call him earlier."

"He knows that already."

"How do you know?" Troy sounded irritated.

"Because she sent him a text message."

"Don't get in the middle of their shit!" he warned me.

"I'm not."

"A'ight. Well, call me back after y'all finish eating."

"Okay."

By the time Troy and I had finished our conversation, Leon had gotten us in the parking lot of Applebee's. Like a gentle-man, he got out of the car and then came around on the passen-ger side and opened the door for me.

"Thank you," I said.

"You're welcome," he replied.

Inside the restaurant, we were shown to our table and the waitress immediately took our drink order. While we waited for her to return, Leon thought it was necessary to ask me about my conversation with Troy.

"So what's up with Troy?"

"What do you mean?"

"I noticed how the tone of your voice changed a couple of times while y'all were talking. So I was just wondering was he all right?"

I knew deep in my heart that Troy wasn't all right. He knew I knew what was going on between Charlene and Leon and he hated when I got involved in other people's shit. Not only that, I knew the idea of Leon and I going out made him feel him uneasy, which was why he asked me had I been keeping it tight. Keeping it tight meant was I keeping my pussy to myself.

For the life of me I couldn't figure out why he had asked me something like that? I hadn't cheated on him the whole time we've been together. Since I was young I had always heard that when your man or woman questions you about cheating means that nine times out of ten they're the ones who were actually doing it. Now if that were the case, I would truly hate it for him . . . because I would pack my bags immediately. The next time he saw me would be at divorce court. So he'd better take his own advice and keep it tight himself.

"Yeah, he's fine," I finally said.

Leon chuckled. "Well, why did he tell you to keep it tight?"

"I'm not sure," I answered him without looking him directly in the eyes. I tried avoiding eye contact with him by looking at my glass. I tend to look as if I'm lying when I look into a person's eyes.

"Come on, you can tell me," he smiled and reached over and grabbed my hand.

I cracked a smiled immediately after I looked up at him. I tried to snatch my hand away from him but he wouldn't let my hand go.

"You know your friend. So I don't have to tell you anything," I told him.

He let my hand go very easy. "Sounds like he's missing you."

"Wouldn't you?" I replied in a flirtatious way.

"You damn right! Shit! Look at you! You're beautiful! You're intelligent. And you're down to earth. You're a woman that every man dreams of."

"Yeah, right. Don't try to blow my head up."

"I'm dead serious," he began. "I remember when Troy first met you. He called me and talked to me for about twenty minutes bragging about how pretty and sexy you were. And then when you paid for dinner on y'all first date, he called me and told me that too."

I started blushing. "You're lying! He told you that?"

"Yeah, he did. And I can't lie, I was jealous."

"Why?"

"Because I had been dating some airhead chicks."

I blushed even harder. It felt really good to hear how jealous he was when he found out about Troy and I relationship. I was even flattered to know how ecstatic Troy was that he'd met me. Men normally didn't run and tell their friends about every woman they had met. Women do it all the time. But I guess I was an exception being as though I had excellent qualities without the baggage.

"Well, you don't have an airhead chick now," I commented, knowing exactly how he really felt about his wife. But the plan was for me to get the attention off me.

"Whatcha got, jokes? I married the biggest airhead there was."

"Oh, stop it, Leon. I'm sure she's a sweetheart."

"She used to be. But that was many moons ago."

"I'm sure it was," I replied sarcastically. I found that men are always trying to make their wives sound like naggers. They always play the victim role too. But if they would only do what they are supposed to do then they would have a good wife. What they say is true, *A happy wife makes a happy house.*

"You just don't understand what I go through," he continued in an effort to convince me about the turmoil in his marriage. But I was no dummy. There were always two sides to every story. And right now I was hearing Leon's side, so I knew he was pouring the drama on really thick.

After I listened to him beat me in the head with all the mess he said Charlene took him through, I ate my food and what was left I got the waitress to put it in a to-go box. On the way back to Leon's house, I got him to drive by my house. It was a last minute request but he happily obliged. He did mention we wouldn't be able to stop because of the "No Physical Contact Rule" that was imposed.

During the entire seven days, we were prohibited to have any physical contact with our significant others or we would forfeit the $10,000 at the end of the week. I wasn't too happy about the rule when the people ran down everything to us. But Troy had me focus on the reward at the end of this journey, so that's what I was doing.

It was around four thirty in the evening and the sun was up for everyone to see it. I sat back in the passenger seat of Leon's vehicle as we drove through my neighborhood. I saw a few people I knew from my community, but I didn't allow them to see me. It would've been somewhat odd for them to see me in a car with another man. And since I wasn't in the mood to explain myself to them, I kept out of sight. I hoped Troy did the same with Charlene, because I really didn't feel like explaining myself to my neighbor, Ashley. She was a nosey bitch and she knew how to put a person's business out amongst the other neighbors. I was surprised that she hasn't gotten her ass kicked yet. But don't rule me out, because in the back of my head, I thought I might be the first to do it.

When Leon got within a few yards of my house, I asked him to slow down so I could get a good look at the house. I only needed to see it because I missed it. So as he slowed down I took a mental picture of the house and the landscape around the house. Everything was exactly how I had left it. The only thing that stood out for me was the fact I wasn't there.

I noticed Troy wasn't there either. So I pulled out my phone and called him immediately. The phone rang at least five times before it went to voicemail. I refused to leave him a voicemail, so I hung up. I didn't say anything to Leon about it, but I wondered why he didn't answer my call. I also wondered where he and Charlene were. I guess I would find out later.

After Leon left my block, he put the pedal to the metal and drove us back to his place in Norfolk.

Leon

As soon as Trice and I arrived back at my house, my Blackberry started ringing. I started not to answer it when I saw Charlene's name pop up on the caller ID. But I knew she would continue to blow my phone up until I answered it.

"Yeah, what's up?" I answered nonchalantly. I let her know right off the bat that I was not feeling the idea of her calling me right now. She caught on to my tone of voice immediately.

"What the fuck you mean what's up? I'm not your homeboy!" she roared.

"I didn't say that you were," I replied. But I was completely annoyed at the sound of her voice.

"Well, why the hell are you talking to me like that? You know I don't play that shit. Talk to me like I'm your wife."

"What do you want?" I snapped at her. She was plucking my fucking nerves so I wanted her to get to the point as to why she called me in the first place.

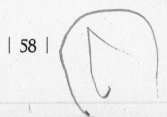

"Leon, don't play stupid! You know why I called you. I mean, you did hang up on me earlier. So, do you think I'm over that?"

"You should be. That shit happened this morning."

"Keep showing off!"

"How the fuck am I showing off Charlene. You're talking really reckless right now."

"Nigga, you're the one talking reckless. But it's all good because when all of this shit is over, I will get some pay back."

"Yeah, yeah, yeah. Are you through?" I replied sarcastically. At that point, I was ready to hang up on her. I had just gotten home from an early lunch with Trice and I wasn't in the mood to argue with Charlene. She knew what to say to press my buttons and I couldn't let her bring me out of my shell right now. I didn't want Trice to see me in rare form. So I politely disconnected the call while she was screaming through the phone. Thankfully, Trice was in the bathroom while all of this was going on. I knew if I would've stayed on the phone and entertained Charlene just a little bit longer, then Trice would have heard all the chaos.

When she exited the bathroom, she rubbed her stomach in a circular motion. "Boy, am I full. That shrimp and spinach salad was delicious. And the glazed chicken breast was even better."

"My food was good too. Too bad I don't have any leftovers," I commented as I led the way to the TV room.

"You can have some of mine," Trice offered me.

"That's good to know," I told her and then we settled down on the sofa.

And right before Trice was about to say something back to me, my Blackberry started ringing again. I let out a loud sigh because I knew it was none other than my worrisome ass wife. She had become more of a pain in my ass gone than she was when she was here. I honestly wanted to ignore the call but again, I knew if I had done that, then she would continue to call me if I didn't answer.

As I pulled my phone from my pocket I noticed it wasn't Charlene calling me. It was this chick I used to fuck named Sabrina. She was a bad chick, pretty as hell with a tiny waist and a fat ass. The only downsize to her was that she was too needy. Plus, the bitch didn't have any money, and she lived with her mama in Young's Park. She was the type of chick that would let a nigga sell her a dream about how much he loved her, he would take her out the projects and give her all the nice things she desired. She was very naïve.

I was able to tell her exactly that and fuck her the same night I met her. And I had to admit the pussy was good. I swear I had not met another woman yet whose pussy could stay wet longer than hers. Not to mention she could suck the skin off a nigga's dick. I almost pulled her fucking weave out of her head that first night.

But as soon as I got my nut off, I was ready to send her on her way. Her conversation game was zero and she had absolutely no ambition. All she talked about was how she needed a car and couldn't wait until her section eight crib came through. Believe me when I tell you that I was completely turned off and I skated from her ass right after I washed my dick off. Too bad she didn't have a bit of common sense. Hell, if she did, she would be a bad bitch.

"Hello," I said as I got up from the sofa. I didn't want Trice to hear another woman's voice.

"Whatcha doing stranger?" she said.

I waited until I reached the hallway house before I responded. "I'm cool. And you?" I replied.

"I'm okay. But I'm missing you though."

I walked out the front door and closed it behind me. "I miss you too," I told her even though I knew it was a lie. I knew I could tell this chick the sky was falling and she'd believe me. She was just that gullible.

"So, when can I see you?" she got straight to the point.

"I can't say right now because I'm out of town," my lies continued.

"Damn Leon, you are always out of town," she whined. "When do you ever come back?"

"I told you how my job keeps me traveling."

She sighed. "I know. But I was hoping that I'd catch you and you'd be able to come and see me."

"I'll be back in a couple of weeks."

"You promise you gon' call me when you get back?"

"Yeah, I promise."

"Well, you better because this pussy needs you. It's been real lonely since you been gone."

I laughed. "I'll make it up to you."

"I'ma hold you to that."

"A'ight. I'll holla at you later."

"Okay."

After I disconnected the call from Sabrina, I hauled ass back into the house. On the way down the hall, I heard Trice talking. The closer I got to the TV room, it became obvious who she was talking to. She sounded irritated, so I made a detour to the kitchen to give her some privacy. While I was in the kitchen, I could hear bits and pieces of her conversation. She tried to talk as quietly as she could but like a noisy neighbor, I had my ears glued to the wall. I knew what was going on.

I knew Troy was starting to have some reservations about this arrangement, because he hasn't called me since *we traded wives*. I had known him damn near all my life, so I knew the type of issues that bothered him and vice versa, which was why he was stressing Trice out.

He knew from day one that I was a womanizer. He and I ran plenty of trains on chicks while we were growing up. He knew I could fuck any chick I wanted. The fact I had his woman in my company I knew was probably making him feel uneasy, if not downright crazy. But as guarded as Troy was, he wouldn't bring that issue to my attention. Troy had a lot of pride . . . and he wouldn't let anyone know his weaknesses or when he was hurt. He knew I wasn't the type of man who would force anyone to talk to me about their problems, so if he didn't pick up the phone to call me, then I wouldn't call him.

After Trice got off the phone, she walked into the kitchen where I was. She stood before me as if she had fifty-pound weights on her shoulders.

"What's wrong?" I asked.

"Troy is acting crazy. He's worried to death about what I am doing. And I keep telling him that I'm not doing anything. But for some reason, it's not registering."

"Can you blame the man? I mean, look at you!" I replied and cracked a big smile.

"Stop it. I'm trying to be serious Leon," she whined.

I grabbed her by both her shoulders. "I know you're being serious. But I've known your husband longer than you. You should know that you ain't gon' win every battle with him. Just give him some space and let him ponder for a while. Then he'll figure it out and snap out of it."

"You think so?"

"I know so. Now let's go watch some TV."

Wifey Extraordinaire

BY KIKI SWINSON

Charlene

I think I cried so much that I developed a fucking headache. I asked Troy for a couple of Tylenol and a glass of water. Within seconds, he was handing me a cold bottle of spring water and two aspirins. I popped the pills in my mouth without even thinking about it. Then I laid my head back against the headrest of the sofa in the den. I closed my eyes and wondered how I could make my life just a little more stress free. I was finally tired of all the hustle and bustle of life. I was even more tired of my cheating ass husband. I knew years ago that this day would come. I admitted I tried to delay putting up with all his shit. But that was over now. It was time to cut my losses, time for a new beginning. When this whole wife swap thing was over, I was gonna get some payback and then I was getting as far away from Leon as I possibly could.

While I was in deep thought planning my escape, Troy tapped me on my leg to see if I was awake or not. I opened my eyes and then lifted my head. "Yeah, I'm awake. What's up?"

"How is your head feeling?" he asked me as he stood up before me.

"The aspirins are starting to work, that's why I had my head back against the chair."

"Well, I'm about to go out to my garage and straighten up a few things, but if you need me, just holla."

"Okay. I sure will," I assured him. I watched him as he walked away.

Fifteen minutes after Troy left to go to the garage, I heard his cell ringing. Evidently he had left it in the kitchen. It rang five times and stopped. I assumed that whoever made the call left him a voicemail. But a minute later, the phone began ringing again. I got up this time. I felt as if whoever was calling him must've really wanted to talk to him. When I got to the kitchen, I picked up the phone and noticed the call was coming from his wife, Trice. I stared at the caller ID, trying to decide whether or not to answer it. I finally picked it up before it stopped ringing and said hello.

She hesitated for a brief moment, before saying, "Who is this?"

I had every right to give her a dumb ass answer for that dumb ass question. *I mean, who in the hell could it be other than me? I was the only woman in her husband's company. Was she trying to be funny or what? She couldn't be that stupid. Or did she make the mistake by asking me the wrong question? Because, if it were me, I would've been straight up with her and asked her why was she answering my husband's phone?* But I guess she wasn't built like me. I was a hood chick and hood chicks didn't play when it came to our men.

"It's Charlene," I finally said.

"Where is my husband?" she asked in an irritated manner.

"He's indisposed right now," I lied. I wanted to see how long she would let me play this game with her. The way I looked at it, being indisposed could mean a lot of things. But since I was at her house with her husband, indisposed meant he couldn't come to the phone because he was busy doing something he wasn't supposed to be doing.

"Indisposed!" she said, her voice screeched. "You tell him to get on the phone now!" she demanded.

I could tell she was getting really pissed off. I started to laugh in her ear and tell her I was only joking, but I was getting a kick out of fucking with her emotions. Besides, I wanted her to get a taste of how I felt when my husband fucked around with my emotions. I was tired of being the only chick with an asshole for a husband.

"I wish I could but he told me if somebody called him to take a message," I replied nonchalantly.

"Girl, I'm not trying to hear that bullshit. Put my husband on the phone right now!" she demanded.

Again, I wanted to laugh in her ear because she was feeding into my drama and I was loving it. But I didn't want to give her the impression that I was being immature, so I held back and continued to pour more fuel on the fire.

"Sweetheart, don't shoot me! I'm just the messenger," I replied calmly.

"Well, I was told by your husband that you're more like a hood rat bitch with low self-esteem and no education!" she snapped.

No this bitch didn't just tell me that Leon called me a hood rat bitch with low self-esteem and no education. I was shocked and completely caught off guard by her comments. I hadn't clocked another bitch in a long time, but I wanted to beat this bitch's ass for disrespecting me. Maybe I shouldn't have been fucking with her the way I was, but now I didn't have a choice, I had to continue the game, especially after she made it personal. I had to come back at her ass real hard now. I couldn't dare let her get away with insults like that.

"Well, my husband might think I'm a hood rat bitch, but your husband thinks I'm a down to earth ride or die chick. As a matter of fact, he thinks the world of me. And just a minute ago

| 65 |

he kissed me in the mouth and told me that I threw my pussy on him better than you could. So you see, Ms. Goodie Two-Shoes, I may be a bitch to you and my husband, but I'm the best thing that your husband has ever had."

"Oh really? So you're saying you and my husband fucked, huh?"

"Oops! I'm sorry! Did I just say that?" I chuckled.

"So this is a game to you, huh?" she said, but I could hear the aggravation in her tone. She was livid with me. And I'm assuming she was heartbroken at the thought of Troy fucking me. Shit, I was heartbroken when I found out about all the bitches Leon fucked. The sisterly thing to do was to understand her feelings. Hell, I didn't or couldn't feel sorry for her in the least bit. People say misery loves company. And they were right. My misery was lonely as hell and company had just walked in the door.

"No Trice, this is not a game. We are all adults, sweetie. So put an 'H' on your chest, baby girl, and handle it. Shit, men fuck around on their wives all the time. It didn't start with you and it ain't gonna end with you. The faster you get over this, the better off you'll be."

"Bitch, you must think I am crazy! See, the difference between you and I is, I come from a good family with strong morals and values. And you come from the slum. So I don't have to deal with a goddamn thing! I know who I am. So bitch, I know my worth. Now if my husband wants to jeopardize our union because of some chicken head bitch with dick breath and sloppy pussy, then that's fine with me. And as far as your husband is concerned, I'm starting to feel really sorry for him because he's a really good man. Not to mention, now I can see why he salivates when I come within two feet of him. He's not used to being around a real woman with class."

"Bitch, please! You ain't got no class! You just like all the other chicks around here."

"Don't let the good girl image fool you Charlene. If you and I walked down the street together, I would get all of the attention. So face it, you can't hold a candle to me. I'm not in your class. And speaking of which, I just now had to remind myself that I am wasting my time with you. You are beneath me."

"Wow! What a coincidence. I'm beneath you and just a minute ago I was beneath your husband while he was on top of me sliding his dick in and out of my wet juicy pussy."

"Well, I hope you made him use a condom because if you didn't, join the club. Because now you got the herpes just like us," she replied and hung up.

Immediately after she hung up, Troy walked back into the house. He startled the hell out of me but I had enough time to stuff his Blackberry down into my pocket. I couldn't let him see it in my hands, so I had to hide it.

I was standing in front of the kitchen island when he approached me. "You seen my phone?" he asked.

My heart started racing. I didn't know whether to tell him I had his phone or act as if I hadn't seen it. But while I thought about what to say, I hoped and prayed that his phone didn't ring while I had it buried inside my pocket. So I quickly told him I hadn't seen his phone and then asked him to excuse me while I went to the bathroom. Thank God he bought my story and moved out of my way so I could pass him.

I rushed down the hallway and into the hall bathroom. After I closed the door behind me, I took his phone from my pocket and turned the power button off. I couldn't let him get a chance to talk to his wife, especially after the conversation she and I had just had. If he found out what I told her this early in the game, he would surely throw my ass out of his house. So I thought of a plan to make him think he either lost his phone or misplaced it until I was able to lure him into my trap. I had already told his wife he and I had sex so I had to find a way to make it happen before she found out otherwise. So immediately after I turned the power off on his phone, I stuck it back into my pocket and left out of the bathroom.

Troy had left the house and made his way back to the garage. I could hear him rambling through some things out there. I figured he thought he left his phone in the garage. That's how I wanted to keep it.

While I was trying to regroup, I heard my phone beep. The beeping sound told me someone had texted me. I looked at the phone to see who texted me and when I realized it came from Leon, my heart jumped and I got an uneasy feeling in the pit of my stomach.

I heard u got u'r rocks off bitch! I hope it was worth it. 'Cause u can't come home. The text read.

My mouth shot wide open. I shouldn't have been surprised. I knew she was going to tell his black ass what I said to her. But the thought of him telling me I couldn't come home really threw me for a loop. At that very moment, I wanted to get him on the phone and curse him out for even going there with me through a fucking text message. He should've been a man and called me. Texting me was a cowardly way of trying to shut me out. I mean, who the fuck he thought he was anyway? I put up with all the bitches he fucked behind my back. So he's got a motherfucking nerve if you wanna ask me. But you know what? I wasn't going to let this shit stress me out.

Trice was gonna have to prove I said all that stuff to her. I wasn't admitting to shit until I got my half of the $10,000. Then I could tell him to kiss my ass all the way to the bank.

Wife Extraordinaire

BY KIKI SWINSON

•·····························•

Trice

I was a big ball of tears when I got off the phone with Charlene. She was a fucking monster with no heart. If I was in front of her trifling ass I would've scratched her fucking eyes out of her head. I mean, how dare she talk shit to me and tell me she had just fucked my husband? Talk about being bold. That ho was definitely a bold bitch. But what really added insult to injury was Troy told her to tell anyone that called that he was indisposed and for her to take a message. I was his wife, not his fucking girlfriend or his mistress. *So how disrespectful was that?*

"I texted Charlene and told her she couldn't bring her ass home," Leon spat as he stood in the doorway of his son's bedroom.

I was sitting on the edge of the bed thinking if I was going to call Troy and confront him. "I thought you were going to call her," I replied.

He stood at the door with his arms folded and said, "I started to. But I didn't wanna hear her fucking lies so I decided not to."

"What would make her be so bold and say all those things to me? I mean, what kind of person is she?"

"I already told you how she was. She's a heartless bitch! And she doesn't care about anyone but herself."

"Well, let's not forget the bastard I am married to. Remember, it takes two, and she didn't get laid by herself," I acknowledged. I said that because Troy had as much to do with what they did then she did. They were both to blame, so why should Leon and I throw all the stones at her.

Leon shook his head with disgust. He seemed as if he was more hurt than I was in spite of all the claims he made about how he wanted to leave her. I had been told that when a man found out his woman had given her goodies to another man or to make it worse, a cat they grew up with in grade school, then that man felt less than a man. Regardless if that man was the biggest ho in the world, his pride and dignity took a major hit. He was no longer the big dawg. Now he was the little pup with a cup to piss in, and not the huge toilet bowl that men pissed in.

Men had pride issues and women were more vocal. Men were logical and tried not to deal with their emotions. Because of this perceived toughness and stowing those feelings internally, their emotions hit them harder. The lion's heart was replaced with that of a pussycat.

"Yeah, I know but she probably came onto him," he said, defending Troy. But I wasn't trying to hear that bullshit. Both of them were to blame.

"It doesn't matter who did what," I stated. "They both are at fault."

"Are you going to call him?"

"For what? So he can lie?" I replied. "I'm not in the mood for lies right now Leon. I swear my heart isn't going to be able to take it. All I wanna do right now is lie down and figure out how I am going to handle this situation when I get home."

I was on the verge of tears. My eyes were filling up very quickly. So I reached up and wiped them with the back of my hand.

"What if he calls you?"

"I'm not gonna talk to him," I said as the tears streamed down my face.

Leon walked over to me and took a seat next to me on the bed. Then he placed his arm around me. In turn, I buried my face in his chest and let all my emotions flow. I sobbed like I had lost Troy to death. And in all honesty, it really felt like a part of me had died.

The feeling of betrayal and infidelity ripped my heart apart at the seams while Leon held me in his arms. I believe the only thing that saved me from having a nervous breakdown at that moment was Leon whispering in my ear that it was okay to cry and that I would be all right. This was death, the death of my marriage, and Leon was the comforter at the funeral.

I believe Leon and I stayed embraced for more than twenty minutes. Him holding me the way he did made me feel as if he was there to protect me, and honestly, I didn't want him to let me go.

"You are going to be all right baby. Watch and see," Leon assured me.

When I finally got myself together and felt I did enough crying, I asked Leon to let me get some rest. He happily obliged and left the room. Immediately after, he closed the bedroom door and I turned off my cell phone. I didn't want to hear from Troy at all. I had heard enough shit from Charlene. Now what I needed to do was have some alone time so I could figure out how to approach this situation when it was time to go home.

Wife Extraordinaire

BY KIKI SWINSON

Troy

I couldn't figure out for the life of me where my Blackberry was. I couldn't remember where I had put it. I thought if I called it using the house phone it would ring and I could locate it. Surprisingly, it didn't ring. As a matter of fact, my phone went straight to voicemail, which led me to believe that the battery had to be dead. Now I knew Trice must have called me by now. And if she got my voicemail, I knew she wasn't going to be a happy camper about it. If you want to know the truth, I wouldn't be happy if I called her and her phone kept going straight to voicemail. And being at my homeboy's house wouldn't make the situation any better.

Knowing how Leon was with a vulnerable woman wasn't a pretty sight...especially if the woman was someone you loved—like I loved Trice. So to keep my mind at ease, I picked up the house phone and tried to get her on the line so I could explain to her that I misplaced my phone and couldn't find it.

Unfortunately for me, her phone went straight to voicemail as well. Now I figured that either she was trying to dial out the same time I was or she turned her phone off. I pressed the redial button and when the line connected, her voicemail came on instantly.

"Wait a minute, what the fuck is going on?" I said aloud, but low enough so Charlene couldn't hear me.

I waited several seconds after I cleared the phone line and dialed her number manually instead of pressing the redial button. But that didn't help because I still couldn't get a connection. Her line went straight to voicemail yet again and I got pretty upset about it. I wanted to slam the phone down but I knew it wouldn't do any good. I remained calm and thought of another way to get in touch with my wife. I placed the phone back in the base and strolled into the den where Charlene was. She was sitting on the recliner watching TV.

"Can you please do me a favor?" I asked her.

"Yeah, what's up?"

"Could you call Leon and ask him to put Trice on the phone for me?"

Charlene looked at me in a weird way as if I had said something wrong. I guess she figured out I really wanted to talk to my wife, so she pulled out her phone and made the call. She put her cell against her ear and waited. Several seconds later she pulled the phone away from her ear and pressed the end button.

"What happened?"

"He must've turned his phone off because it went straight to voicemail."

My heart sunk to the pit of my stomach after hearing Charlene's response. All I could think about was why were both of their phones off. *What in the world could they be doing? I mean, what was going on? Could it be a mere coincidence? Or were they doing something they shouldn't be doing?*

Charlene had her own take on the situation. She gave me this uncertain look and said, "You ain't gotta say a word but I know what you're thinking."

I didn't respond. My heart wouldn't let me. My pride consumed my heart. But that didn't stop Charlene from running her mouth.

"Don't you think it's strange that we can't get in touch with them?" she continued.

I continued to stand there speechless.

"I know it's hard for you to believe it but I know what my husband is capable of doing. So I know what's up. It wouldn't shock me if he had her in our bed breaking her back out right now."

"Nah, I know Trice. She wouldn't do that," I finally spoke up in my wife's defense.

Charlene stood to her feet. "Well, that may be true but don't forget who she's with. Leon is a womanizer. And he doesn't discriminate. So why you're standing here rooting for Trice, she's over my house doing her thing and ain't thinking about you."

I tried to come back at Charlene. But I couldn't think of the words to say, because she had a point. Leon was a dog. He loved the chase of hunting new women, especially if they looked good and were sexy. It didn't matter if they had a man. He welcomed the challenge of taking another man's property.

Unfortunately, homeboy or not, I wasn't an exception.

He showed me that when we were teenagers. I will never forget the time when I started talking to this young girl on our block. She was gorgeous. And she was a virgin. When I told Leon I was trying to get at her, he went behind my back and got there first. I didn't make a fuss about it, because we were homeboys. I never forgot about that.

Instead of feeding into Charlene's antics, I grabbed the cordless phone from the end table next to the love seat and began to dial Trice's number again. I wasn't ready to believe Leon was fucking the brains out of my wife. *No way.*

"Who are you calling?" Charlene asked me. She looked a bit worried. But I had to admit, I was more worried than she was.

"I'm calling Trice again."

Charlene took two steps towards me and leaned her ear near my phone. She didn't have to lean close for long, because as soon as the line connected, it once again went directly to voicemail. I started to leave her a message but I decided against it. I knew she was bad about checking her messages. So I pressed the off button and placed the phone back in its base.

Charlene looked at me and shook her head. "The voicemail picked up again, huh?"

"Yeah," I replied and then I dropped my head.

I took a seat on the sofa and laid my head back against the headrest. I was so devastated at the thought of what could be going on at Leon's house, I wanted to hop in my truck and ride over there to see what was going on. Then something inside of me told me I was being a little paranoid. I knew my wife. I knew she wouldn't dare cross the line and play herself . . . especially with my homeboy. There had to be a perfect explanation of why their phones were off. And sooner than later, I would find out what it was. I took a couple of deep breaths and tried to regroup.

Meanwhile, my eyes were closed. But not for long. I felt Charlene's hand rub my thigh. I lifted my head and opened my eyes. She had the most sympathetic look on her face.

"What are you thinking about?" she asked me.

"I'm thinking about whether or not I should take a ride over to your house."

Charlene didn't like the idea of me wanting to check up on Leon and Trice. Her whole expression changed. "That won't be a good idea. You would be blowing this whole contest up. And then none of us would be able to get our money at the end," she explained.

"Do you think I really care about that money...especially if there's a chance that I could lose my wife in the process?"

"Look Troy, I understand what you are saying. But what if we did go to my house and found out that nothing is going on? We would be looking really stupid and we would also lose our money."

"Wait a minute, why you singing another tune? You were just standing in front of me saying that they were probably fucking in your bed!" I snapped. "And now you're saying that they might not be doing anything? Make up your damn mind!"

I was frustrated and I expressed it. And honestly, I was kinda tired of Charlene. I disliked being around flaky chicks and she was taking the damn cake. This was about money for her. I could use the change. Hell, I was the one who thought of the idea, did the research and contacted the show. But no way was I losing my wife in the process.

"All I'm saying is that I know my husband. I know what he's capable of doing, which is why I am going to leave his ass when all this is over. And if you say you know your wife and she wouldn't fall into Leon's trap then I believe you. But please don't blow this thing up before its time. All I'm asking you to do is leave well enough alone until we get through these last couple of days. And if you find out they got together at the end, you handle it then."

"I would rather prevent it from happening in the first place. You don't have anything to lose. I do."

"You could lose that ten grand."

"Did I tell you I didn't give a damn about that money?" I snapped once again. This bitch had already tweaked my nerves, now she was getting on my last fucking nerves. I was literally about to push her ass on the floor. All this shit she was talking didn't make any sense to me. One minute she was talking all crazy, saying Leon and Trice had to be fucking in her bed because their phones were turned off. Then she changed her story.

I knew what the deal was. She believed they're boning each other but she didn't want me to break it up. She wanted me to confront them about it after our arrangement was over. But I didn't think I could do that. I didn't think my heart would let me wait that long. I mean, I was human with feelings. So what would be the best remedy? Let her stay and risk her sleeping with him. Or call this whole thing off, rescue Trice from the dawg called Leon and cut my losses.

I knew one thing for sure, Charlene wasn't going to let me out of her sight until she could find a way to reason with me.

"Let me ask you something."

"Yeah, I'm listening," I replied.

"If you went by my house and found them having sex, what would you do?"

I thought for a second and then I said, "I don't know."

"Do you think you would attack Leon?" she continued.

I thought about seeing Leon on top of Trice, having his way with her. The thought got me sick to my stomach instantly. "Yeah, I would probably try to kill him with my bare hands," I finally said.

"And if you do that, you know you'll go to jail, right?"

"I probably wouldn't care."

"But you should. Because you would lose everything you've ever worked for. And I don't think killing Leon is worth that. He's my husband and the father of my child and I wouldn't throw my life away behind his filthy ass. So do me and you both a favor and let it go. I can guarantee you that if they are doing anything that they ain't supposed to be doing, it will come out. And you can take that one to the bank."

After Charlene made her point, I sat back on the sofa and thought about everything she said. And the more and more I thought about it, I realized that she had a point. If I went over there, I would definitely end up in jail and I didn't want that. All I needed to do was let this whole thing play out and if something was going on over there between them it would come out.

Once I came to term about my decision to leave well enough alone, I closed my eyes and said a silent prayer to God. I knew I needed God more than ever now . . . because I knew I wouldn't be able to do this alone.

find your inner mermaid

Wife Extraordinaire

BY KIKI SWINSON

Leon

Whether Charlene knew it or not, I was through with her slutty ass. I'd waited on this day for a long time and now it was finally here. I would be free at last of that lazy tramp for good. She couldn't imagine how she made my day by telling Trice that bullshit about her and Troy.

If you wanna know the truth, I wasn't mad with Troy at all. He did me a favor by fucking that grimy bitch. So I was gonna get Trice to remind me to thank him later. Now I knew she was gonna try to take me to court for child support, but I couldn't care less at this point. I would pay that dirty bitch five hundred dollars a month to keep her miserable ass away from me. Other than that, she couldn't and wouldn't get a fucking penny from me. And if she thought she was going to get a dime of the ten thousand dollars, she had another thing coming. When I got through with that ho, she's gonna wish she had never met me. I was going to make her life a living hell by the time I got through with her. I didn't want to talk to her filthy ass, so I decided to keep my damn cell phone off when I wasn't using it.

Trice stayed in my son's room for at least an hour before she came back downstairs. I could tell she had cried the entire time she was up there. I wanted to comfort her when she walked into the TV room, but I allowed her to have her space. I figured if she wanted me to do something for her, she would tell me.

"I tried to get some sleep but I couldn't stop thinking about my conversation with your wife," she said after she entered the room.

"That rat ain't my wife no more."

Trice took a seat on the sofa beside me. "I'm sorry for being so forward, but could you hold me?"

I was shocked by her question . . . and somewhat hesitant. But when I looked into her eyes and saw how hurt she was I couldn't deny her. I reached over and placed my arm around her neck. She immediately leaned into my armpit and laid her head against my chest. The smell of her perfume did wonders for me. It was intoxicating. Not to mention it felt good to have her face pressed against my body.

"I'm filing for divorce when all of this is over," she said.

I looked down at her face and saw a single tear fall down her face from each eye. She was hurt and there was no denying that.

"Don't you think you need to hear his side of the story first?" I asked her. Although Troy had stepped out on me and fucked my wife, I wasn't a hater. I really wanted Trice to think about what she was saying. I had known women to make really bad decisions when they were emotional. Knowing this, I felt Trice needed to think about what she was doing long and hard before she acted, or better yet, reacted.

She lifted her head up from my chest and looked directly at me. "I know exactly what I am doing. And I should've done it a long time ago when I suspected that he fucked around on me a couple of years ago," she growled.

I threw my hands up and smiled. "A'ight! Don't kill the messenger!" I said, hoping she'd smile. But it didn't work. She got more emotional. So I cradled her in my arms.

"You just don't know how hurt I am right now. I don't think I can ever speak to him."

"I know the feeling," I agreed. I was feeling the exact same way. I didn't want to see Charlene's face for that matter. She had done it for me.

Trice and I sat in that position for at least thirty minutes. She talked about how she was going to go on with her life after she and Troy split the money. She even talked about moving back to Florida where her parents had relocated after they retired. I listened to her map her life out while she cried her heart out. I swear I felt helpless as she lay in my arms. I wanted so badly to stop the pain she was feeling in her heart, but I knew there was nothing I could do. I did the only thing I could do—I just held her in my arms.

After a while, she did stop crying. But I had to admit that I had a hand in it. After she dried her tears, she thanked me for being there to listen to her and giving her a shoulder to cry on, and then she kissed me on the cheek. I didn't want it to stop there, so I leaned over and kissed her on the mouth. Her soft, wet lips sent sparks through my entire body. My dick got hard instantly. I believe sparks shot through her as well, because she bit down on my bottom lip very softly and then she stuck her tongue into my mouth.

I looked at her, trying to read her face, to see her expression. But she didn't have an expression. Her eyes were closed and it looked as if she was in another world. At one point I thought the kissing would stop, but it didn't. We kept alternating from kissing to sucking on one another's top and bottom lips. And it became more intense. Before I knew it, she had maneuvered her body from underneath my armpits to climbing on top of me. I found myself lying back on the sofa with her body pressed against mine. She wasn't as heavy as Charlene, so I knew I could manage and maneuver her with no problem. Plus my dick was getting more and more rock hard. I knew my little man down below would be able to handle her too.

"Please make love to me," she begged me.

I mean the words actually came out of her mouth. I couldn't believe it . . . but then again, I did. She was hurting and needed to take her mind off Troy. I guess I was the man who needed to man up for the job. She moaned between each kiss. She was hot as a fucking firecracker and I was ready to light that fire. The warm feeling from her body rubbed off on me and made me feel as if I was on cloud nine. I had to admit that Charlene never made me feel like this. My first sexual experience with her was out of lust, but then over a period of six months I started to have feelings for her.

"Leon, I want you inside of me now," she continued to beg. Without hesitation I turned her over on her back, pulled up her skirt and then I ripped her white satin panties off. Her legs were spread eagle and I had a full view of her fat pussy. Instead of pulling my dick out and ramming it inside of her, I had to stick my tongue inside of her so I could taste it first.

"I gotta taste you first," I told her. Then I dove head first between her legs. I stretched my tongue out as long as I could and licked her entire clit. I moved my tongue around in a circular motion and she began to go crazy. She jerked her pussy back and forth like a wild child. I loved every minute of it. She made me feel as if I was the man. I was in control and that's why I was so in tuned to her.

"Grind that pussy in my face," I demanded. And like a sex slave she did just that.

"Ooowwww, you make me feel so good," she moaned and then she wrapped her legs around my head.

Moments later, I inserted two of my fingers inside of her wet pussy. She jerked instantly, giving me the green light to continue penetrating her. I pushed my fingers in and out at least ten times before she started begging me to stick my dick inside of her. I couldn't lie I wanted her more than she appeared to want me. But I hesitated. I knew I didn't have any condoms on hand. I tried to rationalize how I would be able to fuck her without one. I wasn't trying to get her pregnant or catch something I wouldn't be able to get rid of, so I tried to hold off as long as I could by giving her as much foreplay as I possibly could. But she grew tired and begged me once more to penetrate her.

"I don't have a condom," I told her.

"I don't care. Just pull out when you're about to cum," she instructed me.

Hearing her tell me to pull my dick out when I am about to bust my nut was what I had already had in mind. It was a no-brainer. Going in her raw and catching AIDS or Herpes was on my mind more than anything. Even though I had no intentions on going back to Charlene, I didn't want to walk away from Trice with a medical condition. That wasn't a part of the plan. I had to ask her the one million dollar question.

"Is it safe?" I asked her.

She laid there and looked up at me. "Is what safe?" she asked.

"Have you been tested lately?" I replied.

She smiled. "Of course I have. Six months ago. Have you?"

Relieved by her answer, I smiled back at her. "Yeah, I was tested about ten months ago."

"Well, what are you waiting on? Show me what you got!" she continued and then she pulled me down on her.

It only took me three seconds flat to pull my dick out and slide it deep inside her pussy. The shit was like an explosion. Her pussy was so wet and sweet that I was about to lose my fucking mind. What was so weird was that while I was fucking the hell out of her, all I could think about was how Troy would feel to know I was banging the hell out of his wife. I knew he treasured her because he always talked about how much he loved her. He even talked about how he would feel if he ever lost her. She was his prize possession. But then I had to remind myself of how foul he was for fucking my wife. So Trice was fair game.

That's when a passing thought hit me. What if Charlene lied, which she was very good at. But there was no turning back now.

I dug in Trice's pussy for at least thirty minutes. I had her sexy ass on her back and then I flipped her on her knees. She enjoyed it as much as I did. And right before I was about to drain my wad in Trice's fat pussy, I pulled out and beat my dick against the back of her ass until all my juices filtered out on her ass cheeks.

"Damn! I haven't been fucked like that in a very long time," she said as she reached on the floor for her panties.

I got up from the sofa and stood to my feet with my dick in my hand and gave her the biggest smile my face could muster. But what made me smile even more was when she grabbed me by my belt buckle and pulled me back into her direction. I had no idea what she was about to do until she leaned into me and grabbed my dick in her hand. Before I could say one word, she pushed the head of my dick into her mouth and then she pulled it back out real slow. I was shocked and didn't know what the fuck to say. I was glad she said something first.

"I couldn't let your precious juices drip onto the floor," she told me with a smile.

After hearing her explanation, I smiled even more. She was a bad bitch. Just like that, I was falling for her. My heart was feeling that love spark and that type of feeling didn't come on me that easy. But for some reason, I was feeling this chick. She was everything a man could ever want. I didn't want to get my hopes up, but if she dumped Troy like she said she would, I could definitely see us getting together and making some shit happen.

After all the touchy feeling shit was over, I convinced her to take a shower with me. We got in the shower and played around with each other. I mean, we were acting like teenagers who were sneaking around in their parent's house. It was cool as hell and I enjoyed every bit of it. And right after we got out of the shower, we put on some clothes to lounge around the house and then she got in the kitchen and showed me her cooking skills.

Wife Extraordinaire

BY KIKI SWINSON

Trice

After all that love making popped off I took my ass to Leon's kitchen to see if I could whip us up something to eat. While I looked in the refrigerator, I smiled to myself thinking back on how I stuck Leon's dick in my mouth. I didn't know where that came from. I didn't suck Troy's dick. To do that for Leon really blew my mind. I couldn't for the life of me figure out why I did, but I didn't let it consume my thoughts. I had to switch gears and find us something we could sink our teeth into.

From what I saw, he didn't have much for me to work with, but I was able to scramble up a few things. I whipped up some seasoned ground beef with a little bit of my homemade gravy and then I poured it into a baking pan, along with a can of corn, mashed potatoes and some shredded cheese. When all the ingredients were layered, I had created my famous Sheppard's Pie.

"Hmmm, this smells so good," he commented before he took the first bite.

I sat across from him at the kitchen table so we could eat our food together. "Taste it and tell me what you think," I instructed him in my sexiest voice.

He did just that and after he let the food marinate on his taste buds, he smiled. "Ya Trice, this is so good. Charlene ain't never cooked something like this before."

"You've never had Sheppard's Pie before?"

"Nah, I haven't," he replied as he continued to stuff his face.

While I watched him enjoy my dish, I started feeding myself. During our dinner encounter he and I laughed and talked about everything underneath the sun. And what was so nice about it was that I found out he and I had a lot in common. We both liked staying at home and watching movies. We liked the R&B singer Musiq Soulchild and we both loved to cook. It seemed like he and I were perfect for each other. I even questioned him as to why we hadn't crossed paths before we met our spouses. He didn't have an answer for me, so we laughed it off and tried to make the best out of the situation we were currently in.

After dinner, we got up from the table and retired to the TV room. We watched the tail end of the movie *Brooklyn's Finest*. While he was engrossed in the movie, I wondered to myself how my life would've been if I had Leon instead of Troy. I mean, he seemed like a good guy. I realized he and I had more things in common than my own husband.

Aside from the cheating and the fact he didn't cook, Troy was a good catch as well. I just wished I had guarded my heart from him better than I did. There was no question in my mind on the day we got married that we were going to be together for the rest of our lives. I've been told that money is the root of all evil. Whoever said it was definitely right. Troy was fixated on the idea of the trading spouse arrangement. I wasn't too keen on the idea but normally when he said or did something, I always went along with him. And look where it got us this time.

I knew when all of this was over there would be a lot of regrets. Especially after all of the camera footage had circulated. I could see Troy trying to hide his dirt. But I didn't need to see it. I heard enough from Charlene's big mouth. I didn't have any interest in rehashing anything that happened between them two. And I knew the same would apply to Leon. I couldn't see him caring one way or another to see the footage from my house and I didn't blame him.

I couldn't speak for Charlene and Troy. They probably wanted to see what Leon and I had going on. But I didn't give a fuck? Fuck them! They could both kiss my ass, because it's all about me now. I wasn't playing Ms. Goodie Two Shoes anymore. Those days were long gone.

Wife Extraordinaire

BY KIKI SWINSON

Charlene

Troy hadn't said anything else to me, but I heard him searching high and low for his Blackberry. He literally tore his house upside down looking for his phone. I came really close to giving him his phone back, but I couldn't let him know I had it the whole time. I knew he would have gotten rid of my ass then.

I was still trying to get him to fuck around on his wife but so far he had not budged. I couldn't tell you if that chick had roots on him or not, but whatever it was it had him on lock and key. His focus was on trying to find his phone, so he could see if she tried to call him and left him a voicemail.

While he searched every crack and crevice, I sat back on the sofa and shook my head in disgust. The word sucker was written all over his face. Quiet as it was kept Trice had this poor nigga wrapped around her finger. She was way across town in the house with my husband and he was walking around here like he had lost his best friend. The sight of him on this scavenger hunt was starting to get on my damn nerves. I wanted to tell him to sit his stupid ass down but I decided against it. I was on his territory so I knew it was best to stay in my own lane.

"This is so weird that I can't find my damn phone," he said aloud as he looked underneath pillow cushions on the loveseat and sofa.

I didn't say a word. But I did get up and acted as if I was helping him look for his phone. Meanwhile, my cell phone rang. I took it from my pocket and looked at the caller ID. I didn't recognize the number so I hesitated to answer it. But then I decided against it. I figured it might be somebody important.

"Hello," I said.

Troy stopped looking for his phone and turned his attention to me. He looked directly into my mouth. I guess he hoped it was either Leon or Trice calling to talk.

"Can I speak to Lacy?" the female caller asked me.

"I'm sorry but you have the wrong number," I told her.

When I disconnected the call, Troy's questions began immediately. "Who was that?"

"I didn't get her name. But she asked to speak to somebody named Lacy. I told her she had the wrong number."

"Oh, I heard a female's voice so I thought it was Trice."

"No, it wasn't Trice," I replied nonchalantly and then I laid my phone down on the end table next to the lamp.

Troy dropped his head and walked out the room. I got really bored with him walking around the house as if he had just lost his best friend, so I spoke up.

"Troy, what is the deal with you? You are walking around this house like a chicken with his head cut off. You've got to lighten up. I am about to pull all of my hair out watching you walk back and forth."

"I'm sorry. It's just that I can't function without my phone. And I know Trice has probably been trying to call me. So I need to get my hands on it."

| 90 |

"It wouldn't surprise me if you dropped it when you were out earlier," I chimed in. I was trying to deter him from thinking that he misplaced his phone somewhere around the house. But he didn't take the bait.

"No. That can't be because the last time I remember seeing it was when I was in the kitchen getting myself a bottle of water. I swear I remember setting it down somewhere in the kitchen."

"Well, if that's what you remember then that's where it should be," I told him.

He stood there with a clueless look on his face and said, "I've checked everywhere in there but I couldn't find it."

I sighed. "Well, I don't know what to tell you," I told him and then I redirected my attention to the TV. When he saw I had took my focus off of him, he left the room and continued on with his search.

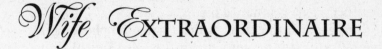

Wife Extraordinaire

BY KIKI SWINSON

Troy

I was about to take my fucking head off. I was so frustrated that I couldn't find my damn Blackberry. This type of shit hadn't happened before. And it wouldn't surprise me if my phone mysteriously got up and walked off by itself. If I found out Charlene picked up and hid my phone all this time, then she was definitely going to feel my wrath. I didn't trust her. I finally understood why Leon was tired of her. I hadn't been with her the full week and I was tired of her. She was indeed selfish. It was about fucking me and getting the money. She didn't give a damn about Leon and I wasn't sure if she cared about their child.

In the meantime, I was gonna use the house phone and try to get my wife back on the line. I didn't know if something was going on or if it was just bad timing. After I dialed her cell phone number, her voicemail picked up instantly. My heart dropped. I couldn't' figure out why her phone kept going straight to voicemail. I knew she had her charger. Because of that, I was nervous. I hope there was a damn good explanation why her phone was turned off.

Instead of calling her again, I hung the phone up and got me a Corona out the refrigerator. I needed something to calm me down. I was getting pretty frustrated and not getting the answers I was looking for wasn't sitting well with me. Immediately after I took the top off my beer, I took a swig and made my way back into the TV room with Charlene.

"Why didn't you bring me one?" she smiled.

"Oh, my bad. I'll be right back," I assured her and retreated back into the kitchen. I retrieved the beer from the refrigerator, opened it and took it to her. She didn't hesitate to gulp it down after I handed it to her. I took a seat next to her and we began to drink together. One beer turned into two and two turned into three. Before we knew it, we had drunk the entire twelve-pack of Coronas. She was toasted and so was I. The alcohol completely took my mind off Trice and the fact she was over another nigga's house.

I guess I needed something to take my mind off her. I was going crazy wondering what she was doing while I was running around here searching for a damn phone. I was okay now—or so I hoped. Those Coronas I drunk got me feeling real nice. They had Charlene feeling really nice too, because she acted as if she couldn't keep her damn hands off me. She started feeling my dick and she wouldn't stop. I had to admit that I wasn't interested in fucking her. But getting her to suck my dick crossed my mind. I started to ask her to pull it out and lick on it. But she beat me to the punch.

"Let me give you some head," she said as she began to get down on her knees.

My dick was already hard. I didn't have to worry about getting erect. I sat and opened my legs a bit. Charlene unzipped the zipper on my shorts and gently pulled my meat out. I had to admit that my shit was proudly standing at attention. She smiled at it and then she started talking to it. It was bugging me the fuck out.

"You want mama to take care of you?" she began to say and then she kissed the head of it. "I'ma make you feel real good."

She licked the tip of the head. Then she licked the head and slid my entire dick into her mouth. The pressure she put on my dick and the warmness of her mouth sent me over the edge. I was about to pull every strand of hair she had in her head but I held my composure. I laid my head back against the headrest of the sofa. I closed my eyes a few times. When she did one of those tricks with her tongue to stimulate my dick I opened my eyes to see what she was doing.

"Damn right, girl, suck this dick," I encouraged her. She seemed as if she enjoyed sucking my meat more than I was. She had my dick soaked and wet. She even spit on the tip of it and then she licked it back off. This was a huge fucking turn on.

I almost found myself wanting to fuck her pussy. That's just how good she was making my dick feel. But I snapped back into reality. I allowed her to suck my dick since that's technically not cheating. Bill Clinton did it and got away with it. I mean, if you look at it I didn't plan on penetrating her and I didn't plan on kissing her, so I was in the clear. I didn't believe she would go back and tell Leon and Trice I let her give me some head. That would be stupid on her part. She would look like the ho. So I thought I was cool.

After twenty-two licks and sucks later, Charlene helped me explode right in her face. She massaged the shaft of my dick until the cum erupted from my dick. I saw her swallow some of it too. I smiled at her because she took me out of my element. I hadn't had my dick sucked in forever. She took me back to the days when I used to fuck with chicks that did all kinds of nasty shit for me. I wished Trice would serve me like Charlene just did me. I believed our sex life would be much better.

Immediately after she drained me for every ounce of protein I had, she stood to her feet and began taking off her shorts, while I was stuffing my dick back into my shorts. Shocked by my actions she asked me what I was doing?

"I'm getting ready to go into the bathroom and clean myself up," I replied and then I stood to my feet.

"What about me?" she asked. By this time she had taken off her shorts and her panties. She kept her bra and tank top on.

"Whatcha want me to do? I just came. I ain't got the energy to fuck you."

"You ain't gotta do anything. Just let me get on top of you. I can make myself cum," she told me and she sounded desperate. But I couldn't help her. My dick had gone limp and it would take an act of God to get it erect again. But who was I kidding? Even if my dick was able to get erect again, I wasn't going to play myself and stick my dick in her pussy. That's where I drew the line.

"So you're telling me I'm ass out, huh?"

"Look, even if I did let you get on top of me, how are you going to get your rocks off when my dick ain't gon' be able to get hard?"

She sucked her teeth. "This is un-fucking-believable!" she snapped. Then she reached down on the floor and grabbed her panties and shorts. I walked by her and carried my ass to the bathroom to clean off. I knew she was furious with me but I didn't care. I had no intentions on fucking her from the beginning. She set herself up for this let down. At the end of the day, she should blame herself.

Wife Extraordinaire

BY KIKI SWINSON

Trice

"**G**ood morning, sleepy head," Leon said to me. I opened my eyes and saw him looking in my eyes. He leaned over me as he sat alongside of the bed. I slept in his bed last night and I had to admit, it felt good. My back felt well rested but my heart sung a completely different song. I realized the alcohol had worn off, so reality reared its ugly face and reminded me about the night I had with Leon.

Every intricate detail ran through my mind and I began to feel really awful. The more I thought about what I had done, the worse my heart and stomach felt. But then I had to remind myself that I stepped out on my commitment to Troy, because he left the door open for me after he stepped out on me with Charlene. I needed to rationalize the entire scenario so I could move forward without the guilt.

"Good morning," I replied and then I rubbed my eyes. They were glassy from the sunlight beaming from the bedroom windows.

"Wanna go out for breakfast?" he asked me.

Without thinking much about it, I said, "Yes, sure."

"Well, get up and get dressed. I wanna take you to this place where they got some good ass breakfast."

I smiled. "Okay."

Leon pulled back the comforter and helped me out of bed. If it weren't for Leon's T-shirt and a pair of my panties I would be naked. He smacked me on my butt when I stood on my feet. I giggled at his child's play because it was cute. I felt like a teenager sneaking around with her boy toy while my parents were out of town.

When I got into the bathroom Leon already had my towel and bath cloth laid out for me. I hopped into the bathtub and took a hot shower. I couldn't believe it but Leon actually washed my back for me. In all the years I had been married to Troy, he never attempted to wash my back, even when we showered together. This was something new and even though it was a small gesture, I found it to be nice. Leon was generally a sweet guy. I thought he would try to get a quickie from me, but he remained a gentleman and kept his hands to himself.

After we both got dressed, we headed out to this breakfast café in Chesapeake. This was my first time at the eatery and I must admit, it had a nice southern appeal to it. It was family-owned and operated and they had superb hospitality. Leon and I both ordered the house special, which was a stack of pan-cakes, our choice of bacon or sausage and two eggs cooked the way we wanted. We talked and laughed while we ate. And for some reason, it seemed as if we didn't run out of things to talk about. I really enjoyed myself.

Once Leon paid our check, we exited the restaurant, got back in his car and headed to the oceanfront. Leon had this brilliant idea for us to go bike riding on the strip. Judging the book by its cover, I never would have imagined he would like to go out on an outing such as this. When I first met him, I'd bet every dime in my bank account that he was a street thug who sat in the house, puffed on a black and mild while he played Xbox 360. This side of Leon definitely caught me off guard.

During our bike ride, we ventured out on the beach area as well as the busy strip. The whole scene was picture perfect. The happy ending to any story. I enjoyed every minute of it.

When the bike ride ended, Leon and I got a cup of ice cream from the Cold Stone and then we sat out on the beach. The scenery was beautiful and I had good company to go along with it. I felt like I was in heaven. A couple of times Leon spoon-fed me some of his ice cream. I thought it was so sweet of him to do.

"I am so glad Troy talked me into doing this wife trading thing, because I am having the best time of my life."

I smiled. "So am I."

He smiled back at me. "So what do you want to do after this?"

"I'm not sure," I replied.

"Wanna go bungee jumping?" he asked me.

I was at a lost for words when he asked me if I wanted to go bungee jumping. I had always been afraid of heights. But the fact he wanted to do something exciting gave me a warm feeling inside my heart. Unfortunately, I had to be realistic. I had always been afraid of heights, so I had to decline his offer.

I did however think of something more adventurous for us to do. When I asked him if he wanted to go play miniature golf, he happily accepted. After we finished our ice cream, he grabbed me by the hand and escorted me down to the golf park. To all the strangers around us, we appeared to be newlyweds. But he and I knew differently. We also knew we had significant others who were spending time with one another, doing God knows what. On the surface it seemed as if we didn't have a care in the world. But we knew better.

Leon expressed his discontent for Charlene. I expressed my feelings of betrayal to Leon about Troy. I felt violated to the tenth power. However, being in the company of Leon, I found myself not thinking about Troy at all. Leon totally took my mind off my no good ass husband. That's exactly what I needed. I even made sure I kept my cell phone off, so Troy couldn't contact me. At this juncture, I didn't want to talk to him.

Wife Extraordinaire

BY KIKI SWINSON

Troy

Before I headed to work this morning, I got up and tried to get Trice on the phone, but her voicemail picked up on the first ring. For the life of me, I couldn't figure out why she had her cell phone turned off. This was unlike her. So I began to get worried. I wanted to call Leon's cell, but I didn't know his number by heart. Since I hadn't found my Blackberry I had no other choice but to wake Charlene up to get his number from her.

I entered my guest room with the cordless house phone in my hand and repeatedly tapped Charlene on her shoulder until she woke up. After four taps she finally turned over and squinted her eyes as she adjusted to the sunlight.

"I need Leon's cell phone number," I told her.

She turned and laid completely on her back. "What time is it?" she asked me.

"It's a few minutes after seven."

She paused for a couple of seconds and then she reached underneath the covers and grabbed her cell phone. After she flipped it open, she quickly closed it back. "Damn, I forgot to charge it last night," she finally said.

"I don't need to use it. I just want Leon's number," I told her.

"I know. But I can't get his number from my phone because it's completely dead."

Frustrated by her response, I said, "You don't know your own husband's number?"

"No. I don't. Because he just got his number changed two weeks ago. So I programmed it in my phone without trying to memorize it."

"Did you talk to him last night before you went to bed?"

"Nope. I ain't got shit to say to him," she barked.

"Well, can you charge your phone up so I can get his number before I leave for work?"

"I'm telling you right now that he ain't gon' answer his phone."

"He may not answer it for you, but I know he'll answer it for me," I assured her and then I tapped her on her arm. "So can you get up and charge your phone?"

Charlene took her time but she slid out of bed and searched for her charger. I left the room and headed downstairs to the kitchen. I made myself a cup of hot tea while I waited for her to charge her phone.

Meanwhile, she joined me in the kitchen. She walked in wearing a white tank top and a pair of thong panties. Her panties hugged her pussy real tight so it looked inviting. She had a three-inch gap between her thighs and that turned me on too. My dick was getting hard by the seconds. But I knew I couldn't fuck with her this morning. Therefore, I immediately took my focus off her and concentrated on stirring the sugar I had just added to my cup of tea.

"Cooking breakfast this morning?" she asked me. Then she paraded herself by me. She walked to the refrigerator and opened the door. She stood there and acted as if she was looking for something. Hell, I knew better. She stood there so I could get a good view of her fat ass. I mean her ass was so big and soft looking. Being a man, I thought about bending her ass over and fucking the shit out of her. I actually pictured sliding my dick into her pussy and fucking the shit out of her while I smack the back of her ass cheeks. Boy, that sounded like fun. However, I quickly snapped back into reality. I allowed her to suck my dick the night before so I refused to take it farther than that. She seemed like one of those fatal attraction chicks who wanted to attach herself to me. Since I didn't need that headache, I answered her question by telling her I wasn't cooking breakfast and I turned my attention back to my cup of tea.

She grabbed a bottle of spring water from the refrigerator, took a swallow and gave me this disappointed expression. "But I thought you were the host around here."

I gave her a fake ass smile. "I got to be at work within the next hour so the only thing I can do for you is make you a bowl of cereal," I told her as I took a sip of my tea.

"You know what I noticed about you?" she asked me.

"What?"

"It seems like every time I want you to do something for me, you always find an excuse not to do it."

"It's not like that," I lied.

"Then how is it?" she pressed the issue as she took another swallow of water.

I took a sip of my hot tea. "You just catch me at bad times."

"So if I asked you to slide my panties to the side and fuck me right now, would you do it?"

I wanted to laugh in her face because she caught me completely off guard with that question. One part of me wanted to tell her I wouldn't fuck her with her husband's dick, because she wasn't worth me losing my wife. But I held my tongue and acted like a gentleman.

"Look Charlene, you're an attractive woman, but I can't get down with you like that. Leon is my homeboy so I can't cross that line," I finally explained.

Charlene's mouth dropped wide open. "You can't cross the line!" she roared. "You already did that when you got me to suck your dick last night."

"That was different."

"How the fuck was that different?"

"It's different because I didn't penetrate you," I tried to explain. Why I tried, I don't know. The more I talked, the more frustrated and angry she got.

She took two steps towards me and slammed her bottle water on the countertop near me. "So you're saying that you hadn't crossed the line with me because I only sucked your dick?"

I nodded in the affirmative.

"Are you in denial?" Her tone was full of venom. "You gotta be, because you received oral sex from me. So the second you let me put your dick in my mouth, the line was crossed. And there's no turning back from that."

"Look, there's no need to be getting upset. So let's drop the whole conversation."

"Yeah, how fucking convenient!" she replied sarcastically and then she snatched her bottle of water off the countertop and made her exit.

I watched her ass jiggle when she stormed out of the kitchen. She had eye candy ass and that was it. Otherwise, no substance. However, that ass was juicy. She was a nice sight to see early in the morning even though our conversation ended on a bad note. I figured she'd be all right, because we only had three days left. When it was all said done, Charlene's ghetto ass would be returning to her house and Trice would be back in mine. I couldn't wait.

Wife Extraordinaire

BY KIKI SWINSON

Charlene

I had to get away from that nigga, Troy, and go to the bedroom before I flipped out on his ass. How dare that bastard try to play me like he did? I'm not a fucking play toy and he needs to know that. He had me sucking his fucking dick last night and had the audacity not to want to fuck me after the fact. And then to add insult to injury, that motherfucker had the balls to tell me he couldn't make me breakfast. He was supposed to be the host. Not me! So what's his fucking problem?

"You think your phone has charged up enough so you can get Leon's number out of it?" I heard him yell from downstairs. Instead of answering him, I closed the bedroom door. I sat back down on the bed and waited for him to come upstairs behind me and asked me that question again so I could tell him to kiss my ass. He definitely barked up the wrong tree this morning. I don't play with niggas . . . especially ones that try to take me for granted.

He better ask my dumb ass husband what I was capable of, because I was a bitch when a nigga rubbed me the wrong way.

Before I left this house, he was gonna wish he'd never met me. I was going to tear his perfect little world apart. And his wife was going to be caught dead in the middle. *Watch and see.*

Five minutes passed and Troy climbed up the flight of stairs and showed up at the bedroom door. He knocked four times and called out my name, but I ignored him. So he took it upon himself to let himself into the room. I knew I would fuck his head up if I was naked when he walked in, so that's exactly what I did.

"Oh, I'm sorry," he said when he saw me as he covered his eyes. He didn't leave the room but made sure he kept his eyes covered while he talked to me. "Do you think your phone charged up enough so that you'd be able to turn it on and get your husband's number?"

I rolled my eyes at him. "No, it's gonna take at least thirty minutes before it's charged up really good."

"Come on now, it doesn't take that long," he griped. I could tell he had gotten frustrated with my answer, because he took his hand from his eyes and gave me this intense look. In my opinion, he looked as if he wanted to choke my ass. So I braced myself and waited for him to make the first move.

"Charlene, I don't believe your phone gotta be charged up for thirty minutes to get it to work," he continued as he rushed towards my phone. He was fixated on getting Leon's number so he could get in touch with his wife. But I wasn't having that. I wasn't about to let him go through my phone as if it belonged to him. That was my personal property and he needed to respect that fact. So I grabbed my phone before he could get it. Since I was able to get to it before he could, he went to the extent of trying to take it from me.

"Girl, stop playing and give me that phone," he demanded.

I was shocked at how aggressive he had gotten over my damn cell phone. He wrestled me down to the bed while I was naked so he could take my phone from me. How fucking crazy was he? He had a lot of nerve.

"Can you get the fuck off me?" I asked him in batted breath. I was tired as hell trying to prevent him from taking my phone out of my hand.

"Give me your phone and I'll get off you," he told me.

Still struggling to keep my dell in my hands, I managed to turn my body over on my stomach. I buried the phone underneath me while he had me penned to the bed.

"I am not going to give you my phone," I told him.

"Well, I'm not gonna get off you until you do."

"That's fine. I can be in this position all day," I told him. Then I started grinding my butt on his dick. He tried desperately to block my advances but he couldn't. His dick was getting hard by the second.

"Hmmm, I feel that dick of yours getting hard on my ass," I continued and then I giggled.

"That ain't my dick."

I laughed aloud at his lie. "Come on Troy. Stop fronting. You know you want this pussy."

"Charlene, give me your phone," he said, trying to dismiss my comment.

"I told you what you gotta do," I replied as I stuck to my guns. I wasn't about to give him my phone. If he gave me some of that big dick he had, then he could get anything he wanted from me.

He hesitated for a moment, then he said, "A'ight. You win. I'ma give you some of this dick. But as soon as I push this meat up inside of you I want you to hand me the phone."

After he agreed to give me a quick fuck, I rested my breast on my hands to secure my phone and then I got on my knees and poked out my butt to give him easy access. I looked back at him while he unbuttoned his work pants. Within seconds, he had his big dick in his hand ready to go for what he knew. I was so ready for him to give me everything he had.

"You ready for this dick?" he asked me as he stood alongside the bed. Before I could answer him, he smacked me on my butt cheeks with the head of his dick. I watched as his dick bounced back off my ass every time he popped it.

"Whatcha waiting for? Stick it in this wet pussy!" I whined. I swear, my pussy was leaking with juices. I wanted him like there was no tomorrow.

"Turn around and lick on it first," he demanded.

I hesitated at first because I was only ready for him to fuck my brains out. I wasn't in the mood to give him head. I figured since I was a thorough bitch when it came to sucking nigga's dicks, I could kill two birds with one stone and get him so hyped up that he'd give my pussy a good workout. I got up from my knees and turned around towards Troy with my cell phone gripped tightly in my left hand. With my right hand I grabbed his dick and leaned in towards it. As soon as I pushed the top half of his penis into my mouth, he reached underneath my chin and tried to snatch the phone away from me. Too bad for him I saw him coming, long before he made his move.

I immediately took his dick from my mouth and jumped back. When I did that, he pushed me on my back but I was able to keep him from taking the phone from me. I placed both of my hands behind my back. Troy wrestled with me to get my hands from behind my back.

"Stop playing and give me your damn phone," he grunted.

To get him away from me, I managed to kick him in the stomach. I was aiming for his dick since it was hanging out of his pants, but he blocked me. After we wrestled for a few more seconds, he got tired and let me go. He huffed and puffed as he crawled off me.

"Man, fuck it! I ain't got time for this shit," he complained as he climbed off the bed. When he stood back on his feet, he pushed his dick back into his pants and zipped up his pants.

I sat there on the bed and watched him as he whined about not being about to get my cell phone away from me. I cracked a smile at him and told him how I felt about his little game.

"When you play childish games, you get played like a child," I commented.

I thought Troy would reply to my comment but he didn't. Instead, he walked out of the room without opening his mouth. When he shut the door behind himself, I laid there and reflected on how he promised to fuck me and reneged on me once again. I felt violated once again and to get his ass back for leading me on, I vowed to make his fucking Blackberry disappear forever.

Wife Extraordinaire

BY KIKI SWINSON

Leon

Trice and I hung out all day at the beach and I could definitely say we enjoyed each other's company. We headed back to my place around four o'clock that evening. As soon as we stepped through my front door, we laid it down. She got her a spot on one end of my sofa and I sat my ass in my recliner and leaned the chair back as far as I could. Before I got good and comfortable, I turned on the TV and flipped to an old *Sanford and Son* rerun. By the time the show was halfway over, Trice was sound asleep.

I found myself staring at her during the commercial breaks. She looked so peaceful and I found her more beautiful than ever. I even went to the extent of getting out of my chair to kiss her on the forehead. When I sat back down in my chair I stared at her some more. The question of why couldn't she had been my wife kept circling my mind. I believed if she was my wife instead of Troy's, then I would have been a happier man. She possessed all the qualities I looked for in a woman. She smelled good. She was classy and was funny. Plus, her pussy was good. I could also tell she was a clean freak, which was what I loved the most.

Charlene was one nasty bitch. She would leave the bathroom tub dirty for at least ten days before she got off her ass and cleaned it. She would also leave the kitchen sink filled with dirty dishes for two to three days. I hate washing dishes. So I had to curse her out for an hour before she'd get in there and handle her business.

I still couldn't believe Charlene cleaned the whole house before she left our house to go to Troy's crib. When I came from work and saw her busting the suds in the kitchen sink, I asked her was she feeling all right. Of course I can't remember what she said, but I was sure it was something slick that came out of her mouth. I shook my head and she went on about her business.

While I daydreamed about the ifs, ands and buts, it dawned on me that I hadn't heard my cell phone ring for quite some time. I remembered turning the power off last night after I talked to Charlene and never turned it back on. When I pressed the power button, the screen lit up instantly. I looked at the LCD screen and noticed I had five voicemails and ten text messages. There was no doubt in my mind that all those messages came from Charlene. I wasn't in the mood to listen to the voicemails so I strolled down the menu bar and pulled up her text messages. I braced myself for every nasty word I was about to read, because her last conversation ended on a bad note.

Nigga u so funny it's pathetic! U always act like I'm da one who fucked up our marriage, the first message read.

U fucked it up a long time ago when u fucked dat bitch, the second message read.

The third text read, U doin' me a fava by tellin me its over. Fuck u! I can do betta!

Afta all dis is ova I'm taking my half of da $ & I'm leavin. So kiss my ass! BITCH!

After reading the last message I pressed the red exit button. I figured I had read enough. There was no need for me to continue to feed into her bullshit. She and I both knew what time it was. Our marriage was over a long time ago. Since she said she's leaving, I was going to let her ass go. So later in life when my son came to me and asked me why we divorced, I was going to tell him his mother left me. And that would be the end of that.

Right after I exited the text message application, I stuck my phone down into my front pocket and watched Trice as she laid there before me. While I stared at her flawless features, I started thinking of the possibilities of *her and I* becoming *one* . . . being together after she divorced Troy. The thought of her being in my life made me feel good. I would be so happy. Now I knew Troy wouldn't be in favor of this and I knew this would fuck up our friendship, but hey, I figured what's good for him was good for me. I mean, it ain't like he hadn't fucked my wife. So he'd get over it one day.

I could see it now. Trice and I could be like Will and Jada Pinkett Smith, without all the money. I could definitely see her as my partner. She seemed so sweet. The fact that we had a lot of things in common gave me the best feeling ever. There was no doubt that she was my soul mate. I could honestly see myself not fucking around on her either. She was the type of chick a nigga would be a fool to mess up with. I swear, I was counting down the days until all of this was over and she broke the news to Troy. Boy, I was going to be sitting on top of the world . . . of course with Trice at my side.

After I felt as if I had stared at her long enough, I got up from my chair. I suddenly had a certain urge for a beer. Since I didn't have any cold ones in my refrigerator, I decided to head out to the local corner store. Before I left the house, I tapped Trice on her arm and told her I was about to go to the store. After she opened her eyes, I asked her if she wanted something while I was out. She told me no.

"Well, if you think of something while I'm out, call me," I told her and then I left.

Troy

On my way home from work I began thinking about how I hadn't been able to speak with Trice for the last couple of days. I thought about wrecking shop a few times. The fact Charlene's dumb ass wouldn't give me Leon's number sent me over the edge. I was really close to telling that bitch to get the fuck out of my crib. But I kept cool. I only had a couple more days with this cunt and then she'd be gone for good, back at her own house driving her husband crazy.

When I merged onto Highway 264 I began to drive the entire seven miles to get to my exit, but I had a sudden urge to make a detour and stop off in Norfolk. So that's what I did.

The idea of going by Leon's place fueled my adrenaline. It gave me an energy blast I hadn't felt in a while. All I wanted to do was see Trice. I didn't have to talk to her. I just wanted to get one good look at her, just to make she was all right. Once I accomplished that mission, I promised I would leave immediately. I knew she wanted me to have the ten thousand dollar cash prize as much as I did, so I knew I couldn't jeopardize losing it.

As soon as I arrived in Leon's neighborhood, I slowed down my truck and cruised down every street until I arrived on the one he resided. My heart immediately started beating uncontrollably. I knew it was a combination of trying not to get caught and wanting desperately to see Trice's face. But as soon as I came within two hundred feet of his house I noticed his car wasn't nowhere in sight. So I instantly became angry. I looked down at my watched and saw that it was a few minutes after seven o'clock, so I wanted to know where in the hell could they be? And since I didn't have the answers to my questions, I decided to pull my truck over and park it at a safe distance from his house. I figured if I waited around for a few minutes, then they'd probably show up.

Meanwhile, as I sat in my truck I realized how frequent police officers patrolled this neighborhood. This part of Norfolk wasn't as hood as the other parts of the city, but it wasn't the nicest. Leon was considered a blue-collar worker. His wife, Charlene, was borderline Section-8 and hood fabulous. Hell, if I called her that she would take it as a compliment.

I remember the day they met. Charlene looked a lot better back then and she had a little bit more class than she did now. I think she switched up on my boy when she started hanging out at Upscale's night club every Thursday, Friday and Saturday night. Leon used to complain about it but it didn't work. She had the attitude that she could do anything she wanted. So when she popped up pregnant, Leon refused to believe the baby was his until she gave him a paternity test. When the results came back, Leon was proven to be the father.

I couldn't imagine the drama, especially when it came to childbirth. The birth of a child supposed to be golden, not drama fueled between the parents because the man refused to believe that he was the father.

I thought their relationship would turn around but it didn't. And the way things look now, I didn't think their situation would ever work out. I did know that I wouldn't let their drama affect me and Trice's marriage. I would die before I let their mess filter over into my household. Hell no! I wouldn't let that shit happen.

After I ran down all the wrong decisions Leon and Charlene made, I saw the Dodge Magnum headlights coming up behind me. The closer the car got to me, the more visible it became. Once the car got within five feet of my car I knew it was Leon behind the wheel. I immediately readjusted my eyes to look in my rearview mirror to see if I saw Trice in the passenger seat, but I couldn't because it was too dark. So I waited for them to pass me and when they did I fixed my eyes on the passenger side door. I knew that I would be able to get a better look from this angle. When the car came side by side with my truck, I looked straight into the passenger side window and my heart sunk in the pit of my stomach.

She wasn't there. That's when I knew she had to be inside of his house. I waited for Leon to park his car and then I called him over to my truck. He had this weird look on his face as he approached me.

"What's up?" he said while he tried to manage three grocery bags in his hands.

I tried to play it cool. I didn't want him to think I was sweating him and Trice. So I reached outside my truck and gave him the proper handshake. "Everything good?" I started off.

"Yeah, I just ran off to the store to get a few things for the house. Trice didn't wanna come. We hung out at the beach all day so she's in the house taking a nap."

"Oh, so she's in the house?"

Leon took a look at his surroundings and then he looked back at me. "Yeah, she's probably still asleep too," he finally said. Then he came back at me and said, "You know if you get caught being around here, those people ain't gon' give you and Trice that ten grand."

"I know. But I had to stop over here because I've been trying to call her phone and I keep getting her voicemail. And then I fucked around and lost my phone and asked your wife for your number, so I could call you and ask you to let me speak to Trice. But she acted like she didn't want me to talk to you."

Leon shook his head. "I told you that bitch was crazy!"

I cracked a smile. "Remember you said that. Not me."

Leon turned around to take a quick look at his house and then he looked back at me. "Want me to tell her to call you if she's up?" he asked me.

"Yeah, tell her to call the house phone," I replied.

"Yeah, a'ight, I can do that," he told me and then he slapped me some dap as if to say he was about to make his exit. But I wasn't about to let that nigga leave without giving me his cell phone number.

"What's your cell phone number again?" I asked him.

He acted as if I had caught him off guard. He stood there and acted as if he had to think about it before he gave it to me. Then after thirty seconds, he finally gave it to me. He said it so fast I had to ask him to repeat it once again. Immediately after he gave it to me for the second time, he reminded me that he needed to let me go so I wouldn't get caught by the people.

I took in his lame ass excuse and watched him walk away from my truck. When he disappeared into the house, I pulled off. As I drove away from his neighborhood, I thought to myself how weird that nigga acted. As long as I've known him he never acted standoffish to me like he just did. I noticed how he tried to blame his behavior on the money we supposed to be getting, but my gut was telling me something was different.

When I got back to my house, Charlene was in the kitchen eating Chinese food she ordered. I gave her the biggest smile I could muster up and said hello. She looked at me as if I was crazy before she spoke back to me. I could tell she wasn't in the mood to talk to me because of what happened earlier, but it didn't matter to me. I was going to get what I wanted to say off my chest.

"I just saw Leon," I told her as I stood three feet away from her.

She stopped chewing her food. "So what?" she spat.

I threw my hands up. "Damn! Don't bite my head off."

"I ain't gonna touch you. But at the same time, I don't wanna hear shit about that trifling ass nigga. I'm sitting here enjoying my food and that's how I would like to be."

"A'ight. No problem," I replied and then I turned to leave the kitchen. But then I thought to myself that I couldn't let her off that easy. She made it perfectly known that she was tired of her husband as well as me and that she couldn't wait to get away from us all. So I had to make mention of that. I stopped in my tracks and turned back around.

"I know you're glad you only have two more days left to be here."

"Trust me, I'm counting down the minutes," she replied and then she rolled her eyes at me and put her attention back on her food.

I smiled and shook my head because I could see how miserable she was and believe it or not, it tickled me. I swear, I was so proud of myself for not sticking my dick in her. That chick was insane. I had always known that when you fuck women who are not emotionally stable, they would ruin a man's life. Boy, did I make a good judgment call with that?

Wife Extraordinaire

BY KIKI SWINSON

Trice

L eon woke me up with a kiss on my forehead. I opened my eyes and he gave me the biggest smile ever. He was such a gentleman. I turned around on the sofa to lay on my back so I could get a full view of him. He took a seat on the edge of the sofa. We were literally side by side.

"I just saw Troy," he told me.

My heart dropped hearing him tell me he'd just saw my husband. "Where?" I didn't hesitate to ask.

"He was parked outside of the house, but he was on the opposite side of the street. And when I got out of my car he asked me to come and talk to him for a minute."

The thought of Troy coming within yards of the house made me feel uneasy. Especially with everything that had happened between Leon and I. So I sat up that instant. "What did he say?" I immediately asked.

"He wanted to know where you were. And then he asked me to tell you to give him a call on the house phone because he somehow lost his Blackberry."

I sucked my teeth. I mean, how dare that bastard ask me to call him after what Charlene told me? Was he on drugs or something? "I'm not calling him," I finally said.

"I kind of figured you wouldn't. But I didn't tell him that," Leon added.

"Did he bring up the shit about him fucking your wife?" I wanted to know.

"No. I didn't mention it. I thought he was going to say something about it. But he acted like nothing went on between them."

I rolled my eyes. I was upset at the fact that Troy would have the audacity to come around here and show his face after all that shit that went on with him and Charlene. And then to ask Leon to have me call him was like a slap in the face. I mean, what kind of fool did he think I was? I know one thing, he could lie all he wanted about what went on between him and Charlene, because at this point in my life I didn't care. I was going to move on with my life and he was not going to be a part of it.

After Leon and I completed our talk about Troy and Charlene, we got up and went into the kitchen. He showed me the items he brought back from the grocery store and then he sat me down at the table while he prepared dinner. I laughed the entire time he paraded around the kitchen because he had a joke for everything. Before I realized it, I had taken my mind off Troy, that is until Leon's cell phone rang.

Leon looked at me immediately after he looked at the caller ID. I started to tell him not to answer it but something inside of me told me to keep my mouth close.

"You know he's calling to talk to you," he said to me.

"Well, I really don't want to talk to him," I replied.

"You know if you don't answer this call, he's going to come back over here," Leon replied and then he held out the phone for me to grab it.

Before I took it, I thought about how I was going to act after I said hello. I knew I didn't want to start a big commotion, so I figured if I played his game and acted as if everything was okay, then he'd get back the same medicine he dished out to Leon earlier. So when it seemed as if the phone was about to stop ringing, I took the phone and pressed the send button.

I tried to say hello, but the words wouldn't come out of my mouth. Troy knew that someone had answered the phone, because he said hello before I could. After I quietly cleared my throat, I finally was able to say hello as well.

He sounded as if he was really happy to hear my voice. But I knew it was all guilt. I said fuck it and played along with his stupid ass game. "Hey what's up?" I responded nonchalantly.

"Nothing much. Whatcha been doing? I've been trying to call your cell phone but it keeps going straight to the voicemail. What's wrong with it?"

"My battery is dead," I lied.

"Why didn't you call the house phone and tell me that?"

"I don't know. I guess, I didn't think about it."

"Whatcha mean you didn't think about it? What's wrong with you? Is there something going on that you're not telling me?"

"No, it's not! And why would you think that?" I snapped because he had a fucking nerve to question me when he was the one who couldn't keep his dick in his pants to begin with. I started to curse his ass out and let him have it. But when I looked at Leon, he placed his hand over his mouth, giving me the signal not to feed into Troy's antics. It was quite obvious to Leon and I that Troy was trying to get me to confess to something, so he wouldn't feel all the guilt from the stuff he and Charlene got into.

"You telling me that you didn't think about calling me to tell me that your phone was dead just doesn't sit well with me. You and I have been married for many years, so don't you think I know when something isn't right with you?"

| 120 |

"What kind of question is that?"

"Just answer it," he demanded. He sounded as if he was about to lose it and snap out on me. But I diffused the situation quickly. I didn't want any drama right now while we were being taped for the show. I wanted this whole thing to be over with before I broke the news to him that I was filing for divorce. So before I answered his question, I took a deep breath and said, "Look Troy, I'm not in the mood to argue with you right now. So can we please drop it?"

"Yeah, we can drop it after you tell me what's going on?"

"There's nothing going on. Now, are you satisfied?"

"Nah, I ain't satisfied because I know you're lying."

"How dare you call me a liar when you're the one who's always gotten caught telling me lies. I have put up with a lot of your bullshit for years. And now you come at me with an assumption because you're feeling guilty about something you've done. You better check yourself before I check it for you!" I roared.

I thought he would come back at me with another fireball to continue with our heated argument, but he proved me wrong and didn't say another word. He and I sat and listened to one another breathe into the phone for at least a minute before we were interrupted by Charlene's voice in the background.

"Are you okay?" I heard her ask him.

"Why the fuck are you bothering me right now?" I heard him snap at her. "I am on the phone trying to have a private conversation with my wife so can you please leave me alone? Then he said, "Hello, Trice, you still there?"

Before I answered him, I thought about how quickly he snapped on her. It didn't sound as if the match made in heaven relationship she bragged about. So at that point I had every intention to ask him what happened between them. However, Leon was in my face, so I decided not to open up that can of worms. So I acknowledged that I was still on the line and told him I had to go. He didn't like that answer too well and tried everything in his power to keep me on the phone.

"Look, baby, I'm sorry if I upset up. But you see, I haven't been able to talk to you in the past couple of days and that wasn't sitting right with me. It really had me thinking some foul shit. And you know when I start thinking crazy I won't let it go until I get some answers."

"Yeah, I know," I finally responded.

"So are we straight?"

"Yeah, we straight," I lied. I told him what he wanted to hear because I was ready to get off the phone.

"A'ight. Well call me before you go to bed tonight. And call the house phone because I misplaced my Blackberry."

"All right."

"I love you."

"I love you too," I replied and almost bit my fucking tongue off doing it. I was really upset with his ass, so how was he going to tell me he loved me and I say I love you back without having mixed feelings. Whether my husband knew it or not, his time with me was coming to an end. And it was a travesty that he didn't see it coming.

After I hung up with Troy, Leon came over and embraced me and told me I handled Troy really well. I didn't know if he was sincere or not, but after he sealed his comment with a kiss on my forehead, I had no choice but to believe him.

Wife Extraordinaire

BY KIKI SWINSON

Charlene

I couldn't believe I let that nigga play me like that while he was screaming at his wife on the fucking phone. Shit, I was only trying to see if the nigga was all right. And this was the thanks I got? Fuck him and her! He was lucky I didn't' curse his ass out. I mean, who the fuck he thought he was trying to show off in front of his wife? That bitch couldn't hold a candle to me, so he better get his motherfucking act together before I fuck his relationship up worse than it is. Leon should've warned that dummy that I wasn't the bitch to fuck with. I was the most scandalous person that walked the face of the earth. I would make a nigga's life so miserable they'd think I had roots on their asses.

Right after I left him, I went to take me a hot shower. I needed to clear my mind and come up with an exit strategy from my no-good ass husband. He and I both knew that we had come to the end of our rope. The thing that lingered in my mind was where I was going to go after we separated? It wasn't clear who was going to live in the house. But knowing

Leon, he'd have the decency to want me and his son to stay there while he find somewhere else to live. He made no secret about how he felt about me so if we didn't have a son together, I'd be out in the street in a heartbeat.

The one thing that concerned me most was how he was going to act when it was time to divvy up the ten grand. I knew there was going to be some problems with him splitting the money down the middle. He had always felt as if he was the overall breadwinner and since he paid the majority of the bills, I knew he was going to want the majority of the money. But I tell you what! I had no plans to sign that check unless I was getting my half. Fuck that. With all the bullshit I had put up with that motherfucker, I deserved to get what was due to me. And I was gonna get it. Or he could kiss that money goodbye, because neither one of us would see it. And that was my final word.

I believed I stayed in the shower for thirty minutes and when the water started turning cold, I shut it off and got out. I wrapped a towel around me and headed back to the guest bedroom. I had a strong mind to lose the towel and parade around Troy butterball naked, but I figured it would be a waste of time. He'd act as if he didn't see me or even worse, he'd tell me to get out of his face and go and put some fucking clothes on as if I looked disgusting or something. He was a class A asshole and the way I was feeling tonight, I wasn't in the mood for any of his bullshit.

After I slipped my night clothes on, I started getting my things ready for the day I left this damn house. I had less than forty-eight hours and I couldn't wait.

Leon

After Troy called my cell phone to talk to Trice that first time, he called at least three times after that. To keep the drama down, she called him once but she didn't stay on the phone long, because she knew I was listening to their conversation. I knew it was only a matter of time before shit would hit the fan, but I was ready to go head-to-head with Troy to let him know where I stood with Trice. I wasn't sure whether he would get physical with me, but I was ready to go for what I knew. I mean, as long as Trice stuck to her guns and professed her love for me, then I had to be the man in the situation and have her back. As I thought about what could go on from this point, I watched Trice as she packed up her things to leave the house. She only had one more night to be here and then she had to go.

"Think I can get me some of that good loving your last night here?" I asked her and then I smiled.

She smiled back at me as she placed folded shirts into her luggage. "Didn't I just give you some this morning when you woke up with a hard-on?"

I walked up behind her and placed my arms around her waist. And then I thrust my dick against her soft, fat ass as I pressed my lips against her neck. "You know I can't get enough of you," I told her.

She continued to fold and place her things into her baggage. "You're not falling in love with me already are you?"

I hesitated for a second because I really didn't know how to answer that question. I wanted to burst out and tell her yes. But then I figured that would be the wrong move considering she hadn't told me how she really felt about me. I mean, she told me she loved being around me and that she could see herself with me, but the words *I love you* never came out of her mouth. So what was a brother to do?

And as I pondered on an answer, she said, "Don't tell me you're scared to tell me how you feel about me?"

Hearing her come back at me so quickly got me on the defense. "Look, I'm a grown ass man, I'm not afraid of anything."

"Well, answer the question," she pressed the issue.

I hesitated some more. "Yeah, I feel love in my heart for you."

She looked back at me and said, "That's good to know."

I was shocked by her answer. I honestly wanted to hear her tell me she loved me back. So I paused for a second and then I said, "Is that it? That's all you got to say?"

She gave me another one of her irresistible smiles and said, "It's not good for a woman to tell a man how she feels because he'll take it and run with it."

"And who told you that crap?" I asked her.

She started folding her things again. "It's a known fact."

"Says who?"

She turned her face towards me and kissed me on the cheek. "Don't' get all worked up over nothing. All you need to know is that I have strong feelings for you and as long as you do right by me, we're going to be all right."

"Strong feelings, huh?"

"Yep."

"Well, you better do right by me too. Because I got a lot at stake."

"And I don't?" she replied sarcastically.

"I didn't say that you didn't. All I'm saying is that, if we're gonna continue to see each other, then we're gonna have to be straight up about everything and we can't let our exes come between us."

"You're not going to have no problems with Troy once I tell him what's up."

"And you're not going to have any problems with Charlene either."

"Yeah, right. As soon as she finds out that you and I are seeing each other, the baby mama drama is going to come at me full force."

"Nah, trust me. That ain't gon' happen."

She sucked her teeth. "Yeah, we'll see."

"You're right. We shall see."

Wife Extraordinaire

BY KIKI SWINSON

Troy

I was so fucking happy that today had finally come. Within the next hour or so I was going to be reunited with my wife. I had already planned a nice day out for us, so I knew she would be thrilled, especially when she found out that I was taking her to her favorite restaurant. And then afterwards, I had planned to bathe her in a hot bubble bath. My goal today was to get our relationship back on track so we could move forward with our life. And instead of me paying a few things off with the ten thousand dollars, I was going to take Trice on the honeymoon she never had when we first got married. After all, she definitely deserved it.

I raced around the house making sure everything was back in its proper place before I left to go and pick her up. I heard Charlene rambling around in the guest room trying to get her things ready so we could leave. I had to admit that it was like music to my ears. In the beginning it was cool having her in my house, but when I saw how much of a sleeze bucket she was, I knew she was going to be a problem. I would say I got a nice dick suck out of the deal, but other than that she was a fucking headache and I was glad her time here had come to an end. After I straightened the pillow up on the sofa in the TV room, I yelled upstairs and asked her was she ready to hit the road. "I'll be down in a minute," she replied.

"Yeah, a'ight," I said and then I waited at the bottom of the staircase for her. I wanted us to walk out the house the same time. After my Blackberry disappeared, my gut told me she had something to do with it. There was no way in the world my phone was going to get up and walk out the house by itself. I'd never had problems with losing any of my other phones. Now all of a sudden I couldn't find a phone that I had just recently purchase a little over a month ago. I knew one thing, if I ever found out that bitch had my shit, I was going to make sure she paid for it one way or another.

Finally, after waiting ten minutes, Charlene appeared at the top of the staircase with her bags in hand. She looked at me like she wanted me to help her bring her things downstairs, but I dismissed her expression and walked towards my front door. After I opened the door so we could leave, she sucked her teeth and proceeded to drag her things down the stairs. She huffed and puffed until she reached the bottom step. Then she rolled her eyes at me as she dragged her bag past me.

"You could've helped me bring my bags downstairs. I mean, that's what any gentleman would've done," she commented as she headed towards the truck.

I started to make reference to her comment, but I figured it'd be a waste of my time and energy so I ignored her dumb ass, locked my front door and followed her to my truck. I was in a good mood because I was about to see Trice. There was no way I was going to let this ghetto bunny ruin a motherfucking thing for me. Fuck that! Her miserable ass had to go back to where she belonged and I couldn't wait to get her there.

The entire drive to Norfolk took me less than fifteen minutes because I put the pedal to the metal. I felt as if I couldn't get Charlene home to Leon fast enough. It was time for us to do the switch-a-rue again. I was delivering his wife back to him. So he needed to give me my wife back. When I pulled up in front of his place, I didn't hesitate to blow my horn. I wanted Trice to hear my truck horn without any problems.

"Need help taking your bags in the house?" I asked her. I knew she probably thought I had bumped my head being as though I didn't help her take her things out of my house. But this time it was different. Trice was inside her house, so I figured if I helped Charlene take her things into her house. That way, I could help Trice bring her things out to my truck and we could leave immediately after that.

"Nope, I don't need your help!" she snapped. Without saying another word, she snatched her bags from the back seat of my truck and dragged them up the sidewalk towards her house. I hopped out the truck behind her and followed her to her front door. It didn't bother me that she didn't want me to help her with her bags. My main priority was Trice. So as soon as she stepped foot through the front door, everything else went out the window.

I watched Charlene as she entered the house. I started to follow her inside but I figured that as soon as Trice saw her she'd know that I was outside and would come out to meet me. After Charlene walked inside, I walked up the steps and waited by the front door. Two minutes later, the door opened and out came Leon. I smiled at him and gave him a handshake. "What's good?" I asked him.

He stepped out on the porch area and closed the front door behind him. "I'm good. But I know shit around here is about to fall apart," he commented.

I knew he was referring to his wife. She was definitely a major drama queen. But that was his mess, not mine. I really didn't care to talk about her. I was more interested in the whereabouts of my wife. So I played it off by laughing, cut it short and asked him if he knew if Trice was ready to go or not?

"She's already gone," he told me.

I was shocked. "What do you mean she's already gone?" I asked him.

"She left out of here in a cab about forty-five minutes ago," he replied. "I thought you knew."

"Hell nah, I didn't know. I was under the impression that when I dropped your wife off, that I would be picking her up."

Leon gave me the dumbest expression he could muster. "Yo' Troy, I swear I thought I heard her telling you she was going to take a cab home."

"When was this?"

"About an hour before she left."

"I don't know who the fuck she could've been talking to because it sure wasn't me. The last time I spoke to Trice was this morning."

"Well, I don't know who she could've been talking to either. All I know is that she told someone she was catching a cab home. And then a few minutes later, she called a cab."

I was disgusted to no end hearing this punk ass nigga tell me my wife left his crib in a fucking cab. What kind of bitch ass move was that? I didn't let his stinking ass wife come home in a cab so why did he let my wife do it? I had every intention to flip out on this buster ass nigga, but I left well enough alone and bailed on his retarded ass. I didn't even say good-bye when I bounced off his porch. I threw up the deuce sign and kept it moving.

Wife Extraordinaire

BY KIKI SWINSON

Charlene

When Leon came back in the house, I thought he was going to fire into my ass about what I told Trice. But he went straight upstairs and acted as if I wasn't even in the house. As much as I didn't want to fuss with him this evening, I was somewhat upset that he wouldn't confront me. I mean, I did tell Trice that I fucked her husband. So why wasn't he grilling me about it? Did he not care? Was he really done with me? Well, whatever was on his mind, it was clear that it wasn't about me and now I knew everything was downhill from here. And things were going to get worse before they got better.

Once I unpacked my bags, I climbed onto the couch in my TV room so I could wind down. I heard Leon rambling around in our bed and then he got quiet all of a sudden. I muted the TV and waited to hear more movement so I could figure out what he was doing up there. But it had gotten so quiet I could've heard a straight pin drop to the floor with no problem. A minute later I heard some mumbling and then it stopped. Then

| 132 |

I heard Leon giggle for a few seconds. I knew then he was either on his cell phone or watching TV. Since I hadn't heard any sound come from the TV I figured he had to be on the phone. So I jumped up from the couch and snuck up the staircase to see if I could find out what was really going on.

When I reached halfway up the staircase, I heard him whisper a few words. They weren't quite clear but my suspicions were confirmed that he was talking on the phone to someone and he didn't want me to hear his conversation.

I knew I talked a lot of crap and I professed that I hated my husband, but this was not the way I wanted this thing to go down. I was tired of being the one with the aching heart, which was why I told Trice I slept with her husband. I got tired of sitting on the sidelines and hearing the rumors about Leon and his fucking tramps. I nearly came close to having a nervous breakdown one time, so it felt good not to be on the receiving end this time. I wanted to fuck up his pride and let him see how I felt when I used to catch him cheating. But apparently he wasn't fazed by what I told Trice. The more I thought about it, the motherfucker probably fucked her to get back at me.

Realizing I may have created my own hell storm, my heart began to ache and I got this huge knot in my stomach. I wanted to turn around and head back downstairs but my heart wouldn't let my body make the turn. I wanted to find out what was going on behind my bedroom door and that's what I did.

When I reached the top of the staircase, I tiptoed to the bedroom quietly, pressed my left ear against the door and waited patiently for him to say another word. My heart started beating like crazy and then I heard him laugh.

"Come on now, Trice, you gon' play me like that?" I heard him say.

From the moment I heard her name that knot I had in my stomach started flipping around uncontrollably. I had also developed a bad taste my mouth. I mean, why in the world was he talking and laughing with Troy's wife on the fucking phone? Did he fuck her while she laid her stinking ass up in my house? Or did she get played like I did and was only able to suck his dick? Whatever happened, he liked it enough to have her laughing and talking to his grimy ass on the phone.

It took everything within me not to kick this fucking door down, but I figured that if I cool down and listened to his conversation a little longer, I'd have more ammunition for his ass during our divorce proceedings. So I took a deep breath and tried to remain calm while I let his sorry ass dig his hole a little deeper.

"Just say the word and I'll be there in a heartbeat. I told you my marriage with Charlene is over. I'm not even attracted to her anymore. It's been over a month since we last had sex. So that ought to tell you where my head is with that situation," I heard him say and then he fell silent.

While I had a chance to soak in everything he'd just said, my mind started running around in circles. I knew that there wasn't a chance for us to patch things up but I had no idea that he wasn't attracted to me anymore. For him to tell her we hadn't had sex in over a month was like a slap in the face. What the fuck was he trying to gain by telling her our business like that? She was the fucking outsider, not me. What the fuck was his problem?

Once again I found myself trying to remain calm so I could finish hearing everything Leon had to say to her. I've been told that when you go snooping around looking for something, you always get more than what you bargain for. So while I continued to eavesdrop on this nigga's conversation, I heard him interrupt her.

"Hey baby, hold on a minute. Somebody is trying to call me on the other line," I heard him say.

"Hello," he said, after he clicked over on his other line. Then he fell silent. "Nah man, she ain't called here," he said and then he fell silent once again. "Troy, if I knew man I would tell you. All she did was hop in the cab, said goodbye and then she left," he said and then he fell silent again. "A'ight, I'll let you know if I hear something," he concluded.

When I heard him say hello all over again, I knew he had clicked back over to the other line, so he could finish talking to that bitch Trice. At that point, I wanted to bust his motherfucking bubble. I wanted to see his facial expression and let that asshole know that I knew he was on the phone with Trice and I heard his entire conversation with Troy. I didn't know how he would react but I was willing to see.

But first I wanted to see if he was going to tell her that her husband had just called. From what I heard, it sounded like Trice was somewhere other than with her husband. Because why would he be calling Leon and asking him if he heard from her? Not only that, if she wasn't with Troy then where the hell was she? I knew one thing, Leon knew where she was and as soon as I got the chance, I was going to make sure Troy knew it.

"That was Troy on the other end," I heard him say. "Nah, he's gone now. But he did ask me if I heard from you," Leon continued and then he paused. "Come on now, how would I look telling him what hotel you're at?" he whispered. Trice evidently said something and he replied, "Look, I got everything under control on this end. You just handle your end."

I so wished I could get my hands on that bitch's neck. She was fucking up my marriage. Yeah, I lit the fire with my conversation with her and lying on her husband, but what kind of bitch find refuge in another's man arms that damn fast?

I knew she was talking but I didn't know what she was saying. Then Leon questioned her, "So, when you gon' break the news to him?"

When I heard him ask her about when she was going to break the news to him, I knew Leon was referring to her husband. The type of news she planned to break to Troy was beyond me. Then I figured it had to have something to do with them. If that was the case, then shit was going to get really ugly.

The way Troy felt about Trice, I knew he wouldn't be a happy camper when he found out my husband was keeping information about Trice from him. If he found out they fucked each other during their time together, big shit would hit the fan in the worst kind of way. And the way I saw it, somebody was going to get it.

While Leon continued to chat with Trice, I began to weigh my options about whether or not to burst into the bedroom. I could either curse him out and go upside his head, or I could act as if I wasn't eavesdropping and kill his ass softly by calling Troy up and telling him everything I knew. I mean, calling Troy and giving him the scoop about their little affair would be icing on the cake for me.

I could sit back and watch Leon get his ass kicked and then I could see Trice and Troy's marriage destroyed right before my eyes. Everybody would feel violated just like me. That would be a win-win situation across the board for me. Raining on Leon's parade was the best revenge I could ever get since I endured all those lonely nights while he stayed out and fucked random bitches. And doubly getting back at Troy for being an ass when I lived with him and his high and mighty wife for being an overall bitch for being just that—a bitch.

Hell yeah! I was gonna finally get the payback I deserved. But before I walked away from the bedroom door, I had to find out which hotel she was staying. I knew when I told Troy she was in a hotel room, he was going to ask me where. So I waited at the door just a little bit longer to see if Leon would slip and mention her whereabouts.

"I'll tell you what. Get some rest and as soon as I take care of my business here, I'll head over there," I heard him tell her and then he paused. "Whatcha mean?"

I had no idea what the hell he was talking about. Plus I hated the fact I couldn't hear Trice's responses or conversation. One-sided conversation truly pissed me off.

"Trice, you ain't that far. Remember, it only took me about fifteen to get you from here to Newtown Road. But if I don't get there by the time you get up, just walk next door to Ruby Tuesday and get you something to drink," he told her and then he said a few more words. It sounded as if he was giving her some type of instructions. A few minutes later, it sounded as if he was trying to give her a remedy to get rid of a headache.

I knew one thing, I was getting a headache listening to them. I also felt as if I had heard enough information to call Troy, so he could tear their whole world apart, and in turn, upset his own world.

So I walked away from the bedroom door, raced back downstairs, grabbed my cell phone from the coffee table and grabbed Troy's Blackberry from my purse. I searched for his home number in his Contact log and found it underneath the name *home*. I wasted no time dialing the number. While I waited for him to answer it, I listened for Leon's every movement. I figured since he wanted to be sneaky and talk to Troy's wife behind his back, I was gonna do the same fucking thing by talking to Troy.

Finally, on the fourth ring, Troy answered, "Hello," he said.

I cleared my throat. "Troy, this is Charlene."

"What's up?" he asked me. I was surprised he was in a calm mood when he heard my voice. I was expecting some smartass comment.

"You just called Leon a few minutes ago, asking about Trice, right?"

"Yeah, why?"

"Because, while you were on one end asking him if he talked to her since she left, she was on the other end," I whispered to avoid Leon from hearing my conversation.

"You bullshitting me!" he roared.

"Nope. I am not bullshitting you. As a matter of fact, he's up in our bedroom talking to her on the phone now. I stood on the other side of the door and heard his entire conversation with her."

"You mean to tell me that nigga talking to her right now?" he spat and I could tell that the more he thought about what I had said, the angrier he was becoming.

"Yep. I started to blow his cover and bust into the bedroom on his ass, but I decided not to, because it wouldn't have done any good. He probably would've shined on me while she listened. So I figured it would be better if I didn't say one word to him. I want him to think that I don't know shit."

"So why did he lie to me?" Troy asked me.

"Can't you read between the lines?" I raised my voice just a little. This fool couldn't be this damn whipped. "They are fucking around just like I told you there were. And pretty soon she's going to break the news to you. But right now, she's at the Springhill Marriot Hotel on Newtown Road, trying to figure out what she's going to do about the situation."

"How you know she's at the Springhill on Newtown Road?"

"Because he told her it would only take him fifteen minutes to get to her and that if he didn't get to her by the time she got up, go next door to the Rudy Tuesday. The only hotel in this area that takes fifteen minutes to get there and has a Ruby Tuesday next door on Newtown Road is the Springhill Marriott. Now am I right or wrong?" I questioned him because I had my facts together. He was the one who needed to screw his head on tight. Because whether he wanted to believe it or not, his wife was fucking my husband and from the way things look, they're planning to see each other again.

"Where is Leon now?"

"He's still upstairs in our room."

"Is he still on the phone with her?"

"I think so. Why?"

"Because I want to talk to that nigga. He's got a lot of explaining to do," Troy replied. He sounded like he was grinding his teeth. I couldn't believe how thickheaded this damn man was. *Did I really have to tell this lovesick dumbass everything to do?*

"No. That's not a good idea. Because he might deny it. What you need to do is go up to that fucking hotel and wait around and see if he shows up. That way, you'll be able to catch their monkey asses in the act."

Troy paused for a couple of seconds and then said, "Yeah, you're right. I'm gonna go up to the hotel and wait for him to show up."

"Don't kill nobody," I warned him. I was serious when I said that. These type situations had a way of messing with the mind and confusing the heart. They say there is nothing like a woman scorn and I agreed with that. But equally as bad or worse was a man whose woman was fucking another dude. These was the muthafuckas who killed the woman, her lover and the damn kids too if they happened to be around. Plus, I didn't want any blood on my hands.

"It's too late for all that. But I appreciate you calling me with this."

"No problem. My husband needs to be taught a fucking lesson."

"Yeah, I'm gonna be the one who does it," Troy replied prior to hanging up.

As soon as our call ended, I laid my phone down on the coffee table and smiled. I honestly felt like jumping up and down because it seemed as if I had scored a victory. Troy was on his way up to the hotel where Trice was hiding out. In another hour or two, Leon would be heading that way too. When everyone met up, fireworks were going to go off and I was going to be on the sideline laughing my ass off. Yeah, it really felt good to know I was about see someone else get hurt other than me. When they said misery loved company, they weren't lying.

And the more I thought about it, Leon's worthless ass was worth more to me dead than alive. So if Troy killed his monkey ass I would be sad and hurt . . . and that was the truth, but that shit would only last until the insurance check came.

Wife Extraordinaire

BY KIKI SWINSON

Troy

My heart felt as if it was dangling from my chest, barely hanging on by the thread. My adrenaline was pumping as if I was running a marathon. So as I raced to get to the hotel, all I could think about was how that nigga, Leon, betrayed me. That motherfucker lied to me and he's fucking my wife on top of that.

Did he know I would kill his ass?

The way I felt I could really do some damage. When a man loved his woman and found out she cheated on him with another man, that man could literally rip a man's heart from his chest. What was even worse was our pride was tested as well.

Women were emotional, men were logical. There was no doubt women hurt when their men cheated on them. However, because of our sense of logic and egotistical ways, cheating hurt us men more. We didn't think it could happen to us. No man believed his woman could or would cheat on him. Even if the relationship was bad, we as men still possessed that air of dominance that my woman won't do something as stupid as cheating. Knowing that another man slid his dick inside of something we deemed so precious was damaging to our minds. Most men couldn't come back from that. And the way I felt, I didn't think I would be able to do it myself.

Charlene told me Leon said it would take him fifteen minutes to get to the hotel. However, it only took me ten minutes. I didn't remember if I exceeded the speed limit or ran any red lights. All I knew was I had to get there in a hurry and that's what I did.

When I entered the parking lot, I parked my truck on the side of the hotel. My plan was to stay out of sight, so Leon wouldn't see me when he got there. But I still had to be in a good position so I could see all the cars come and go. After I shut off my truck engine, I sat there in complete silence and wondered to myself how I was going to approach this situation.

I wondered about my number. How many men had come before me, sitting outside a hotel, motel, restaurant or house trying to see what was up with his woman or wife? How many men were in this heartbroken fraternity? Who believed in his woman, only to learn she was a liar and breaker of vows. How many men had to endure this powerful heartbreak before me and how many would endure this same heartbreak after me?

My manhood had been challenged. A spear had pierced my heart. Men were logical and we tried to fight our emotions. Emotions made us crazy. That's why men were from Mars. Mars represented the ego and the unknown. A man learning about his woman cheating on him could beat the shit out of the wife and lover or even kill the assholes. And that was what I was battling with. What would I do?

My first thought was to curse her out and maybe smack her ass one good time. But then I figured if I did that, then she would have every right to call the police on my ass and leave me for good. That was my logical side and I was somewhat happy that I still possessed some logic in my soul.

So was that what I wanted? I mean, I wanted to get my point across but I didn't want to go to jail in the process. Damn, what should I do? That thought was beating me up. Meanwhile, I contemplated about how I was going to handle things. My heart spoke to me and convinced me not to wait for Leon because it could and probably would get really ugly. Logic was seeing its way through to my brain but seeing the both of them together and having an image of the two of them together would probably make me beat the shit out of both of them.

Anyway, I needed to talk to Trice on my own and then I'd be able to draw my own conclusion from there. So without giving it anymore thought, I took my keys out of the ignition and got out of my truck. I had to see her face. I wanted to know firsthand why she was here and why she felt like she couldn't come home.

I put on a smile when I walked up to the front desk. There was a young black lady waiting for me as I approach the desk. She didn't look a day over twenty-four so I knew I could manipulate her into giving me Trice's room number.

"Welcome to the Springhill Marriot," she said.

I looked at her name tag and said, "Hi Nancy, I suppose to be meeting my wife here but when I last talked to her I forgot to get her room number."

"I'm sorry, sir, but I wouldn't be able to give you that information."

"Look, I understand that you have to enforce company policy, but I just talked to her not that long ago and if this would help," I said and then I took my ID card out of my wallet. Three seconds later, I was showing it to her. "Her name is Trice O'Neal. See we have the same last night."

"She took the ID out of my hand and looked at it." And while she looked it over, I chimed in and made her focus on the fact I had the same last name as her and that if she looked in the system she'd noticed that our addresses were the same.

"Does she have a cell phone?" she asked as she handed me my ID back.

"That's the thing, she told me she was charging it, which was why we were talking on the hotel phone," I lied. I kept a straight face though. I wanted to come off as honest as I could. "Look, sweetie, I don't want to get you in trouble, so why don't you call my wife's room and ask her if it's okay for you to give me her room number," I continued and then I gave her the most sympathetic expression I could muster up.

She thought to herself for a moment and then she started punching keys on her computer keyboard. A second or two later she looked back at me and said, "Your wife is on the sixth floor in Room 611."

I smiled at her and said, "Thank you so much, sweetie."

I almost jumped for joy when they young girl gave me Trice's room number. She had no idea what she had just done.

As I made my way to Trice's room, the palms of my hands started sweating like crazy. So I rubbed them along the sides of my jeans. But by the time I approached her room, my hands felt drenched all over again. I knew that trying to keep them dry was out of the question. When I was involved in some kind of drama, this always happened to me. I knew I had to block it out and continue to do what I came here to do.

I lifted my sweaty hand to knock on the door, but the sound of Trice's voice stopped me. "Leon, why you playing?" she said and then she giggled.

My heart pounded like crazy and then it sunk in the pit of my stomach after I heard her call Leon's name.

"You know I want to but it's gonna take some time," she continued to talk and then she paused again. I was wondering what Leon was saying to her. I tried to block out the hurt I was feeling, but I couldn't. I wanted to kick the door in but I didn't want to bring any attention to myself. The young girl downstairs had already given me the room number when she wasn't suppose to, so I knew I had to be on my best behavior. "I don't care where we go and eat, just as long as it's seafood," I heard her say. And from that statement I knew they were making plans to go out to eat. But I couldn't let that happen. So I knocked on her door that instant. "Hold on. Somebody's knocking at the door," I heard her say.

I heard her footsteps as she approached the door. When she pressed her face against the door to look through the peephole, the hole got dark. I knew I startled her by coming there unexpectedly. But this was the only way I was going to be able to get to the bottom of all this madness. Leon was forging a wedge between me and my wife and I couldn't let that happen. When I saw the light reappear through the peephole, I knew she saw me and had backed away from the door.

"Trice, open the door," I demanded calmly. But she refused to answer me. So I knocked a couple more times. "Trice baby, please open the door so we can talk." Again she refused to answer me. By now I knew she had told Leon I was at the door, because it had gotten completely silent in the room. The hotel didn't have a balcony so I figured she'd be in the bathroom trying to figure out what to do. So I knocked on the door a few more times.

"Trice, please open the door, baby. We need to talk. I'm not leaving until we do," I told her. I figured I had to let her know that she didn't have any other option but to answer the door because I wasn't going to leave until she did.

Finally, after begging and pleading with her for over five minutes, she opened the door. To see her face was truly a relief. She acted as if she didn't know what to say to me. The fact she opened the door for me led me to believe that she was willing to hear what I had to say. I smiled at her so she could feel a little more at ease. She held her cell phone pressed tightly against her right ear as she stood in front of the entryway of the room. She made it painfully obvious that she didn't want me coming no further than where I was, so I didn't press her into letting me come in.

What bothered me was that she acted as if she didn't want to end her phone call. I figured Leon told her to keep him on the line so he could hear our entire conversation. But I wasn't trying to have that. She was my fucking wife. Not his. So he needed to get the fuck back before I turn into something they wouldn't want to see.

"I'm listening," she started off, giving me this nonchalant facial expression.

"Are you on the phone with someone?" I asked her, even though I already knew the answer.

She hesitated and then she said, "You said you needed to talk to me. So what is it Troy?"

I was on the verge of snatching the phone out of her hand so I could have a man-to-man with that nigga, Leon. But I decided against it. I wasn't ready to deal with him yet. I wanted Trice to explain her side before I questioned Leon.

"Can you hang up the phone first?" I asked her as nice as I could.

"No, I can't hang up."

"Who the fuck are you talking to?" I snapped.

She sucked her teeth as if she was more frustrated than me. "Look, Troy, just tell me what you need to talk to me about," she replied.

"Not until you hang up the phone."

"Why is this phone bothering you so much?"

"Because you're my wife and I want to talk to you privately!" I roared and then I took a couple of steps towards her.

"You didn't think of me as your wife when you were fucking the hell out of Charlene," she spat. I could tell she was really angry because spit snot out of her mouth with every word she spoke.

I was shocked more than anything. I mean, who could've told her that I fucked Charlene?

"Who the fuck told you that dumb ass shit? Leon?" I asked. I wanted to know who could have told her that lie. I knew I

| 146 |

hadn't fucked Charlene. And Charlene knew I hadn't fucked her, so where did this bullshit come from. I needed to know.

"No, Leon wasn't the one who told me," she answered me as she continued to hold her cell phone against her ear.

"Well, who told you Trice? Because whoever said it, lied. I didn't lay a fucking finger on her," I tried convincing her.

"That ain't what Charlene said," she blurted out.

"Nah, I don't believe that. She couldn't have told you that bullshit."

"Well, she did," Trice assured me as her eyes became glassy. I could see the hurt in her eyes.

"That's not truth. So, when could she have told you this?" I asked because I needed answers. At this point, I couldn't care less if that nigga was on the phone. I wanted him to hear every word I had to say, because the way things were looking, that lie about me fucking Charlene had to come from his ass.

"Look, Troy, stop it. I am up to here with your lies," she said as she took a few more steps backwards. She grabbed the door handle and acted as if her next step would be to close the door on me. I couldn't have that, so I walked towards her until I was right dead in her face. Without even thinking about it, I immediately snatched her cell from her. She tried her best to get it back from me, but I was stronger and taller than her. I was able to keep her at arm's length with my left arm while I used my right arm to put the phone up to my ear.

She started screaming and jumping up in the air, hoping she could grab her phone back from me. But she didn't have a chance. "Give me my phone back Troy."

I ignored her and kept her back from me long enough to say what I had to say to this nigga. I had a lot of shit I had to get off my chest. "Leon, this is Troy," I began to say.

"I know who it is," he replied confidently.

"A'ight. Good. Now tell me why the hell is you talking to my motherfucking wife on the phone? What, y'all fucking now?" I roared.

| 147 |

"That ain't for me to say homeboy. You gotta ask Trice that question," he told me and this time he sounded a little cocky.

He gave me the impression he was the motherfucker and I was some chump ass nigga from the street. I quickly straighten that out. "Yo' nigga, let me tell you something. I don't know whatcha bitch ass told my wife, but I'ma tell you that you ain't got enough balls to bring that shit over here to me."

"Troy, you think I'm scared of you? Nigga, I will kill you. Whatcha forgot how I roll?"

"Nigga, do you think I give a damn how you roll? This is my motherfucking wife! I got papers on her. So do yourself a favor and get the fuck off the phone and tend to your own greasy ass wife."

"I don't give a fuck about no papers. She said she don't want your monkey ass no more. She told me she wanted me. Now you get the fuck off the phone!"

Hearing Leon tell me that Trice told him she didn't want me anymore felt like I had been hit with a ton of bricks. It hurt me to my heart for another man to tell me that my wife didn't want me anymore. I swear, if Leon was in front of me right now I would kill his motherfucking ass. But since he wasn't there, I had to turn my focus to Trice.

"You told this nigga you didn't want me anymore?"

Trice's eyes became more glassy as ever. As soon as a tear dropped from her right eye, she said, "Yeah, I said it because when I called you the other night, Charlene answered your phone and told me that you were busy taking a shower because you had just finished fucking her."

"Wait, you called and she answered my phone?"

Trice nodded.

I thought for a second and then I said, "That bitch! She had my phone the whole time."

"What are you talking about?" Trice asked me as if she was confused.

I ignored her question and put my focus back on Leon. "Yo' Leon, stay the fuck away from my wife and tell your bitch I said she owes me a phone." After that, I ended the conversation—I pushed the damn end button. I started to smash her phone against the wall but I didn't want to scare her. I needed to sit down and act as calmly as I could so I could explain what really happened while Charlene was at our house. I couldn't afford to have my wife thinking that I fucked that nasty bitch. So I laid all the cards down on the table.

After I convinced her to take a seat on the bed, I laid all the cards down on the table. I even told her the truth about me letting Charlene suck my dick, which was probably why she stole my phone and acted like she hadn't seen it.

"I love you so much Trice. And if you left me, I wouldn't be able to move on," I told her.

Tears started rolling down her face, one after the other. She kept looking at the door and then she would turn to look back at me. I knew she wanted to tell me something, but didn't know how. I figured it had something to do with Leon. And I kind of knew what it was, but I didn't want to hear her say the words. So I put my finger up to her mouth.

"Look, whatever you did, doesn't matter. So, just keep it to yourself," I told her. I knew my heart wouldn't have been able to handle it.

Wife Extraordinaire

BY KIKI SWINSON

Leon

I grabbed my pistol from my sock drawer and headed downstairs. Charlene smiled at me on my way out the house. I knew the bitch was up to something, I just couldn't put my finger on it. Since I didn't have time to find out what it was, I gave her the middle finger and told her I was leaving her dumbass and that I'd be back in an hour to pack my shit.

"I don't give a fuck! Carry your ass on nigga!" she spat.

I started to call her a grimy ass whore, but I refused to waste my energy and my breath. She was a lazy, washed up bitch with bad credit and a bad attitude. I had something better with a lot more class waiting for me to rescue her from her loser husband at the hotel. So I bounced and didn't look back.

I hopped in my car and sped towards Virginia Beach as if my mind was going bad. The fact I had my burner in my pocket I knew I would be all right when I ran up on Troy. I had to admit he had somewhat of an edge on me, because he was bigger and taller than me. But I knew when I bust him in the ass with one of these iron clad missiles that would bring him down to size. I knew I had to go there and let him know I had fallen in love with Trice and I wasn't going to leave there without her.

When I pulled into the parking lot, I parked my car directly in front of the hotel revolving doors. Immediately after I turned off the ignition, I jumped out and rushed inside. I heard some lady say good evening but I ignored her and proceeded towards the elevator. My heart pounded with each step I took. But I blocked it out. I was there to set the record straight with Troy and that's what I intended to do.

I knocked on the door as soon as I walked up to it. I thought Troy was going ask who it was, but he snatched the door open as if he was expecting me. Troy stood about four inches taller than me and was about fifty pounds heavier. When he spoke, his tone matched his body type.

"You still a hardheaded nigga I see," he said sarcastically.

"Where is Trice?" I asked.

Before he could answer me she stuck her head out from around the corner of the room. She looked like she had been crying. So I wanted to know was she all right. "You all right?" I asked her.

Before she could answer me, Troy stepped in front of her, blocking my view of her and told me told me to get lost. But I wasn't having that. "Can you move out of her way so she can answer me?" I asked nicely. I was trying to give that nigga a get-out-of-jail free card but he was pressing his fucking luck.

"I ain't going nowhere nigga. But you are!" he roared as he rushed towards me. At that moment I knew I couldn't let him grab a hold to me or I'd be finished. So before he could lay a finger on me, I pulled out my pistol and aimed it at him.

He stopped in his tracks and laughed at me. "Oh, so you pulling out burners on niggas now, huh?" He said. "You know you gon' have to use that right?" Then he lunged at me.

| 151 |

I couldn't tell you why I did this, but as soon as he got within arm's reach of me, I closed my eyes and pulled back on the trigger. I lost count but I think I shot the gun twice. I knew the power behind these bullets would stop him in his tracks but I was wrong. And when I realized how wrong I was, Troy was on top of me and I heard Trice in the background screaming her poor little heart out. She screamed for someone to come and help break up Troy and I.

I was lying on my back while he was on top of me. He snuck a couple of blows to my head while I struggled to keep the gun in my hands. I managed to fire two more shots. When I did, I heard a loud thud immediately after. Troy heard it too.

Both of us took our attention off each other and look inside of the room and noticed that Trice was lying on the floor in a pool of her own blood. Troy got off me and rushed to her side.

"Oh no, you shot her!" he screamed as he tried to lift her up from the floor.

I panicked. I knew at that very moment that I was in a world of trouble. My freedom would be snatched away from me as soon as the policed arrived. I wasn't trying to go to jail. I had so much to live for out here on the streets. I mean, if Troy would've let me talk to her then none of this shit would have happen. It was his fault. Now I had to take the rap for it.

With the gun in my hand, I got up from the floor somewhat paralyzed. I really didn't know what to do. I knew I didn't want to go to jail, especially since I had no intentions on shooting Trice. I loved her. If Troy would've stayed out of our way, then I would be in a better place right now. But since it didn't happen that way, I had to come up with another plan.

"Police! Drop your weapon and put your hands up!" I heard a male voice yell from behind me.

I turned to see if my ears were deceiving me and when I saw five police officers dressed in uniform and strategically positioned, my heart dropped. I started to bust a couple shots at them but they were too far from me and spread out, and I wouldn't get a good shot.

I looked at Trice one last time. I saw her losing consciousness, but Troy kept talking to her hoping he could keep her alive. She looked so pitiful and I didn't want her to die. She didn't deserve it. All she wanted was for a man to love her. And I wanted to be that man. However, Troy wasn't trying to let me take his place without a fight. Unfortunately, Trice got caught in the crossfire. If I didn't move out of her way and let the officers call the paramedics, then she wouldn't have a chance in hell of surviving. So I put the barrel of the gun underneath my chin.

"Put the gun down!" the same officer yelled.

I wasn't trying to hear him. I had nothing else to live for. I hated my wife and now my life as well. I knew I wouldn't be much of a father figure while I was in jail, so I pulled the trigger. Click. Click. Kiss my ass! I forgot I only had four bullets in my gun to begin with.

When the police officers noticed I had run out of ammo, they rushed my dumbass and threw me down to the floor. At that point, I knew my life was over.

They handcuffed and hauled me out of the hotel quicker than I could count to ten. While I sat in the back of the police car, I was able to see the paramedics roll a stretcher inside and come out twenty minutes later with Trice scrapped to it. They had an oxygen mask covering her nose and mouth so I knew there was a chance that they might be able to save her. I guess I would find out soon enough.

BY KIKI SWINSON

Charlene

I was restless and curious about what was happening at the hotel. I borrowed a friend's car that lived on the next street over and made my way to the hotel. I was surprised when I saw the police cars and the ambulance. *What the fuck happened?*

The ambulance meant someone was hurt. The police represented it was bad.

I felt indifferent to the whole situation. I didn't want anyone dead. If anyone did have to die, I hope it was Leon, so I could get the insurance money. I did hope this ruined Troy and Trice's marriage—they didn't deserve to be happy. Both were phony as hell.

As I walked closer to the crowd, I saw my dumbass husband, Leon, sitting in the back of the police car in handcuffs looking pitiful and miserable as hell. *What the fuck?* I shook my head. Dumb, stupid fuck.

Then the paramedics rushed the stretcher out with Trice on it, with an oxygen mask on her mouth and other stuff hooked up to her. Troy was by her side. He got in the ambulance with her along with a cop as well.

I looked at Leon and he finally turned his head my way. He had tears in his eyes. We looked at each other and I moved my mouth to say sorry muthafucka. And he did look sorry. As sorry as anybody I have seen in a long time. I spit on the ground and wiped my hands together, signifying to him I had wiped my hands of him. He was on his own. I looked forward to keeping the money from the show for myself and my child.

Two weeks later the executives from the show informed me that none of us would receive the ten thousand dollars. Evidently, because I had disconnected the cameras that automatically disqualified us, and they wanted to distance themselves from all of this drama. I talked to several attorneys and none of them would take my case, unless I gave them twenty thousand upfront. I didn't have that kind of money. Of course, the show executives did pay for Trice's hospital care. I still hated that bitch.

I heard she and Troy stayed together and for the life of me I couldn't understand why. Why would he want to be with a bitch who fucked another man, his so-called homeboy?

Several months later at Leon's trial, it came out that Leon and Trice were fucking all over the place and sleeping in the same bed. A show executive confirmed this on the witness stand. I laughed internally at the hypocrisy of it all. That asshole Troy thought his wife was so damn pure, and wouldn't fuck this pussy. When I testified, I played the hurt and scorn wife and the women on the jury ate it up. I didn't give a fuck if they gave him the chair. I was glad when Trice said she loved her husband, Troy, and what happened between she and Leon was a mistake. I loved the unhappy and disappointed look on his face. *Damn fool.*

By the way, Leon got twenty-five to forty years for at-tempted murder, assault and illegal weapon possession. *Dum-bass*. At least he would be eligible for parole for good behavior at the twelve and half year point. He could forget about ever trying to see our child again. One of the cops even said the mu-thafucka tried to commit suicide but the gun was out of bullets. *Real stupid dumbass.*

And for me. I was hating life. Of course we lost the house and I had to get a job. I raided the bank accounts before Leon could get to them and pay attorney fees. That's why his ass was stuck with a young ass public defender who didn't know shit.

That's what his ass get for me having to shake my ass every night at a rundown, nasty as hell strip joint.

BONUS STORY

Ex-Wife Status

BY AMALEKA MCCALL

Ex-Wife Status

BY AMALEKA MCCALL

PROLOGUE
When It Was All Said and Done

Police sirens wailed in the distance like a flock of screaming geese. Someone had called the police. They must have heard the gunshot blasts. There were only two, one singular shot directly to each of the victims' heads. It was finally over. Crystie had flinched when the gun erupted in her hand, but it was more of a physical reaction, rather than an emotional or mental one.

Aside from the small flinch, Crystie hadn't done much else in response to her deed. There was no screaming, no hysterics, no immediate feeling of regret—nothing. Even when she saw all the blood and brain matter, she didn't cringe and barely moved, much less screamed. She was numb, numb from all of the mental anguish she'd endured trying to keep things together. Numb from the way he'd treated her. Crystie's self-esteem and mental stability had taken several blows over the past year. Now there she stood, blood speckled on her legs and hands, a hot burner clutched in her hand, and two dead bodies resting at her feet.

"Police! Drop the weapon!" the first arriving police officers screamed.

Crystie heard them coming, yet she still hadn't moved. She couldn't move. Something had her rooted to the floor. She smiled at the sound of the police officers' voices. It was a goofy, maniacal type of smile that was a nervous reaction she'd had since childhood. Crystie couldn't help the expression, nor did she mean it. She knew damn well that there was nothing to smile about.

In response to the weapons that were trained on her, Crystie let the gun fall from her hand. It skittered onto the shiny hardwood floors with a scratchy noise that made her skin crawl. Finally, she could feel something. It was her blood rushing as her heart thumped wildly. Crystie now realized she was in a world of trouble. She opened her mouth to speak, but no words came out. It was only a matter of seconds before she was being manhandled and thrown roughly to the floor. She landed on her stomach with a thud as the wind was knocked out of her. Several cops laid hands on her, and not soft touches either. They were treating her like she'd just assassinated the president.

"Search her for weapons!" one of the officers barked. Crystie knew she didn't have anything else. She had only purchased one gun—a .40 caliber Glock.

As she was being lifted off the ground to be placed into the squad car, Crystie looked over and stared into his eyes, the familiar eyes that she had fallen in love with years ago. His eyes seemed to glare back at her—cold, glassy, and dead.

"You made me do this. You pushed me to the limit," Crystie mumbled almost incoherently as she kept staring into the dead, dilated pupils of the man who was once the love of her life, the father to her children, and most importantly her husband.

"This shit is like an episode of *Snapped*," one officer said loudly, breaking up Crystie's reverie.

"Looks like she just went off. This is one of the worst crimes of passion I've seen in a while," another officer commented. They had no idea just how bad it was.

"I wonder what happened? I mean I've heard that breaking up is hard to do, but damn. What would drive her to do some shit like this—cold blooded?" the other officer asked.

Crystie was pushed into the backseat of a squad car. She started rocking back and forth as she thought about the officer's questions. She began to remember just what had driven her to her breaking point.

Ex-Wife Status

BY AMALEKA MCCALL

CHAPTER 1
The Beginning of the End
One Year Earlier

The sound of the doorbell ringing roused Crystie Bale from a sound, drug-induced sleep. Opening her eyes in response to the annoying ringing, she looked over at the empty spot on the other side of her bed where her husband Quinton should've been lying. For some reason she was expecting him to be there, but the neatly tucked sheets and untouched pillow quickly brought her back to reality. Crystie dreamed that Quinton had come back home.

The bell rang again, jolting her. She rolled over with her face drawn tightly into a frown. Somebody was really ringing her damn bell. Crystie squinted her eyes to look at the cable box to verify the time. It was only eight o'clock in the morning and she wasn't expecting any visitors. Besides, the sleep sedatives she'd been taking since her separation from Quinton had not yet fully worn off, so Crystie still felt tired and drained.

The bell rang again, this time with more urgency.

"Wait a fuckin' minute. I know these Jehovah's Witnesses done lost their damn minds," Crystie said as she threw her legs over the side of the bed. She grabbed her robe and headed down the steps toward the front door of her home. When she made it to the bottom of the stairs she didn't bother to peek out of the small glass window next to the door. Instead, she just snatched open the door and got ready to curse out somebody. Crystie opened her mouth, but before she could utter a word, the person standing in front of her beat her to the punch.

"Mrs. Crystie Victoria Bale?" a tall, slender man asked as he looked at her.

"Who wants to know?" she snapped, surveying the man suspiciously.

"Here you go, ma'am," the man said, extending his hand to give Crystie a thick manila envelope addressed to her, but with no return address.

Crystie grabbed the envelope without thinking, her eyebrows furrowed in confusion. "What's this shit?" she asked, surveying the sealed envelope.

"It's a package, ma'am. Now if you'd just sign here," the man said, rushing her. Crystie scribbled her name without reading the form. Her mind was still fuzzy with sleep.

"Who sent this?" Crystie finally asked, turning the package over in her hands a couple of times. But the man was already down the front steps of her home before she could fully get out her question.

"Consider yourself served," he called out, smirking as he climbed into his white pickup truck and pulled away from the curb.

Crystie opened her mouth, but he was gone before she could even formulate a response. She noticed her nosey neighbor across the street watching her. "Fuck is you looking at?" Crystie grumbled and slammed her door.

Once inside, she ripped the seal on the envelope, pulled out a set of papers, and began reading. A hot feeling came over her body when she read the words PETITION FOR DIVORCE. She felt like someone had punched her in the chest and knocked the wind out of her. As she leaned against the door for support, she let her eyes run rapidly over the words on the paper.

"Oh my God," Crystie gasped as she read further. Quinton was filing for divorce. A tennis ball sized lump formed in the back of her throat and she gripped the papers so tightly that the edge of the paper cut her finger. As soon as tears formed in her eyes she heard her kids moving around upstairs.

"Mommy!" Tiana, Crystie's three-year-old called out. Crystie could also hear her two-year-old daughter Tamia calling for her as well, but Crystie couldn't move. She was paralyzed with shock and disbelief at what her husband was doing.

"How dare he!" Crystie groaned, holding her chest as if she was having a heart attack.

After everything she had been through with Quinton, after everything she had sacrificed for the sake of their marriage, for his career, this was how he was repaying her? Crystie's mind whizzed with thoughts of all she'd given up. She felt dizzy just thinking about her past.

The day she met Quinton, Crystie was rushing down the train station steps at Fifty-ninth Street and Columbus Circle. She was coming from school and had to get to her night job. Quinton was coming up the stairs and they ran dead smack into each other.

"Excuse me," Quinton said as he grabbed Crystie's shoulders to keep her from sending them both barreling down the stairs.

"I'm late! I'm so sorry!" Crystie huffed to catch her breath as she watched the doors to her train close.

Quinton flashed a beautiful, straight toothed smile and told Crystie it was all right. "Calm down, pretty. There will be another train. C'mon, I'll walk with you," he said. Quinton paid a second fare, since he had just exited the turnstiles, and he walked Crystie inside to wait for the next train.

At first Crystie was skeptical of Quinton, as she was of all men. But when she realized he was just trying to be a gentleman, the gesture made Crystie mushy inside. She never really trusted men too much. She didn't trust anyone really, except her cousin Lydia, who was also her best friend.

"You didn't have to follow me back inside and use another metro card swipe," Crystie told Quinton.

"It's not a problem. It's not every day an average old dude like me runs—literally—into a beautiful woman like you," Quinton replied.

Crystie blushed so hard that she couldn't even look him in the eye. She peeked down the tracks, but there was no train in sight. She checked her watch and shifted her weight from one foot to the other. She hated being late, but at least that day it would be worth it.

"So I can't keep calling you the beautiful woman that ran into me, so what's your name?" Quinton asked.

"Crystie," she replied, lowering her eyes as if she had done something wrong.

Quinton smiled. "I'm Quinton," he told her. He stuck out his hand for a shake.

Crystie lightened up a little bit and shook his hand. He took her hand, pulled it up to his lips, and kissed the top. The kiss sent a hot feeling down Crystie's spine. Crystie felt an instant connection with Quinton. She never believed in that bullshit love at first sight, but that day she thought she could understand when people said they fell in love at first sight.

Quinton was tall, dark, and handsome. It was a cliché, but it was very true when it came to him. He stood six feet two inches tall, and his skin was the color of espresso. He had an athletic build and his thick, curly crown of hair was perfectly shaped at his forehead and sideburns. Crystie felt kind of awkward because he was so gorgeous, and she had never even thought of herself as cute. But he told her several times how beautiful she was during that short meeting.

"Can I get a number to call you?" Quinton asked as another train came bolting into the station.

Crystie didn't hesitate to comply with his request. She gave him her cell phone number, and she also took his, although she didn't plan on calling him.

Quinton watched as she got on the train, smiling the entire time. Crystie stared at him until she couldn't see him anymore. She didn't even realize that she smiled during her entire train ride while thinking about Quinton. That evening at work Crystie couldn't concentrate. She kept replaying the episode with the hunky stranger over and over in her head. To her great surprise, Quinton called her that same evening. He told her exactly what she'd been thinking too.

"I could not stop thinking about our chance meeting," he said, his voice a deep baritone that made her pulse quicken.

That was the first of many conversations. Quinton took Crystie to a quaint, trendy eatery in Manhattan for their first date. They spoke about everything from politics to rap music. It was more than Crystie could've asked for in a man. Quinton then rode with Crystie back to Brooklyn, although he was from the Bronx. He did and said everything right.

After several weeks of dating, they were finally alone together at his place. That night Quinton awakened every nerve ending in Crystie's body when he touched her. He explored her body like a meticulous surgeon.

Crystie was rigid at first, because she had never really had what she considered a good sexual experience. As a child she had been felt up and molested by an older cousin, and she had given up her virginity in the eighth grade to a boy that spread that information all over the school. Sex wasn't high on Crystie's to-do or to-like lists. But when Quinton touched her, kissed her, and whispered sweet things in her ears, he put her at ease.

When he entered her for the first time it sent her reeling into a place that she never wanted to come back from. It was more than love that she felt. Crystie thought she might be infatuated with Quinton. He seemed to feel the same way about her, and they started spending a lot of time together.

Crystie began to slack on her studies at John Jay College of Criminal Justice. Before she met Quinton, she had never been late to a class, much less missed one. But after they started dating, Quinton would beg her to stay with him and miss classes. Crystie was too in love to protest, so her studies fell to the wayside.

They had been together for eight months when Quinton told Crystie, "I want you to be in my life forever. I'm not ready to get married yet, but when I am, I know you will be my wife."

A few tears dropped from Crystie's eyes due to the sheer happiness she felt. "Oh, Quinton, I love you so much!" Crystie responded, throwing her arms around his neck and hugging him tightly. It was at that moment, although she didn't say it, that Crystie surrendered her entire self—body, mind, and soul—to Quinton.

"I love you too," Quinton said. No man had ever loved Crystie. She had never known her father, and her uncles and cousins certainly didn't love her.

That night Quinton made love to her again. It was the first time he took off the protection, and the first time Crystie let herself go fully. She performed oral sex on Quinton for the first time, and he exchanged the favor. In Crystie's mind, she would've done just about anything for the man of her dreams.

Several months later Quinton moved in with her. One day soon thereafter, he came home excited. Crystie was in bed, since she had just gotten home after a day at school and then working a late shift.

"Crystie! Crystie! Where are you, baby?" Quinton yelled.

Tired as hell, but wanting to be responsive to her man, Crystie bolted upright in the bed and forced a smile onto her face. Quinton came barreling into their bedroom waving an envelope in his hand. He bounced onto the bed and put the envelope in Crystie's face.

"What? What's that?" she asked, looking at him like he was crazy. She already felt excited for him just seeing his eyes all lit up.

"It's my acceptance! I got into the business program at Baruch! That shit is super competitive, but I finally got it!" Quinton yelled.

Crystie started clapping. "Yay! Oh, baby, I'm so happy for you!" she sang, grabbing him for a hug and kiss.

Quinton was too excited to kiss her. He hopped off the bed and started walking in circles. "You don't know what this means, Crystie. We are set! We will be on our way. That fucking program turns out the best marketing, finance, and company executives in the nation. Can't you see me as the VP of a Fortune 500 company?" Quinton asked excitedly.

Crystie nodded her head vigorously. She could actually see her man exchanging his baggy jeans for a suit and French cuff shirts. Crystie was so happy for him. She had learned over the months they were dating that Quinton had come from rough beginnings, even worse than her own. He was in foster care starting at age two, and since he was never adopted, he found it very hard to focus and stay in school. He aged out of the system at eighteen and worked odd jobs while studying to get his GED. Crystie was proud of him and she admired him.

"You are going to be the best VP in the world, baby," Crystie said. She got off the bed and embraced her man. That night he made passionate, excited love to her right on the bedroom floor. Crystie was deeper in love than she could ever have anticipated.

Crystie completely stopped going to college after Quinton got his acceptance and started business school. He somehow convinced her that quitting was the best thing to do. Head over heels in love, Crystie gave up her dream of being a forensic scientist just like that. She walked out of school and never looked back. Instead she worked two jobs while Quinton studied for his business degree. Crystie was their only source of income while Quinton went to school full-time.

Crystie believed she was working hard for their relationship and for what he promised her in the future. She believed him when he told her that once he graduated and landed a job at a big marketing firm, she wouldn't ever have to work again.

Sometimes Crystie felt neglected after Quinton started school. He would spend a lot of time at the library or at school, but Crystie remained loyal. She worked, cooked, washed his clothes, bought his metro cards, and paid the mortgage and maintenance fees on the condo they'd purchased in Brooklyn in addition to helping him buy his textbooks. Crystie would often be dead tired after working in the morning and going to her evening gig, but when Quinton wanted to make love to her or asked for her help with research papers, she would never tell him no. No matter whether she was tired, sick, or just really didn't feel like it, Crystie gave Quinton her all, despite Quinton not always showing his appreciation.

One night Crystie was in bed when he finally came home from studying at school. She heard him slamming around inside their tiny apartment, but she was too tired to move.

"Crystie!" Quinton called out, his tone angry.

Crystie moaned in response, and Quinton stormed into the bedroom.

"You didn't make nothing to eat?" he yelled. "Or at least bring something in?"

Crystie couldn't believe his nerve. She had been working like a dog. All he did was go to school. Shit, the least he could do was get food. She had gone to bed hungry herself.

"I didn't get anything because I was too tired," she said instead of voicing her thoughts. "But I can get up and make you something."

She didn't think he would really expect her to get up, but he did. That night was the first real sign of selfishness Crystie had ever seen in Quinton. There would be many more signs of that in the years to come.

Only part of the fantasy that Quinton had sold Crystie worked out the way he said it would. Sure, Quinton graduated from Baruch at the top of his class and landed the big job at one of the premier marketing firms in New York. He had even told Crystie that she could stop working her two jobs, and Crystie quit immediately. She was content being at home for Quinton. She did all of her duties and finally he asked her to marry him. It wasn't a romantic proposal. By then Quinton had stopped being sweet and romantic. But it was a proposal nonetheless.

He took Crystie to dinner at Peter Luger in Brooklyn. She hated steak, but she was still overjoyed. He slid the small ring box across the table just as Crystie lifted her glass to her mouth and taken a gulp of her soda. The sight of the box made her almost choke.

"What's this?" she asked.

Quinton gave her an annoyed look, but he didn't say anything. Instead her waited for her to open the box.

"Oh my God, Quinton!" Crystie said, cupping her hands around her mouth.

"I want a simple wedding," he said immediately. "We don't need to spend a lot of money to feed a bunch of people that don't matter."

He had some nerve. Crystie had been noticing that Quinton was real careful about his spending when he was the one making the money. But when Crystie was the breadwinner, they would often spend money frivolously.

With the help of Lydia, Crystie planned a very small, intimate wedding. Most of the attendees were her friends and some of her family. Quinton didn't have many friends and he certainly didn't have a family.

After they were married, Quinton still wanted Crystie to stay home. They started a family right away. After the birth of their first daughter, Quinton and Crystie seemed to be the couple to envy. Although Crystie dealt with some of his cruel ways in the privacy of their own home, to outsiders they seemed happy and in love, and they were living what appeared to be every woman's fantasy. That was until it all backfired.

Crystie became a Stepford wife—cooking, cleaning, caring for her husband and child all while keeping a smile plastered on her face. And then she made the biggest mistake of her life. Crystie gave up who she was. She changed her style to be more "wife" like. Her jeans were looser, she hardly ever wore heels anymore, and she made baggy sweat suits her regular wardrobe. She no longer worried about her hair being done or her nails being filed. She no longer cared about her disappearing waistline. She was so fully focused on taking care of Quinton and building a home that she no longer remembered the woman she was when she'd met Quinton.

She was once a beautiful young woman with an hour-glass shape, a fresh face that required no makeup, and a good head on her shoulders. When Quinton met Crystie, she had style and class, and she always made sure she kept her nails manicured and toenails painted. She worked out five days a week to keep a flat stomach and small waist.

Quinton seemed enamored with her in the beginning. He was super attentive, and especially sensitive to her feelings. He would often tell her how beautiful she was and he would do little sweet things for her like leaving rose petals on her pillow. When she surrendered her own education to help finance his business degree, he seemed to fall deeper in love with her. But after Quinton graduated and they started living real life, things changed. It seemed like once Crystie had given up who she was to be a mother and a wife, Quinton began to lose respect and admiration for her.

Quinton began to treat Crystie even worse after the birth of their second child. He was upset when Crystie told him she was pregnant so soon after their first child. Crystie knew she had gained weight with the pregnancies, but she wasn't prepared for the level of betrayal she felt when Quinton told her he couldn't bear to have sex with her because she repulsed him.

"Look at your stomach," he said. "You expect my dick to get hard looking at that shit? It looks like brains, all those fuckin' nasty stretch marks."

Crystie cried for two days after that. He never apologized to her either. It was as if he thought he was justified in that level of disrespect.

Yet Crystie didn't let Quinton's cruelty and neglect deter her from trying to be a good wife. She joined Curves, got her nails and hair done, and even purchased a hot little lingerie number from Frederick's of Hollywood. But none of those things worked or helped. Quinton still barely touched her, and when he did, it was so mundane and routine that Crystie often buried her face in her pillow and cried afterward.

After a while Quinton moved up in his company and started traveling and spending long nights at the office. His neglect rose to an all new level. Still, Crystie tried even harder to please him. She would cook extra big meals, clean the house so it was spotless, and tried to dress and look as sexy as possible. But nothing worked. She started to grow frustrated and angry. Sometimes she would express her displeasure with his treatment, but that would always turn right back against her.

After months of arguing, Crystie agreed with Quinton when he said he would live at the condo they owned before they bought their house. With Quinton in their condo, and Crystie in the house, she thought they could rebuild their relationship like two people dating. Crystie convinced herself that all Quinton needed was space and time to miss her and the kids and he would come running back to them. But things hadn't worked out that way at all.

After he moved, Quinton barely visited Crystie and the kids, and when he did, he always seemed to be in a rush. It was

| 171 |

always some business meeting, business trip, or business deal that took precedence over Crystie and the kids. Every once in a while he would have sex with her during one of his cameo appearances. But the way Quinton performed in bed made Crystie feel like he was providing her with sympathy sex.

Although they'd now been separated for over six months, Crystie had never expected this—not divorce papers.

"Mommy, why you crying?" Tiana asked, her little angelic voice breaking up Crystie's romp down memory lane.

Crystie opened her red-rimmed eyes to look into her daughter's eyes, whose face resembled Quinton's down to the one dimple in her left cheek. Crystie hadn't even realized her kids had come downstairs and were now standing in front of her while her mind raced backward down memory lane. She inhaled and tried to pull herself together for the kids.

"I'm OK, baby. Are you guys hungry!" Crystie asked in a phony display of happiness, trying to sound excited so she could put her kids at ease.

"Yes!" her two beautiful little girls sang out innocently. Crystie pulled herself up from the floor and dragged her feet into the gourmet kitchen. It seemed so much bigger and lonelier now.

As she prepared each of her kids' favorite meals, Crystie lapsed into tears each time she thought about the way Quinton had done things. She felt so betrayed. He didn't even have the decency or respect to talk to her about his plans. He never told her he wanted a divorce. In fact, Crystie was under the impression that Quinton wanted to work things out. Although he had never said he wanted to work it out, Crystie had held out hope that he was coming back home as soon as he got the space he needed.

Crystie slammed down her fists on the granite countertop and bit into her lip just thinking about being all alone with two kids. She felt nauseous and her legs got weak as she waited for the girls' waffles to be ready in the microwave. The thought of divorce had not fully settled into her mind yet. She could not believe Quinton was leaving her just like that. She had nothing of her own except the two kids.

She gripped the side of the counter now as she thought about her situation. She gripped harder the more she felt her life slipping away from her. Crystie managed to pull herself together enough to feed her kids and put them in the bathtub where they usually played for about an hour.

She sat on the closed toilet seat to watch them play in the water. She usually played with them or sang songs, but not today. She was in a daze. Every time she thought about what was going on, her mind slipped back to the past. Some memories were good and some were bad. But as she searched in her mind, nothing stuck out that warranted a divorce.

While she sat there half watching the kids, Crystie pulled out the divorce papers again for the tenth time since she'd been served with them. This time her mind was coherent enough to read them carefully. As she read, some of the words stuck out to her, like "irreconcilable differences, infidelity, and cruel and unusual treatment." Crystie could feel her blood pressure rising the further she read.

Quinton was actually saying that *she* was responsible for the demise of their marriage. That was just like him to blame her for everything, another habit he had picked up over the years. No matter what the issue, Crystie was always responsible.

"Oh hell no!" Crystie mumbled mindlessly as she stepped out of the bathroom with the crumpled papers still waded between her balled fists. She did not even think about leaving the kids alone in the tub, which she never did, not even for a minute. Too angry to remember the kids, Crystie stomped into her bedroom and picked up her cordless house phone. She blocked the number and dialed Quinton's business cell phone number. At this time of day Crystie knew he had no choice but to answer an unknown call because he would probably think it was a client.

She bit into her lip as she waited for him to answer.

"Hello?" His deep voice filtered through the phone.

Crystie felt a flash of nerves, but they quickly turned to pure anger. "You motherfucker!" she yelled. "I cannot fucking believe after all I gave up, after all the shit I did for your ass, you have the fucking nerve to file for a divorce!" Crystie boomed into the phone, which was uncharacteristic for her. She was usually calm and collected, and she damn sure had taken a lot of Quinton's shit over the years. The impending divorce had sent her to a different place, though.

"Now is not the time to talk about this," Quinton responded calmly.

That response just pissed off Crystie even more. He sounded so smug and composed while she was frazzled and a mess. She could picture him with a smirk on his face and his arms folded.

"Don't tell me it's not the fucking time!" Crystie shrieked. "Our marriage is on the line here! What am I supposed to do, Quinton? What did I ever do to deserve this but try to love you and take care of you!" Crystie shrieked, her voice cracking. Everything was spinning. She felt like she was on one of those amusement park rides where the floor falls out. She couldn't help the tears that started flowing down her face in buckets. She clenched her fists tightly and the vein in her neck throbbed fiercely.

Crystie was mad at herself for letting Quinton hear her cry, but she just couldn't contain her pain. She did not remember feeling so off kilter and crazed since the day she realized her mother wasn't coming back after leaving Crystie her with grandmother, who already had a house full of other grandkids.

"Crystie, we have been over for a while now. You and I both know this. Don't act like there was any love left," Quinton continued in his smooth, calm voice.

His words were like a gut punch and Crystie flopped down on her bed, exasperated. What the fuck did he mean there wasn't any love left? That was certainly not how she felt. She still loved Quinton with every fiber of her being. Crystie didn't think anything could change that. His words were cruel. She felt overwhelmed with anxiety, like she'd just found out someone close to her had died. What would she do without Quinton? Crystie had admitted to herself long before this that she loved him more than she loved herself.

"Please, Quinton, don't do this. I'm begging you. I will do anything you want. I will lose weight. I'm sorry I had another baby. We can work this out. Puh-lease!" Crystie pleaded, her words muffled by her sobs. She didn't know which of the things she mentioned had caused her husband to want to leave, but she was willing to fix them all. "Please, Quinton, give us another chance!" Crystie cried, her words barely understandable. She was a blubbering mess. She didn't care if her hysterics made Quinton mad, though. She just couldn't help letting out her feelings if it meant it would save the most important thing to her in the world—her marriage.

"Tsk." Quinton sucked his teeth in disgust. "Crystie, you're better than this. Pull yourself together. You finally have to be your own person. I don't see us being together ever again. It's over," Quinton said with a snide undertone.

"But why!" Crystie screamed, letting her raw emotion be known. *What nerve he has telling me to be my own person after he completely destroyed who I was years ago,* she thought. But Crystie didn't voice her thoughts. She didn't want to say anything else that would piss him off. She just wanted to beg him to come back home and work things out.

"Look, just face it. Once again I'll say it. It is over," he said, putting emphasis on each word. "You knew this when I moved out. You're far from a dummy, Crystie. You can start over. I have to go. I will be by to pick up the girls for a visit later this evening. Please have them ready," Quinton said with finality.

Crystie felt like someone had slapped her around, or maybe even punched the shit out of her. Her body ached with an overwhelming feeling of adrenaline and anxiety.

"No! No! Quinton, don't do this!" Crystie screamed in one last-ditch effort to convince him to change his mind. Her efforts fell on deaf ears. Nothing she did would make him change his mind.

"Get yourself together. You sound like a mess. And like I said, have the girls ready," he snapped.

Crystie's mood switched gears like she was a stick-shift car. A pang of pure anger flashed in her chest and replaced her previous feeling of sorrow. Crystie searched her mind for something to say or do that would make Quinton hurt as much as he was hurting her.

"You will not see your kids if you do this! I'm warning you, Quinton Bale!" Crystie boomed, her emotions hanging out there like a sore thumb. Quinton was quiet. "Do you hear me?" Crystie screamed.

Then she heard something that made her heart feel like it would burst. It was like her worst nightmare had come true. Crystie could hear a woman's voice in the background talking to Quinton. Crystie pressed the phone closer to her ear so she could hear better. She had to be sure her ears weren't deceiving her.

"Quinton!" Crystie screeched. He didn't answer, but Crystie could tell he was trying to keep the woman in the background away from the phone. Crystie heard a bit of shuffling and fumbling. She was fully focused and honed in on the sounds in the background. "Who is that?" she asked. "I know you can't have a fucking woman in my condo!" Crystie screamed, her voice high-pitched and jagged. "We are still fucking married, Quinton! So that's it! That's what this is all about. Just like that? Out of nowhere! It's a bitch that is making you do this! I can't believe you would betray me like this! After all I've done!"

Crystie cried again. The tears came flooding back again. She felt defeated and weak. He was cheating on her.

"How could you disrespect me like this?" she asked. "How could you give up on what we have and our kids? Don't you think they deserve better than their father leaving them over a bitch? I guess you want your kids to be statistics just like we were, huh? No father around! " Crystie cried some more, trying to appeal to any mercy Quinton might have.

"Look, I have to go. Either you let me get the kids or you don't. It's all up to you, but I won't fight you," Quinton replied.

Before Crystie could formulate a response, the phone went dead. He had hung up in her ear, one of the things she considered most disrespectful, right up there with spitting on someone.

"Quinton! Quinton!" Crystie screamed into the dead phone. He was really gone. Flabbergasted, Crystie dialed his number back over a dozen times, but he refused to answer his phone. After her thirteenth call it began going straight to his voicemail. Crystie threw her phone across the room in frustration and anger, sending the back cover and the battery pack flying in opposite directions.

She started pacing, trying to figure out what to do next. Suddenly she heard coughing, gagging, and splashing noises coming from the bathroom where her babies were taking their baths. A rush of heat came over Crystie and she was moving before her mind really even registered anything like danger.

"Oh my God! The girls!" Crystie shrieked as she was spurred into action and her legs started moving. She raced down the long hallway between her bedroom and the kids' bathroom. Crystie almost fainted when she reached the doorway of the bathroom. Her eyes grew as wide as dinner plates and her throat was desert dry as a feeling of fear and panic gripped her tightly.

"Tamia! Oh my God!" Crystie screamed.

With one swift move she was at the side of the bathtub snatching her baby out of the bottom of the deep, porcelain tub. The tub was almost completely filled with water. The girls must have been playing with the faucets and turned on the water after Crystie walked out.

"Tamia, baby! C'mon, breathe!" Crystie belted out frantically. Crystie started shaking her youngest child. The baby's eyes were rolling as she fought to breathe. Crystie continued to shake her. She didn't know what else to do. She didn't even think about shaken baby syndrome or the damage she could've inflicted on her baby by jerking her so roughly. All Crystie was focused on was getting her little girl to breathe properly.

"Tamia! Please!" Crystie screamed, shaking the baby even more violently than before. Tiana was still standing in the water screaming. Crystie couldn't comfort her other child. She had to save her baby.

"C'mon, baby!" Crystie belted out, hitting her two-year-old on the back. Suddenly the baby started coughing and throwing up water. Crystie had never been so happy to see vomit in all of her life. A sense of relief swept over Crystie's panicked and rushed emotions.

"Oh, thank God! Baby! My baby! I'm so sorry! Mommy is so sorry!" Crystie cried. Tiana was trembling, her teeth chattering. She was afraid. Crystie helped Tiana out of the tub and wrapped both of her kids in their cartoon character towels. The close call was enough to get her back to reality.

"Mommy is sorry," she said again. "It's all my fault. Everything is my fault. Neither of you deserve this kind of life," Crystie said, holding her babies tightly. Crystie and her kids sat on the wet bathroom floor for the next half hour while Crystie wondered what to do next.

CHAPTER 2
The Calm Before the Storm

Crystie had finally calmed down from her baby's near drowning scare. Although she was collected, she was far from cool. She threw on an old sweat suit that was half a size too small and caused her flabby stomach to protrude over the waist line. She hand combed her short, tapered hair and tried to get it to look like something. When she glanced at herself in the mirror, she didn't even recognize the person staring back at her. She had changed over the years so much, and she hadn't ever taken the time to notice just how much. Even her hair was short now when it had been almost down to her butt when she met Quinton. She had dark rings under her eyes now where before she had flawless, blemish free caramel-colored skin.

Looking at herself caused another wave of anxiety to come over her. She envisioned Quinton's new woman to be gorgeous, in shape, and everything that she was not. Picturing different women with Quinton had been driving Crystie crazy. She had the sudden urge to see Quinton, to confront him, but more importantly to see who he had left her for.

"Tiana and Tamia, let's go!" Crystie called out to her kids urgently. The two little girls came bounding out of their room. Crystie had dressed them to look like a mess too. She was clearly not focused. The kids had on bottoms and tops that didn't match and she hadn't bothered to redo their ponytails, so their hair was fuzzy and sticking up in places. She never took them outside like that, but today she was in a rush.

"Let's go see Daddy!" Tiana sang out. Crystie cringed. Just thinking about what the divorce would do to her kids caused Crystie's stomach to suddenly cramp.

"Yes, let's go see Daddy," she told her kids.

Crystie strapped both kids into their car seats and slid into the driver's seat of her Cadillac SRX. Even the car reminded her of her husband. He had bought her the car and told her he had chosen that particular cross between a car and a minivan because it was a "soccer mom" car. Crystie had been too over-joyed that she had a new car to even think about his words. She hadn't thought anything of his statement at the time, but now the car represented everything Crystie didn't want to be—some boring suburban housewife waiting for her husband to dole out her allowance so she could go buy a pair of "mom" jeans and a cardigan.

Crystie made it to Brooklyn from Long Island in record time. She sped through the streets of Brooklyn until she was finally in front of the condo building she used to live in with her husband. She pulled her car into the inside parking lot and drove around to what used to be her personalized parking spot. Crystie immediately noticed a silver Lexus LS 400 with perso-nalized plates reading DARCY G parked in the spot. Crystie's heart began hammering against her chest bone.

"This can't be the same spot," she whispered. Quinton wouldn't be stupid enough to have his bitch park in Crystie's spot. She craned her neck and squinted her eyes to make sure the number on the parking spot was the same one she remem-bered.

"Thirty-five seventy-six," she whispered. It was definitely her spot. Then she noticed Quinton's car right next to it and that was all she needed to confirm her suspicions. He had this bitch already living with him in a place Crystie had slaved to purchase. It was yet another blatant slap in Crystie's face by her husband. Without even thinking, Crystie grabbed the car door handle and scrambled to get out of the car. When she lifted her foot off the gas the car lurched forward and almost hit the intruding Lexus that was occupying Crystie's old parking spot.

"Fuck!" Crystie cursed and threw her car into park.

Focused on her mission, Crystie fumbled with the door handles again and raced out of her car. She was so furious that she left her sleeping children in the backseat of the car. She was definitely losing it. This would be the second time her mind had gone so blank that she forgot about her kids.

Crystie took the stairs from the parking lot that led into the condo building two at a time to the fifth floor. While she raced through the building's stairwell, a memory of a hot and heavy petting session she and Quinton had when they first moved into the building came flooding back to Crystie's mind.

Quinton stopped her from going up the steps and spun her around to face him. Crystie giggled and tried to pull away from him, but Quinton held her tightly. He placed his mouth on top of hers and forced his tongue between her lips. She relented and kissed him passionately. Then Quinton lifted her shirt, pulled up her bra, and took mouthfuls of her breasts right there. Crystie sighed and let the hot feeling take her over. She wanted him to fuck her right there. Quinton got her so hot and heavy that by the time they reached their door, she was already half naked and she didn't care who was watching them.

The memory threatened to send Crystie's heart into overdrive. Flinging the exit door open violently, Crystie raced through it and sped down the carpeted hallway until she reached the familiar door—her door to be exact. She didn't have her keys to the condo anymore. Quinton had taken them from her in exchange for keys to their new home in Baldwin, Long Island. But it didn't matter if Crystie still had keys. Quinton would've surely changed the locks.

Crystie banged on the condo door like she was the police. "Quinton! Open this fuckin' door!" Crystie screamed. She didn't care about the noise ordinance that was enforced in the ritzy building. "I know you're in there with that bitch! Open this fuckin' door! I am your wife!" Crystie boomed. She could hear some of the neighbors moving their peephole covers to see what was going on.

Quinton pulled back the door wearing the most evil scowl Crystie had ever seen. She knew he'd open the door because he hated to be embarrassed. Quinton was always worried about what white people and other ritzy black people thought of him. But Crystie knew where he really came from.

"What are you—" he started to say, but Crystie didn't allow him to finish. She pushed him so hard in his chest that he stumbled backward. He wasn't expecting her brute force, so he was unable to brace himself in time. Crystie came barreling into the condo like a bat out of hell.

"Where the fuck is she, Quinton?" Crystie growled as she stormed into the living room of the condo. Crystie whirled around like a crazed madwoman, looking in every direction for the bitch responsible for breaking up her marriage.

"You need to leave," Quinton said, grabbing Crystie's arm roughly.

Just then a young, beautiful Hispanic looking woman came sauntering out of the bedroom. Crystie was stopped cold. The woman's beautiful butter-colored face, long, dark, silky hair and slim, shapely legs made Crystie feel horrible. Crystie felt like dying right there on the spot. She felt so ugly and fat compared to the siren sauntering around in front of her that Crystie wished she could blink herself out of there that very instant.

"Honey, is everything OK?" the beautiful woman asked Quinton, her face crumpled in confusion.

Crystie's eyes hooded over when she noticed that the woman was wearing a John Jay College T-shirt Crystie had bought Quinton years ago when all he wore were T-shirts and jeans. All of Crystie's feelings of insecurity quickly converted to blind rage. Crystie's vision became clouded and she began seeing red spots in the corners of her eyes. Her chest began heaving in and out. She viewed the woman as the enemy now. Not only did this bitch ruin her marriage, but she was in Crystie's home taking her place in Quinton's life.

"Is everything OK?" Crystie yelled. "You got some nerve, bitch!" Crystie barked, moving in the woman's direction with her finger pointed menacingly.

"Crystie, you just need to leave," Quinton said, trying to pull her toward the door.

The woman looked Crystie up and down and smirked. That was enough to send Crystie over the top.

"Arrgghh!!" Crystie screamed, breaking free from Quinton's grasp. Crystie charged into the woman with full force. The woman screamed, but it was too late. Crystie was too thick and too strong for the puny little woman to handle. The woman fell backward on her ass so hard she let out a little squeak when she hit the floor. She was unable to break her own fall or put her hands up in time to block Crystie from getting at her.

Crystie was on top of Quinton's new love within minutes. She was like a wild animal just let out of captivity. She wound her hand up in the woman's beautiful hair and began punching her in her pretty face. Crystie wasn't going to have any mercy on the bitch taking everything from her. She felt like she was at war fighting for her territory.

"He's married! I'm his fucking wife, you home wrecking whore!" Crystie growled from someplace deep inside her. She sounded animalistic and she acted just as badly.

| 183 |

Quinton rushed over to the two women's tangled bodies and tried to pull Crystie off of his beautiful new woman, but Crystie was relentless. She had a grip on the woman's hair so tight that each time Quinton pulled her, the woman screamed out because Crystie was almost pulling out the woman's hair almost by the roots.

"Crystie, you are going to jail! I am calling the police!" Quinton belted out after he was finally able to pull off his scorned wife from his lover. Crystie had a handful of the woman's hair and she had blood from the woman's nose all over her sweat suit.

Quinton dragged Crystie over to the door kicking, scratching, and screaming. He pushed her out into the hallway, but it was no easy task. Crystie had taken some of the skin off of Quinton's chest and arms with her nails. She could hear the woman speaking to the police.

"This shit is not over, Quinton Bale! It's not fucking over!" Crystie screamed through tears. Quinton slammed the door. With the sound of the door slamming, Crystie was brought back to reality.

"My kids!" she yelled, her body quaking with fear and anxiety. She had forgotten all about them. Crystie took off running toward the parking garage. When she got downstairs she noticed the garage security guard standing by her car shining a flashlight inside while he peeked through the windows.

"I'm here! I just had to get something quick!" Crystie called out breathlessly, trying in vain to straighten out her mangled clothes and hair. The guard looked at her strangely. He noticed the blood on her and her wild hair. He turned his flashlight toward her.

"The police are on the way, miss. I can't let you leave," the guard said.

This toy cop can't be serious, Crystie thought. He just didn't know what kind of mood she was in right then.

"I didn't do anything," Crystie said. "Move the fuck out of my way." The guard stood his ground. He was going to be a tough guy with no gun, no handcuffs, and just a flashlight. Crystie could hear sirens in the distance. Desperate to leave before the police arrived, and still totally out of control, she punched the security guard in his face. Her blow caught him off guard and he doubled over.

"Ahhh, bitch, you crazy!" he belted out, holding his cheek.

Crystie pushed him to the ground, hopped into her driver's seat, and screeched out of the parking lot just in time. The police cruiser whizzed right past her. With tears running down her face and a sense of relief that she hadn't been arrested, Crystie drove away from the building as fast as she could.

Feeling lost and dejected, Crystie drove straight to her cousin Lydia's house. Lydia had been her best friend since childhood. They grew up in the same household, raised by their grandmother. Lydia's mother was on drugs and Crystie's mother left one day and never returned. The girls stuck together ever since.

"Please be home. Please be home," Crystie chanted as she pulled up to Lydia's house. When she saw her cousin's car outside, a sense of relief washed over her.

With her hands shaking, Crystie dialed her cousin's house number. When Lydia picked up, Crystie just started hollering into the phone. She was crying so uncontrollably Lydia couldn't even understand what she was trying to say. Crystie finally managed to tell her cousin that she was right outside. Lydia rushed outside to the car.

"Oh, God, Crystie, what the hell is going on?" Lydia gasped when she saw Crystie's physical appearance.

"He is leaving me!" Crystie broke down and wailed. Her screaming had caused the kids to start crying.

"What? Who?" Lydia asked.

"He's leaving me! It's a bitch! Oh, God, what am I gonna do, Lydia!" Crystie screamed some more, this time louder and with more emotion behind her words.

"Shhhh. OK, calm down, girl, you scaring these kids. C'mon, let me take these babies inside," Lydia told Crystie as she started taking the kids out of their car seats.

Crystie followed Lydia and the kids inside the house. She watched helplessly as her cousin fed her kids and set them down to watch cartoons. All Crystie could do was sob and sob. She looked and felt pitiful. Her kids didn't even want to be near her because she had already acted so crazy in front of them. When the kids were settled in front of the television in Lydia's living room, Lydia grabbed Crystie by the hand and led her into the kitchen. Lydia pulled out a chair and helped Crystie sit down.

"Tell me what is going on, Crystie. You drive over here unexpected. You look a mess, you were screaming like a nut, what the hell?" Lydia asked.

Crystie couldn't even hold eye contact with her cousin. She was terribly embarrassed. She had no choice but to be honest about everything. The one thing she didn't want to do was lie to Lydia any more than she already had over the past year. Crystie broke down and told Lydia everything about what she had been going through with Quinton. Lydia did not know that Quinton had moved out and had never suspected Crystie and Quinton were having any problems. Crystie had always wanted everyone to think her life was charmed and enviable. Although she loved her cousin to death, Crystie always wanted to be the one doing better than all of the cousins she had grown up with. She always felt like she had something to prove.

"Crystie, you could've called me a long time ago. Why did you hide this?" Lydia asked, a little perturbed that her cousin hid what was going on for so long.

"I was sure he would come back. I was sure it would work out. I just didn't want to turn everyone against him and then shit work out between us. I hope you understand. I was embarrassed." Crystie sobbed.

"Oh, honey, I'm so sorry," Lydia said sympathetically, touching Crystie's hand.

She reached out and embraced her cousin. She held Crystie and let her cry. Lydia told her she would be there for her through everything that was happening. It wasn't any different than when they were kids. Lydia would try to protect Crystie.

After about an hour of straight sobbing, Crystie was finally calm. Lydia made some chamomile tea for them and they were talking about Crystie's options and the things she should ask for during the divorce proceedings. It had taken Lydia a while to convince Crystie to accept that Quinton was leaving, but when she finally did convince her, she told Crystie to take his ass to the bank if he wanted to just up and leave her with two kids and a mortgage.

As they discussed things, Crystie's cell phone began ringing. She looked at it and her eyes grew wide. A quick pang of excitement mixed with fear flitted through her stomach. She looked over at Lydia like a terrified, yet excited child.

"It's Quinton," Crystie said to Lydia before she decided to answer the phone. Secretly Crystie was hoping Quinton was calling to say he had made a big mistake, he was sorry for everything, and that he was coming back.

"Are you going to answer it?" Lydia asked. Crystie slowly picked up the phone and answered the call.

"Hello," she croaked out, her throat desert dry and her heart beating like crazy.

"Just so you know, there is a restraining order against you. If you come within three hundred feet of this building, you will be arrested. You are lucky I have a real woman who didn't press charges on you because of the kids. Now stay the fuck away from me!" Quinton barked into the phone.

He was speaking to her like she was a stranger in the streets. Crystie was awestruck at how he'd changed. She didn't even recognize him anymore. Crystie's previous feelings of hope and excitement were quickly squashed by her husband's cruel words.

"Fuck you! Fuck your bitch too! You don't know who you fucked with, Quinton. I gave up everything! I have nothing, and if I can't have it all, neither will either of you! You wait and see!" Crystie screamed at the top of her lungs.

"Shhh." Lydia tried to quiet Crystie to protect the kids from being upset all over again, but it was too late. Both little girls were standing in the doorway of the kitchen crying as their mother screamed like a maniac. They had never seen their mother act like this before, and they were scared. Crystie could feel herself changing inside in more ways than one.

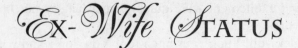
CHAPTER 3
What's Yours Is Mine and
What's Mine is Mine

It had been two days since the scuffle with Quinton and his woman, and Crystie was trying her best to make life normal for herself and her girls. She decided to do some food shopping and then a little retail therapy. Shopping always made Crystie feel better in the past, especially when all of the money was Quinton's, like now.

Crystie pulled into the Pathmark parking lot and unloaded her kids. She put them into the shopping cart and pushed them into the store. As soon as she walked into the store she noticed her pastor's wife. Crystie tried to avert her eyes and act like she didn't see the boulder-shaped woman, but there was no use. There was only one set of doors in and out, and Crystie had literally run dead into her. *Shit*, Crystie thought. She hadn't been to church in a while and certainly did not feel like explaining why to the phony ass first lady. Crystie plastered a fake smile on her face and proceeded further into the store.

"Crystie? Crystie Bale? Is that you and those beautiful little angels?" Loretta Jenkins sang out. As usual her face was painted with so much makeup that she resembled a clown, and although it was a weekday, she was dressed like she was going to church. The woman wore so much perfume Crystie could smell it coming off of her even from a distance. Crystie took a deep breath and kept on smiling so hard her cheek bones ached.

"Hey, Mrs. Jenkins. How are you?" Crystie asked, sounding just as phony as the pastor's wife.

"Oh, I am just fine. God knows it too. Crystie, what is going on? I haven't seen you in service in a month of Sundays, and then I turn around two weeks in a row and see Quinton, but instead of you and those angels being his escorts, I notice some other woman who looks young enough to be his daughter with him just as proud as a peacock with all her cleavage showing up just like a heathen," Mrs. Jenkins said, her words coming out rapid fire like she had been dying to tell someone's dirty secrets.

The information threatened to make Crystie's knees buckle. *That disrespectful motherfucker,* Crystie screamed inside her head. It was bad enough she was already ashamed of her impending divorce, but now her husband was setting out to publicly humiliate her. In Crystie's opinion it was totally unnecessary for Quinton to take his mistress to their church when Crystie could barely get him to attend with her and the kids.

Crystie felt her heart sink into her stomach as Mrs. Jenkins kept on going on and on about how she was surprised to see him with such a beautiful woman, yada, yada. Crystie felt like her bowels were going to release right there in the store at the first lady's feet. Swallowing the lump in her throat, Crystie gripped the shopping cart rail tightly. She knew she had to play it off and pull it together. There was no way she'd let Quinton win again by showing that she was caught off guard by Mrs. Jenkins's revelations.

"Oh, didn't you know? I filed for a divorce months ago. So Quinton is free to have whomever he wants, and frankly it's probably better for the both of us. See, Quinton and I just grew apart. Quinton had become so cruel to me and the children. You wouldn't even believe he was the same man. I know Pastor Jenkins teaches against divorce, but sometimes you have to know when to say when," Crystie lied, trying hard to fight back the tears burning at the backs of her eye sockets.

"Oh, I didn't know," Mrs. Jenkins said, placing her hand against her chest in a clutch-the-pearls manner. "Well I hope it all works out for you and those little angels," she continued, flashing a fake, denture clad smile.

"I'm fine. We're fine. Just fine," Crystie said, returning an even faker smile, minus the false teeth. The kids started squirming in the cart. That was Crystie's cue to get the fuck away from the lady. Besides, her stink ass perfume was making Crystie gag.

"Well, it was nice seeing you. Let me go. As you can see, the natives are getting restless," Crystie said, nodding her head toward her kids. Crystie's insides were on fire and she wished she was a genie that could blink herself right out of the store.

"Take care of those angels now," Mrs. Jenkins bellowed.

Crystie nodded and pushed her cart away from Mrs. Jenkins. She rushed four aisles down into the cereal aisle. It was the one with the least people in it. Once she felt the coast was clear, she stopped the cart and let her tears finally run down her face. A few passersby coming through the aisle looked at her strangely. A few others looked like they wanted to ask if she was all right, but none dared to say anything to her.

Crystie cried in earnest for a few minutes. She still could not believe the audacity of Quinton to take his new eye candy to their church, flaunting her in front of all of their friends. That church was where Quinton and Crystie had taken their vows, where they had worshiped as a couple and as a family. It was where Crystie had drawn her strength when everything was on her while Quinton leisurely went about his business at school. One blow after another, Crystie just didn't know how much more she could take. One thing was for sure, she knew she could never step foot back in that church again.

Finally composing herself, Crystie wiped her face and smiled at her kids. They had gotten so used to seeing her cry the past few days that it didn't even alarm them anymore. Crystie walked through the aisles and started picking up things for the house.

She was in such a routine with what she purchased that each time she touched something, Quinton was the first thing that came to her mind. Pleasing Quinton was always paramount for Crystie in everything she did, even food shopping. She was used to purchasing foods that he liked, such as, wheat bread. Crystie always hated wheat bread, but it was the only kind she purchased because Quinton liked it. If she ever purchased something he didn't eat, Quinton would complain incessantly, so Crystie learned over the years to condition herself to eat the things that he liked. But today, with a devilish feeling coming over her, Crystie picked up white bread instead of wheat. After that she had to catch herself over and over again picking up things Quinton preferred over what she actually liked. She made herself buy all of the things that she had missed over the years just because Quinton hadn't liked them. This time her shopping cart was filled with things Crystie liked.

When she made it to the counter to pay for her groceries, the kids started whining and crying for the candy that was lined up at the side of the register. Feeling emotionally and physically drained, Crystie didn't have it in her to argue with them or to hear their crying, so she just allowed them to pick up whatever they wanted. Tiana and Tamia chose all types of chocolate bars, gum, and bags of chips. Crystie couldn't care less. Normally she didn't let them eat junk food, but today whatever would keep them quiet was what Crystie was going to allow. She just wanted to go back home, climb into her bed with her sedatives, and sleep away her pain.

Crystie loaded all of her items onto the register's conveyor belt and watched as the cashier scanned her food. She looked around, hoping she wouldn't see anyone else that knew her or Quinton. She couldn't take anymore news about Quinton flaunting his woman around town. When all of the items were finished being scanned Crystie started placing her bags in the cart as she waited for the girl to give her a total.

"One hundred thirty-seven dollars and twenty-five cents," the cashier said dryly. Crystie dug into her pocketbook and handed the girl her debit card.

"Debit or credit?" the cashier asked.

"Either. It doesn't matter," Crystie answered as she reached over to make Tiana sit down in the cart before she fell out. Crystie was distracted, so she didn't notice that the girl had swiped her card several times.

"Do you have another card? This one is not working," the cashier told Crystie.

Crystie crinkled her face in confusion and looked at the girl like she was crazy. "What do you mean not working? That is a debit card connected to my bank account. It can't be declined," Crystie replied, chuckling sarcastically and nervously at the same time. She knew there was money in the bank. Quinton made a decent salary, so there was no way that their account could be so low that her card would be declined.

"It's saying declined," the girl replied, annoyed.

"Swipe it again then!" Crystie growled, urgency lacing her words. She felt flushed as the heat of embarrassment began to rise from her neck and spread across her face.

"Miss, I have swiped it at least six times. It is de-nied," the girl snapped, putting emphasis on denied.

There were people grumbling on the line behind Crystie. The kids had already bitten holes into the candy wrappers, trying to open the candy. Tiana had even gotten a piece and started eating it, which meant Crystie had no choice but to pay for it. Her heart started racing and sweat dripped down her back as she dug into her bag, trying to scrape up enough cash to at least pay for the candy. Crystie didn't have credit cards or any other bank cards. Quinton had given her one card and one card only, the debit card associated with their joint account. This had never happened to her before. Even when she considered herself dead broke, she had always known her spending limits.

"I don't know what could've happened. I have money in my account," Crystie croaked nervously as she handed the girl a bunch of change she had dug out of her purse. The cashier looked at her like she was crazy. "That's for the candy. I don't have enough for the groceries," Crystie said, on the brink of tears.

Embarrassed and wanting to melt away, Crystie frantically took the bags out of the shopping cart and set them on the floor. People behind her mumbled and made mean comments. When she was finished unloading the cart, Crystie pushed her shopping cart out of the store at top speed. She raced over to her car, loaded the kids into their car seats, and got in. Flustered, she pulled out her debit card and examined it. Locating a number on the back, she dialed the number for the bank's customer service line.

When a representative was finally on the line, Crystie began screaming at the woman about how the bank had wrongfully denied her charges. Crystie wouldn't let the woman get a word in edgewise. When the woman finally got Crystie to calm down, she said something that Crystie thought would send her over the edge.

"Mrs. Bale, your joint account owner has emptied this account and closed it. That is the reason you were unable to make a purchase today," the customer service representative said in the light, airy voice representatives all seemed to use when trying to keep irate customers calm.

The words exploded inside Crystie's ears like small bombs. "What? I . . . I . . . don't under . . . understand. Wouldn't we both . . . ha . . . have to agree to close it?" Crystie cried into the phone in total disbelief.

"No, ma'am, I'm afraid not. When the account was opened, a Mr. Quinton Bale added himself as the sole signature authority, and you were just an additional cardholder, which means he had all of the power over the account, and all you had authority to do was purchase with the card you were issued and make deposits. That is the way Mr. Bale set up the account," the woman said empathetically. She could hear in Crystie's voice that things weren't going so well.

"Thank you," Crystie replied, almost whispering as she hung up the phone. "Why, God? What did I do to deserve this?" Crystie asked aloud as she sobbed. She realized then that Quinton was playing for keeps. He had left her with nothing—literally.

Quinton bent down at the side of the bed, kissed Crystie on her cheek, and stroked her head, rousing her from sleep. Crystie looked at him strangely at first, not expecting him. When she realized it was him and that he was really there, she smiled.

"I'm sorry, Crystie. I made a big mistake. I never meant to hurt you. Will you forgive me?" he asked, still stroking her hair. Crystie began to cry, but they were tears of joy. She didn't want to scare him away with any other emotions, so she turned over and sat up. She grabbed her husband tightly and inhaled his scent. In her mind Crystie told herself she would never let him go again.

"Yes, Quinton, I forgive you. I never want us to be apart again." She cried into the skin of his thick neck. His cologne mixed with his sweat was intoxicating. She inhaled him some more.

"I love you, Crystie," Quinton said, lifting her up off the bed in a tight embrace. She straddled him, locking her legs around his waist. It felt so good to have him touch her again.

| 195 |

"I love you too, Quinton," Crystie replied.

Quinton lowered her back onto the bed and began kissing her deeply, passionately, more passionately than she ever remembered. He moved from her mouth to her neck where he ran his tongue slowly down the length of her throat. Quinton knew all the right places to touch her in order to awaken her sex drive. Crystie squirmed and moaned because his touch, his kiss all felt so good.

Quinton moved lower until he had his hot mouth on her breasts. He took each one into his mouth, gently at first, then he began to suck more rigorously. Crystie let out a soft moan. He had her in a frenzy now. She could feel sticky wetness dampening the inside of her thighs.

"I missed you," Quinton said as he devoured her areola.

"Oh, Quinton, I never want to be away from you again," Crystie said almost breathlessly. Quinton stood and began frantically removing his clothes. Crystie could tell he couldn't wait to feel her again. He had already removed her underwear. Crystie's legs shook in anticipation of what was to come—feeling her husband's thick, hard manhood deep inside her again.

Quinton climbed onto the bed and used his knee to part Crystie's trembling legs. She felt like it was her very first time having sex. That was how nervous and filled with anticipation she was.

He mounted Crystie roughly. He couldn't resist.

"Yes!" she croaked out. Quinton took his dick in his hands and stroked it, teasing her by rubbing the tip up and down on her clitoris. "Please give it to me. I need it. I want it so bad," Crystie begged, arching her back and hips to receive him. With one swift motion, Quinton drove his ten inch dick deep into Crystie's slick, wet, wanting pussy.

"Aggh." Crystie moaned loudly. She hadn't felt her husband in months. It hurt so good. Quinton thrust in and out of her with vigor. His skin slapped against hers and she could feel *an orgasm welling up inside her. "Fuck me! Fuck me!" Crystie screamed.*

She was in heaven. This was just where she wanted to be forever.

"You feel much better than any other woman. I will never leave again!" Quinton screamed out. His sweat dripped onto Crystie's face and chest and she loved every minute of it. Anything that came from him she wanted to feel and even taste.

"Oh, Quinton, I'm about to cum. I feel it . . . oh, God!" she screamed out in ecstasy. Quinton fucked her harder and harder the more she screamed. "Oh . . . oh . . . ohhhhhhhh!" Crystie yelled as she came.

"I'm about to cum too, baby!" Quinton huffed. Crystie began moving her hips, fucking him back. That was something she had never done in the past. Crystie had been sexually conservative after they'd gotten married. But now she wanted to please him so he'd never leave her again. "Come on, baby, cum for this pussy." Crystie panted.

"Awww, shit . . . I'm right there . . . I'm right there," Quinton said.

"Come on, please!" Crystie panted some more. The headboard was knocking against the wall. They had knocked it loose.

"Here it comes!" Quinton screamed. "Agggh!!" He let out a scream.

Crystie jumped up with her body covered in sweat. She looked around, looking for her husband. All she saw were her kids. Crystie could swear she could smell Quinton in the room, but he wasn't there, and she soon realized he hadn't been there. She flopped back down when she realized she had been dreaming. Quinton hadn't really come running back to her and fucked out her brains. She had been fantasizing.

Crystie felt slightly embarrassed that she'd had a wet dream as she felt her damp panties. Then she heard the knocking noise she had heard in her dreams. She was so drugged up on sedatives that she hadn't even realized that Lydia was pounding on her door, ringing her bell incessantly, and blowing up her cell phone. When she finally came around, Crystie looked over at her two kids who were sprawled out on her bed sleeping soundly as well. She had given both of them a double dose of children's Motrin to put them to sleep.

Crystie reached over on her nightstand and retrieved her cell phone. She picked up the line after she noticed the screen flashing Lydia's name.

"Hello," she rasped into the phone. She felt like shit and really didn't want to be bothered.

"Crystie! Oh my God! You had me so worried about you and the kids! Please open the door. I'm out front!" Lydia gasped.

Crystie closed her swollen, red-rimmed eyes. She was in no mood for company, but she knew if she didn't open the door, Lydia would not leave. Crystie felt a deep sense of disappointment that her dream hadn't turned out to be true.

As she sat up in bed, she immediately felt a severe, painful pounding in her head. She felt like she was having the worst hangover ever and she didn't even drink. She dragged herself out of the bed and took the stairs one by one. Feeling slightly dizzy, Crystie pulled back her front door, cringing at the sunlight she let in with her cousin. Lydia rushed inside and grabbed Crystie in a tight embrace. Lydia's shoulders slumped in relief when she saw that Crystie was all right.

"Don't you ever fucking scare me like that again!" Lydia yelled.

"What were you scared of?" Crystie grumbled. Lydia didn't answer, and Crystie didn't return her cousin's embrace. Instead she let her arms hang limp while Lydia squeezed her tightly.

"Like I said, don't fucking scare me like that again!" Lydia yelled.

"Shhh, the girls are still sleeping," Crystie whispered, her voice sounding like she had a frog lodged in her throat.

"I was so scared. Shit, the last time I saw you, I swore you was gonna drive off a cliff or some shit. You better always let me know where you are. Anyway, I came by with some information. Look, I've called around to a few of my divorced friends. I got the names of two attorneys who are supposed to be the best in the city," Lydia said, digging into her purse to retrieve business cards.

Crystie dragged herself into her living room and flopped down on her loveseat. She stared at her cousin blankly. The last thing she wanted to discuss was divorce lawyers. She wished Lydia was there to give her advice on how to get her man back instead.

"Girl, do you hear me?" Lydia asked. "C'mon, you gotta pull yourself together and call one of these attorneys. It's the only way you will get what you deserve for all the years you put in. You didn't fuckin' practically take care of his ass for him to turn around and leave you with nothing," Lydia told Crystie.

She was right, but Crystie wasn't ready to listen to reason. "Lydia, I don't even have money to feed my kids. He took all of the money out of our joint account. The mortgage on this house is due. I . . . just . . . I don't even have money to sustain us, much less pay some expensive ass divorce attorney to fight for some shit that ain't mine to begin with," Crystie confessed, her lip quivering.

She steeled herself and took a deep breath. She knew Lydia would probably offer her money, which would just make her weepy and teary-eyed yet again. After the incident in the supermarket, Crystie told herself she would not shed another tear unless it was a tear of joy.

"You can't be serious," Lydia said. "This motherfucker wants to play dirty, I guess. Crystie, I'm telling you in New York a man can't just walk away from his *wife* and take everything. I will be your witness in court. You gave up everything for your marriage. You depended on him solely for support. I'm sorry, but that bastard is going to have to fuckin' pay," Lydia spat.

Crystie shook her head. She didn't know if she had any fight left in her.

CHAPTER 4
I'll Have My Day In Court

Crystie looked at herself in the mirror one last time. She didn't look bad if she said so herself. Admittedly, she looked better than she had in weeks. Lydia had paid for her hair to be done and Crystie had used her Bill Me Later online credit account to purchase an Anne Klein suit and some Nine West pumps from Macy's. They weren't the high priced designer threads and shoes Crystie was used to wearing when she lived off of Quinton's money, but they would serve their purpose for her court appearance.

"You look fine, girl," Lydia said. "Now stop staring at yourself and let's go. Deilia is going to keep the girls and I'm coming with you to court. I can't wait to look that motherfucker in his eyes and let him know that I know the real Quinton Bale."

Crystie turned away from the mirror and looked at her cousin. She was so grateful to Lydia for being there for her. Crystie knew that without Lydia she would've probably fallen apart even worse than she already had.

Crystie looked Lydia directly in the eyes. With a stoic expression on her face, she spoke to her cousin. "Lyd, if something happens to me, I want you to be the one to take care of the girls," Crystie said solemnly, not even batting an eye.

"Bitch! Where you think you going? To criminal court to be sentenced to death?" Lydia joked. The tension and the mood in the room was heavy and thick with sadness. "You're going to divorce court to take that stupid bitch ass nigga for everything he is worth. Now stop talking all crazy and shit before I have you committed." Lydia laughed. She had always been good at lightening the mood.

Crystie smiled half heartedly. "I mean it though, Lyd. I'd rather them be dead than to ever be with him," Crystie finished, her tone serious.

"Girl, you talkin' mess. You're going to be around until we are both wearing Depends and dancing at Tamia's wedding!" Lydia laughed, grabbing Crystie by the hand and walking her out of the bedroom.

The drive to downtown Brooklyn to the family court was solemn. Lydia and Crystie didn't say much. Neither of them dared to bring up the topic of the divorce or Quinton. Crystie was clearly preoccupied with what was to come. She felt like huge bats were flitting around in her stomach.

"You get out, and I'll go find parking," Lydia said when they pulled up to the Adams Street courthouse building.

Crystie grabbed her purse and opened the car door. Lydia stopped her for a minute. "Just remember—" Lydia started.

"I know, I know. I'll have my day in court," Crystie interrupted, finishing her cousin's sentence. They both forced a smile.

When Crystie finally walked into the small courtroom she felt cold all over. Lydia had made it upstairs just as they were called into the courtroom. She grabbed Crystie's hand and whispered a few words of encouragement to Crystie. Crystie nodded and walked slowly toward the end of the table where her attorney sat. Lydia had been gracious enough to retain the top divorce attorney for Crystie, a debt Crystie swore over and over that she would pay back, although her cousin had told her to stop talking about the money each time Crystie brought it up.

Quinton sat smugly next to his attorney. His girlfriend sat next to him on his other side. *The audacity of this bastard to have this bitch here,* Crystie thought. She bit into her lip in an effort to control her emotions.

Unlike in criminal court, the judge was already seated on the bench, so there was no "all rise" or gavel banging to begin the proceedings. The judge began with the perfunctory spiel about the parties being present in the matter of Bale v. Bale, blah, blah, blah. Crystie was only half listening to whatever the judge was talking about. Her focus was on Quinton's eye candy bitch, whom Crystie felt was totally out of place for being at the proceedings. Crystie couldn't help but to keep cutting her eyes at Quinton and his woman.

Leaning in and whispering to her attorney, Crystie expressed her displeasure with the woman's presence at the divorce proceedings. Crystie's attorney totally agreed that the woman being there was completely inappropriate, so he stood and asked the judge to have Quinton's girlfriend removed from the courtroom as she was party to adultery and a direct party to the demise of the marriage. Crystie felt elated and vindicated when the judge agreed. But she felt deflated all over again when Quinton kissed his girlfriend passionately on the lips before she was escorted out of the room.

The divorce proceedings seemed to go on for hours. Crystie's lawyer would ask for something, and Quinton's lawyer would strike it down. Quinton's lawyer would ask to be absolved of giving Crystie something, and Crystie's lawyer would argue its necessity. Crystie and her attorney tried to argue to the judge that she had given up working and attending school for the sake of her marriage. Quinton's attorney countered by arguing that after Quinton was established at the firm, Crystie had numerous opportunities to return to work prior to the birth of their children, but she had chosen to be a house-wife. Crystie's lawyer argued that Crystie had very little post high school education, aside from a few college credits, and no real skills, which made it nearly impossible for her to find gainful employment that would benefit them as a family.

The arguments flew back and forth between the lawyers at the behest of their clients, and so did the requests and denials for alimony, child support, and full custody of the children. Crystie was on her feet when she heard Quinton's attorney ask for custody of the kids on behalf of Quinton.

"He doesn't even visit them!" she shouted. "They barely know him aside from just seeing him and calling him Daddy!" That was the last straw. She had heard enough from her soon-to-be ex. There was no way she was going to sit and be quiet while Quinton tried to bring up the topic of taking her kids from her. No fucking way!

The judge ordered Crystie to sit down and refrain from further outbursts. With six hours of back and forth without reaching an agreement, the judge finally granted a temporary order of alimony and child support to Crystie. At first Crystie felt a sense of relief when she heard that she would be getting some financial help from Quinton, but her relief was short-lived. The judge entered the small amount of nine hundred dollars a month, causing Crystie to start screaming again.

"He makes well over two hundred thousand dollars a year! I can't even pay the mortgage on the house with that! I can't feed my kids! He fucking emptied the bank account and took everything! That's how much of a man he is," Crystie screeched, shooting daggers at Quinton with her eyes.

The judge gave Crystie one last warning about her lack of self control and her loud screaming outbursts. Before she knew it, the proceedings were put on hold. The hearing was adjourned for eight weeks. That meant two months of mortgage that Crystie had no clue how she'd pay with the bullshit amount of money the judge had ordered Quinton to pay.

Quinton smiled and shook his attorney's hand like he'd just won a million-dollar settlement. He made Crystie sick to her stomach. Even if he ever wanted her again, Crystie didn't think she could ever accept him back.

She stormed over to where Quinton stood milling about and laughing with his attorney. "Quinton! I can't fucking believe you!" Crystie screamed. He turned toward her, wearing a look of shock that quickly dissipated and turned into disgust. Before he could react, Crystie was on him and slapped his face so hard his head snapped from left to right.

"Mrs. Bale, I will have you arrested if you come near my client again!" Quinton's lawyer growled, grabbing Crystie by the arm to restrain her. She wasn't deterred in the least bit.

Crystie's attorney and Lydia rushed over to the scene to break it up.

"You are such a fucking man, Quinton Bale, a real man! You would take food out of the mouths of your children all for some high class ho bitch! You will rot in hell for this shit, Quinton. I will see to it," Crystie screamed as her lawyer and Lydia dragged her out of the courtroom.

CHAPTER 5

What Goes Around Comes Around

Crystie held the first alimony/child support check in her hand as she sat in front of the bank. She had not had her own bank account in years. Quinton had convinced her early on to let him open a joint account, which he told her would be the easiest way for them to "share" money, although at the time all of the money going into the account came from her. They had combined their separate accounts—his fifty dollars with her two thousand dollars at the time.

Crystie had always been good at saving her own money. She worked at several different fast food restaurants throughout high school, and instead of buying a bunch of bullshit with her money, she saved half of everything. That was how she was able to get an apartment and move out of her grandmother's house as soon as she turned eighteen. When she met Quinton, she had money in the bank and he barely had any.

Now she sat with a measly nine-hundred-dollar check in her hand, when she had over three thousand dollars in bills associated with the house alone. Crystie didn't know how the judge, a female, could have ever allowed something like that when clearly Quinton was bringing home nearly eight thousand dollars each month.

After she opened a new checking account with the money Quinton had sent, Crystie drove out of the bank parking lot, heading in the opposite direction from Lydia's house, where she needed to go to pick up the kids. As she drove, Crystie didn't know what was urging her forward, but she drove until she was finally in front of Quinton's building. She had a need right then. Crystie didn't know if it was a need to see him with the woman again, or a need to confront him. She really didn't understand this overwhelming urge to be at the building when she knew damn well they had an order of protection against her.

Crystie attempted to get into the parking lot with her key card, but as she expected, her card had been deactivated.

"That's all right. I'll wait right here," Crystie whispered.

Crystie tapped the steering wheel as she waited. Not really sure what she was waiting for, she still refused to move. She waited and waited some more. Finally Crystie looked down at her watch and realized that she had been waiting for over an hour. All she wanted was a glimpse of him, or maybe it was the woman that Crystie wanted to see again. She still wasn't sure why she was there, yet she continued to wait.

After another thirty minutes Crystie sat up in her seat when she noticed the now familiar silver Lexus swing out of the building's parking garage. Her heart jerked in her chest as she read the plate that said DARCY G. Crystie recognized the car and the plates that had been invading her former parking spot and also her marriage. *That's the bitch right there!* she screamed inside her head.

Crystie put the car in drive and slowly pulled out behind the Lexus. With her mouth as dry as the desert, and her heart hammering against her sternum, Crystie followed Quinton's girlfriend, whom she assumed was named Darcy. With every turn, every stop, and every block, Crystie kept Darcy in her sight. She didn't even notice that she had been biting her lip until the metallic taste of blood filled her mouth.

Finally the woman who Crystie blamed for her failed marriage pulled up to a Fort Greene store front. MANE ATTRACTION the sign above the store read. From the looks of it, it was an upscale hair salon. Crystie had even passed there once or twice before while driving to Lydia's house.

Crystie stopped her car far enough away not to be noticed, but still close enough where she could see Darcy get out of her car. Quinton's girlfriend sauntered up to the store's gates, fished around in her bag, and after a few minutes she pulled out a set of keys. Crystie watched carefully as Darcy unlocked the big silver padlocks and pulled the store front gate up to reveal a huge, tinted, and etched glass window. That was when Crystie noticed the etching on the glass. It read DARCY'S MANE ATTRACTION.

Crystie squinted to see inside the salon. It was beautifully put together with mirrored walls and from what Crystie could see there were neat beauty stations, hanging plants, and what looked to be artwork hanging on the walls.

Crystie felt sick. She wanted to throw up. She was immediately jealous of the woman and even more angry at Quinton than she was before. Here she was struggling to make ends meet and Quinton had an executive salary and his girlfriend was a business owner who drove a Lexus and carried a two-thousand-dollar designer bag. Crystie felt stupid and less than. She felt like the scum of the earth in comparison to Darcy.

Suddenly Crystie knew that she had to speak to Darcy face to face, woman to woman. Their last meeting didn't count, since Crystie had been too violent to get her point across. Crystie put the car in park and removed the key from the ignition. Some unknown force was moving her and she was following its lead. She grabbed her purse and rushed up the block to Darcy's salon. As she tugged on the grand brass door handles and stepped inside, the door chimes made a tingling sound that reminded Crystie of a fairy waving a magic wand.

"Just a minute!" Darcy sang out from somewhere in the back of the salon. Crystie wasn't able to see her and she knew for sure Darcy hadn't seen who it was in the salon yet. Her chest heaved and she felt lightheaded as she waited. She wanted to rehearse what to say to the woman, but nothing came to her racing mind. Although Crystie wanted to turn and run back out of the salon, she was rooted to the floor. For some unknown reason, she needed to be there.

"Can I help y—" Darcy started to say, but her words went tumbling back down her throat like oversized marbles when she saw Crystie standing there.

Darcy's face paled and she began backing up with her hands out in front of her in surrender. Quickly remembering the ass whooping Crystie put on her the last time they met, she scrambled for her cell phone to call the police.

"I'm not going to do anything to you," Crystie managed to say. The words and questions suddenly came rushing to her tongue. "I just want to know how you can sleep at night with a clear conscience. Quinton is my husband. He is a father. We are married and we've been together for years. As a woman, how would you feel if you were in my place? Knowing your marriage was ending because of another woman, knowing your kids would be left without their father because of another woman," Crystie said. Her voice was rising and falling like waves crashing against rocks. The woman's eyes were as big as saucers and she didn't say anything.

"Don't you know breaking up something that God put together is a sin? Haven't you ever heard that what goes around comes around? Do you have any morals or scruples? I mean you've been to church, *our* church to be exact. Haven't you learned anything? Why couldn't you find a man of your own?" Crystie asked, her voice cracking in places as she fought not to break down and cry.

"Look, I'm sorry about everything that has happened to you, but I'm just as much a victim as you are. I didn't know Q was married until the day you showed up at our condo," Darcy said almost apologetically.

"Q? Our condo?" Crystie repeated for clarification, making the quote signs with her fingers. "Did Q tell you that it was my fucking blood, sweat, and tears that purchased that condo while he went to school and did absolutely nothing? Did Q tell you that I sacrificed my entire college career and sense of self just so he could be a success, only to have him turn around and pick up somebody like you that has no regard for the sanctity of marriage or our kids? No! I bet he didn't tell you any of that while he was flaunting you at his big business dinners and at our fucking church, did he?" Crystie growled, her voice rising ten octaves.

"I'm sorry about all of this, but he lied to us both. We met after his company did the marketing plans for my business. He never said he was married. I mean where were you when he was taking me on all of the trips, buying me all of the expensive gifts? I mean he would spend a week at a time with me. Why would I have believed that he was married? Didn't you ever question your own husband? I'm sorry, but I can't help who I fell in love with," Darcy said, making sure she kept a safe distance between herself and Crystie. "He is with me now, and I am willing to be a part of the kids' lives if that makes you feel any better."

That was the wrong thing to say to Crystie after questioning her common sense when it came to Quinton. Crystie knew that Darcy was right. She had been so busy trying not to rock the boat that she let Quinton tip the fucking boat over and cheat on her. The truth definitely hurt.

As Crystie started advancing toward Darcy like a lion toward its prey, she squinted her eyes into slits and spoke through clenched teeth. "You may have won the man with your hair extensions and your fake tits, but I'm fucking warning you, if you ever come around my kids for any reason, trust me, you will regret it. I would die before I let you and your Q play house with my fucking kids," Crystie said, pointing her finger so close to Darcy's face that Darcy almost fell backward trying to avoid getting poked in the eye. "Now you tell Q that I said that shit. Also remember, you reap what the fuck you sow," Crystie finished, turning and storming out of the salon.

She could hear the woman behind her scrambling for her telephone. *Call your Q and tell him. Tell him he will regret the day he left me,* Crystie thought as she headed back to Lydia's car.

Crystie didn't sleep the night after she confronted Quinton's girlfriend. The woman's words kept replaying in Crystie's head. Maybe it was all her fault for being such a passive wife. She had beat herself up all the way to Lydia's house and all the way home. That evening she took her sedatives, but they only put her to sleep for a few short spurts at a time, and then she'd jump up in a cold sweat.

She kept obsessing about the situation—what she did wrong, what she could've done better, what she shouldn't have done, or what she should have done. It was literally driving her crazy. To top it all off she had to admit to herself that she missed her husband and the security of having him around. Even when he had moved out, Crystie knew he would be back, so she never worried and she still felt secure. She hadn't felt this lost and lonely since her mother had abandoned her as a child. Crystie had always seen Quinton as her savior from her past, just as much as she was his savior to him from his past.

Now she tossed and turned thinking about how fast things had spiraled downhill in her marriage. She was also obsessing about her financial situation. The mortgage was due and there was still six weeks until the next court date where she would find out if the judge was going to increase the alimony and child support payments. Frustrated and restless, Crystie threw back her bed covers and got out of bed. She looked in on her kids several times between her fitful bouts of sleep and wakefulness. She peeked at them again for the tenth time and watched their little chests rise and fall. It was like she was making sure they were still alive, still hers. She loved them so much, and they were the one thing she didn't now regret about her relationship with Quinton. She loved him for giving her such beautiful children. Her girls were all Crystie had left, and they were the one thing Crystie would fight for to the death.

After she'd checked in on the kids, Crystie roamed the house aimlessly. A few times she even thought she heard voices whispering shit to her.. She wandered through her kitchen and decided to read the pile of accumulated newspapers that she hadn't touched in weeks. Quinton had subscribed to the *New York Times* when he still lived there. He loved to read the business section. She picked up the prior day's paper and began turning the pages. All of the news about war and crimes depressed her even more, so she flipped to the entertainment portion of the paper. She skimmed it and turned to the announcements section.

As she read the birth and marriage announcements of strangers, something caught her eye. It was a small square box under the announcement section. It had hearts surrounding the box and it read: "Marketing Exec and Upscale Salon Owner Announce their Engagement. Congratulations, Quinton and Darcy, from all your friends at the Mane Attraction Salon and Spa." It was like someone had kicked Crystie in the chest, or maybe the feeling was more like she was having open heart surgery while she was still awake. The pain was unbearable. Time seemed to stand still and she was having trouble breathing properly. Crystie's ears began to ring. She stared at the small black print for what seemed like an eternity. The words started jumping around on the paper, seemingly taunting her.

"Engaged? We're not even fucking divorced yet, and he gets engaged," Crystie gritted through clenched teeth. She had been biting down into her jaw so hard blood filled her mouth.

Still dressed in her pajamas, Crystie mindlessly raced out of her front door and climbed into her car. She didn't even think about her sleeping children being left alone. Crystie sped onto the highway, not sure exactly where she was headed. She was driving with her hands at ten and two o'clock, and her back was completely straight. A few times she ignored traffic laws, and she also cut off some people. She had tunnel vision, which was dangerous for driving.

Before she knew it, she was in front of Darcy's salon once again. The gate was pulled down and the locks were on. Crystie wished she would have caught the gate up. She wanted to bust every window out of the place. She wanted that bitch Darcy to hurt. If Darcy and Quinton were in front of Crystie at that moment, she probably could kill them both and think nothing of it.

Crystie jumped out of her car, scrambled around to the rear, and let up the hatch door. She frantically dug around in the space behind the seats where she usually threw the kids toys, emergency umbrellas, and stuff like that. Crystie knew just what she was looking for—a can of white spray paint she'd purchased when she and Quinton had sprayed fake snow and frost on the windows of their home for Christmas. Crystie remembered how she and her husband had worked so hard together to decorate the house for the kids.

Crystie finally located what she was looking for. With her heart pounding, she grabbed the can of paint and rushed over to the salon's gates. She sprayed the words HOME WRECKER, SLUT, DICK SUCKER, DIE, DEAD WOMAN, ADULTERER, and BITCH all over the salon's silver gate. With her chest heaving wildly after she emptied the can of spray paint, Crystie reached back into her car and grabbed the newspaper section that revealed Darcy and Quinton's secret. She twisted the paper into a long wad, dipped the tip into her gas tank, and retrieved a small flare lighter from her trunk. She set the gasoline soaked paper on fire. With the paper burning quickly in her hand,

Crystie walked up to the gate and threw the burning paper in front of the salon, as close to the building as she could get it.

"I hope both of you bastards burn in fuckin' hell," Crystie growled.

Then she jumped back into her car and sped off. Although it was the wee hours of the morning, Crystie did notice a few people walking the streets. She wanted to get out of there before anyone took her license plate number or saw her face. When she was about ten blocks away she pulled over and put the car in park. With all of her windows rolled up she screamed at the top of her lungs and slammed her fists against her steering wheel. She screamed and screamed until her head hurt. Exhausted, Crystie collapsed with her head lolling onto the steering wheel. She sobbed pitifully.

Crystie didn't know how long she'd been there, but before long she noticed winks of the sun coming through her windshield. She looked out of the windshield at the sky strangely. It was then that Crystie realized that she was in her car and something had definitely happened to her. It was the first time she had lost touch with reality since the episodes she had as a child. Looking around wildly and realizing she was in her pajamas, Crystie lurched around to check the backseat of her car.

"My kids! Oh my God! Where are my kids?" she shrieked, whirling her head around. She sped out of the spot she was in and headed back to her home. It was not until she burst through her front doors to find her girls screaming and crying that she realized she had left them all alone . . . again.

It was the first time, but would not be the last that Crystie let the situation get the best of her. She realized that something inside of her was slowly coming apart, and she didn't know what to do about it.

CHAPTER 6
Losing It All

L ydia was the one who answered the door when the NYPD showed up to Crystie's house to question Crystie about what had happened at the salon. Lydia told the police that Crystie was out running errands, and that when the incident allegedly occurred Crystie had been home the entire time with her children.

"These kids are babies," Lydia said. "Ya'll can't possibly be accusing my cousin of some early morning vandalism. Does that even sound right to you when she has babies? You just said the witness got a glimpse and said the person was alone. Look, I think this is all a ploy by her ex-husband to paint her in a bad light so he can get away without giving my cousin anything," Lydia told the police. "I mean, come in, take a look at the kids."

The cops observed the kids from the door. When they realized that the children were very young, they agreed that Crystie leaving them alone to drive from Long Island to Brooklyn to vandalize the salon might just be a far stretch. They had seen these types of tit for tat divorces in the past. Usually they just dealt with mothers accusing fathers of molestation or fathers accusing mothers of neglect and abuse. This was certainly different, but not that far from what could've happened. Satisfied for the moment, the police officers gave Lydia their card and asked that Crystie call them when she returned home.

When they were gone, Lydia gave Crystie the signal. Crystie emerged from her bedroom closet where she had been cowering while her cousin covered for her ass. Crystie was embarrassed, but relieved at the same time that her behavior had not cost her much more than flushed cheeks.

"Crystie, you gotta get a grip. This shit ain't cool at all and it damn sure ain't worth losing your freedom and your kids over. You are so fucking lucky that bitch's security cameras were there just for show and weren't working. I mean what the fuck would you have done if those shits had caught you fucking up her store? Get it together," Lydia scolded.

"I know. I know you mean well, Lydia. I'm sorry for putting you in this whole thing. Everything you do is appreciated. I'm OK now," Crystie lied.

"You have to think before you act, Crystie," Lydia emphasized again. Crystie just looked on dumbly. "I don't trust leaving you with these kids, Crystie. I'm dead ass serious. Are you sure you're going to be OK until I get back from work?" Lydia asked.

Crystie smiled and hugged her cousin. She was putting on a good act, but really she just wanted to be alone. "I got it all out of my system. I'm sure. I pinky, dinky, doodle swear," Crystie said, laughing as she repeated something that she and Lydia used to say to each other as kids.

Lydia looked at Crystie with skepticism, but love. "OK, I'm trusting you," Lydia replied, finally relenting. "But no more wigging out spray painting and setting fire to people's shit," she continued, waggling her finger at Crystie and then chuckling to lighten up the mood. Crystie forced herself to laugh. Inside she was crying and coming apart, but she put up a front to put Lydia at ease. Lydia finally took Crystie's word and left her alone.

Crystie gave the girls something to eat and then put them down for a nap. She decided that she would just relax and watch some television to clear her mind. That was her plan until she checked her mailbox and retrieved a notice that the mortgage company was about to proceed with foreclosure on the house.

"Agggh!" Crystie yelled. "How much can one person take? What the fuck am I supposed to do?"

She picked up her phone and dialed Quinton's number without even thinking. She didn't know what she would say to him, but she dialed the number anyway. When it began to ring, she hung up. Crystie redialed at least ten more times. She never spoke to him, and he kept pressing ignore. Eventually he turned off his phone so it would go straight to voicemail. Crystie still continued to call. She just kept dialing, listening to his voice, letting the voicemail pick up, and listening until his voicemail cut her off. Crystie just wanted to hear his voice over and over again. She did it until her phone battery died and she was no longer able to make any more calls.

After that was out of her system, Crystie spent almost an hour on the phone with the mortgage company trying to negotiate a deal that would work out for her. She didn't know the first thing about refinancing, loan modifications, or the like. When she had put the Brooklyn condo in her name, it had been all Quinton. All Crystie had done was sign on the dotted line. She wasn't even sure she still owned the damn condo with the way Quinton had been sneaking behind her back doing grimy shit.

After being transferred almost ten times, Crystie was finally put in contact with a foreclosure specialist, only to be told that Quinton was listed as the sole owner of the home and that Crystie had no authority to negotiate on his behalf.

"Even though I'm his wife and I am living here with my children?" Crystie asked incredulously. The foreclosure specialist apologized to Crystie, but told her that only Quinton could save the house from foreclosure.

Frustrated and angry, Crystie broke yet another telephone by sailing it across the room. She paced for almost an hour, feeling aimless and helpless. She glanced over at the ever growing pile of household bills that littered her kitchen table. She hadn't paid the light, gas, telephone, or cable bills. She was getting doubled up bills for just about all of them. The kids had been whining and crying because they couldn't watch new episodes of *Dora the Explorer* and the *Backyardigans* on Nick Jr. Crystie had tried putting on DVDs for them, but they'd seen all of the movies she had in the house at least twenty times. She felt like the walls of life were closing in on her.

Crystie stomped up the steps into her bedroom and flung open the doors to her walk-in closet. Inside she searched the top of the closet rack for her wedding album. She pulled down the thick, white, engraved book and carried it down to the kitchen. Placing it on top of her pile of bills, Crystie opened it. The very first picture was of Quinton, alone. Crystie should've known he was a selfish piece of shit when he had instructed the photographer to put his solo picture first in the album. It wasn't supposed to be that way. After all, she was the bride and everyone knew the bride was the center of attention at a wedding, but not at their wedding.

Crystie remembered how much attention Quinton craved during their special day. He had showed her up several times, dancing alone to garner attention, going around to greet guests and collect money cards without her. She wondered what other signs of her husband's selfish personality she had overlooked over the years.

Crystie flipped through the pages of the wedding album some more. She found herself involuntarily smiling at the images of her happy day. She reminisced about the good aspects of her wedding day and how she'd been so proud that they had paid for everything and didn't owe a soul after it was all over.

Crystie stared at a picture of her and Quinton kissing as they shared their first piece of cake. Cake was smeared on her chin and she remembered now how Quinton had wiped it with his finger and then liked his finger clean. Suddenly a flood of tears dropped from her eyes.

"What happened, Quinton? Why are you going this?" She sobbed. Blinking rapidly, Crystie stared at the pictures some more. All of a sudden she started seeing flashes of Darcy's face replacing her own in the pictures. She blinked and wiped her eyes roughly. The images were still there. Darcy and Quinton kissing, Darcy by herself, it was all too much for Crystie to handle. She frantically flipped the pages because she knew this was her wedding album. But each time she turned a page, it was Darcy's face she saw staring back at her, and not her own.

Crystie dropped the photo album like it was burning hot. She pushed back from the table like a poisonous snake had just bitten her and rushed around the kitchen, pulling open her kitchen countertop drawers one by one, leaving them hanging open as she pillaged through them. Knives, forks, spoons, and coupons clattered to the floor as Crystie rummaged like a madwoman. She exhaled loudly as she finally clasped her hands around a pair of garden scissors. The thick steel cutters were just what she was looking for, just what she needed to solve this problem. Crystie went back over to the table and began ripping her wedding photographs out of their matted places in the album. The thick glue ripped some of the pictures in half, completely destroying them.

"Bitch!" Crystie hissed as she began cutting the pictures into a million little pieces. "I hate you!" she boomed as she drove a jagged line across Quinton's face in one picture. Crystie continued cutting and slicing until she was completely exhausted and her hands ached. Flopping down into a chair, she threw down the scissors. As she looked down at the mess in front of her, her bottom lip quivered as the severity of her deed set in.

"Oh, no! What did I do? What did I do?" Crystie screamed, putting her hands against each side of her head pulling at her hair roughly. Crystie looked down at the tiny slivers of pictures that now resembled the pieces to a two-thousand-piece puzzle—impossible to put back together, just like her marriage.

Crystie sobbed. She was angry with herself for losing control again. It had been happening more and more often. Taking a deep breath, she roughly wiped her tears away.

"Pull your fucking self together! Stop this shit now!" Crystie whispered harshly to herself. She scrambled out of the chair and ran over to her pantry. Peeling off a large garbage bag from the roll of bags, she raced back over to the table and started frantically sweeping the cut up pictures into the bag. She couldn't risk Lydia stopping by and seeing the complete mess she'd made. She knew that Lydia would think she was losing it again and the lectures would start all over again.

When everything was finally cleaned up from the table, Crystie placed the bag near the back door. Something told her to see if her children were OK, so she checked in on them. They were playing with baby dolls quietly in their playroom, so Crystie came back downstairs and exited through the back door and into the backyard. She placed the bag with the pictures into Quinton's large, stainless steel GrillMaster grill, squirted lighter fluid on the pile, and dropped a match inside. It was definitely a *Waiting to Exhale* kind of moment. She felt sad that she no longer had her pictures, but for some reason she also felt vindicated. She looked around nervously to make sure her neighbors weren't watching while she burned away remnants of her past.

When she was satisfied with the pile of ashes before her, Crystie went back into the house. She washed her hands and changed her smoke scented clothes. Then she picked up her cell phone and called her attorney. Crystie pleaded with him to ask the court for an emergency hearing. She explained to him that there was no way she could wait another three weeks to go to court with the situation the way it was. She even confessed to him that she could feel herself losing it—her mind, her home, her life as she knew it—losing it all to be exact.

CHAPTER 7

Nothing But Death Can Keep Me From Them

Crystie's attorney was able to push up the hearing date, but only by one week. Crystie didn't complain, though. She was going to take what she could get.

When the day of the hearing arrived, she didn't bother to dress up like she did for the first court appearance. She was at the point where she didn't care any longer. She threw on a pair of jeans and a regular polo shirt. Her hair was slicked back in a lumpy, uncombed, cakey ponytail. She didn't bother to put on makeup either, although she knew she had bags the size of pillows under her eyes. Nothing mattered to her anymore. She only went day to day for her children. Crystie told herself over and over that if it weren't for her girls, she might've ended her miserable, worthless life a long time ago.

When Lydia pulled up to pick up Crystie and the kids, she crinkled her face at Crystie's appearance. Crystie slid into the car without saying anything in response to her cousin's incredulous stares. They drove to Lydia's house and dropped off the kids to Lydia's friend who would babysit again. When Lydia and Crystie were back in the car alone, Crystie finally began to speak as Lydia pulled off and began to drive.

"Well off to see what way this motherfucker is going to fuck me over once again," Crystie said, chuckling awkwardly.

Lydia was silent at first, but Crystie's appearance and behavior were just killing her inside. It just wasn't right. In fact, Lydia thought her cousin looked and sounded like she was falling apart. "Girl, why are you dressed like you're going to the store or even worse, like you're going to put the damn garbage out or something? I mean you want to present yourself well, don't you? Do you want this nigga to think you're pining over him and falling apart?" Lydia asked.

"What nobody seems to understand, Lydia, is I don't give a shit about him, the judge, or my life right now. I could give a fuck less what anybody thinks about me and whether I'm pining over him or falling the fuck apart. I mean it's the truth at this point. Whether I was dressed to the nines or naked, if shit is going to go in my favor, it just is and vice versa," Crystie replied, her tone cold and flat.

Inside the courtroom, Crystie's lawyer had the same reaction to Crystie's appearance as Lydia had. He eyed her up and down, wondering what she was thinking. Crystie sat down next to him and folded her hands in front of her. She didn't say a word.

"I think all of the parties are here. We can begin," the judge said. Crystie shot the female judge an evil look. *Fuckin' traitor ass bitch,* Crystie thought.

Quinton's lawyer stood and adjusted his suit jacket. He looked just as smug as Quinton. Crystie figured that was why Quinton had hired him.

"Your honor, my client would like to make the divorce final today," the lawyer said. "We feel there is no need to prolong these proceedings at the expense of either party. We are prepared to present our requests today and trust that you will find in our favor or whatever is favorable to the court."

Crystie finally looked over at Quinton and his lawyer, and that's when she noticed Quinton's best friend Mike sitting on the other side of the room. *What the fuck is he doing here?* Crystie screamed in her head.

Her heart jerked and her stomach cramped at the sight of him. She hadn't seen Mike in two years. She couldn't imagine why he would be at their divorce proceedings. Mike had always stayed neutral when Crystie and Quinton were having problems. He had even been a source of comfort for Crystie at times, allowing her to vent to him and providing her with sound advice when it came to Quinton. But his being there today made Crystie uneasy and overwhelmingly nervous.

"We are prepared to hear your client's request as well as Mrs. Bale's requests," the judge replied.

Quinton's lawyer smiled. "Your honor, my client is asking for an immediate divorce from Mrs. Bale," he said. "His request is not unexpected. My client wants to end his marriage due to his wife's infidelity, which he is prepared to prove today; due to cruel and unusual treatment, which he is prepared to prove today; and finally due to violence and erratic behavior by Mrs. Bale throughout the course of their marriage, which he can also prove today."

Crystie's head whipped around so hard she felt her neck crack. She thought she'd fall out of the chair. Was Quinton fucking serious? She leaned in to her attorney and began whispering harshly in his ear. She told him that it was all bullshit. Quinton was lying. Her attorney shushed her and promised that she would get her chance to speak.

"Go ahead and present what your client has today," the judge told Quinton's attorney.

Oh, my God! He can't continue talking, Crystie thought as a cold sweat broke out all over her body.

"Your honor, as to the infidelity during the marriage, as Mrs. Bale correctly argued during the last hearing, Mr. Bale spent four years working hard, studying for his business degree at Baruch business school," the lawyer began. "After his graduation he was the main and only source of income in the marriage. On occasion, Mr. Bale's employment required that he travel for two, sometimes three nights a week. Mr. Bale has physical proof that during that time, his wife, Mrs. Bale, committed adultery with his best friend, Mr. Michael Short, who is in court today to give a statement to such if necessary. Also, my client has photographs that Mr. Short took while he had sex with Mrs. Bale on numerous occasions," Quinton's lawyer announced proudly.

"You motherfucker!" Crystie erupted. Her ears rang and the room began to spin. Her vision blurred and she felt like she would faint. She jumped out of her seat and pushed away from the table. The chair she was sitting in went crashing to the floor, startling everyone in the room. Crystie covered her face and bolted down the aisle and out of the courtroom. She raced into the courtroom hallway and spun around and around wildly like a lost child. Finally she noticed a sign for the bathrooms and she sped toward the doors. Her chest ached like she was having a heart attack.

Inside the bathroom, Crystie splashed water on her face, but it didn't help. She stumbled into one of the stalls and threw up. Crystie felt like dying. If she had a weapon, she would take her own life right then. She could not believe Mike had betrayed her like that. Mike had sworn that neither of them would ever speak of what had happened. They both knew it was a mistake the minute it had happened.

Crystie and Mike had their one-time sexual encounter after one occasion when Quinton had been extremely cruel to Crystie. Quinton had called her an ugly, disgusting pig. Crystie was still crying when Mike called for Quinton, so she quickly told Mike that she didn't know where Quinton had gone after he had stormed out of the house. As Crystie continued to sob into the phone, Mike told her he'd be right over.

When he got there, he listened to Crystie. He told her she was definitely not ugly and nowhere near a pig. He stroked her hair and hugged her, allowing her to cry on his shoulder. Crystie was weak and vulnerable, and one thing had just led to another, literally. Mike had kissed her on the cheek at first. Then he had swept his lips over hers and the heat between them moved so quickly that before Crystie knew it, Mike had entered her. The entire night was still a blur to Crystie, although she knew they had sex. Mike had sworn to her over and over that he would never utter a word about what had happened. He assured Crystie that he had just as much to lose if Quinton found out as she did, and that he would take it to his grave, as should she.

Crystie had buried that night far into the recesses of her mind. But now here was Mike betraying her in the worst possible way. Crystie didn't remember him taking any pictures. She would never have allowed that. She couldn't believe any of this. As she leaned against the courthouse bathroom wall for support, it was all she could do to keep from fainting.

After a while, Lydia entered the bathroom. She was coming to the rescue as usual. But Crystie didn't want to face her or anyone for that matter.

"There you are! Oh, baby, I'm so sorry," Lydia said, grabbing Crystie and holding her. That made Crystie feel even worse, and all of her tears came flooding back to the surface along with her sins.

"I don't know why Mike would do this. What have I ever done to him?" Crystie cried.

"They are both bastards. I can't believe it either, but you have to go back in there with your head up high. Nothing he says can change the fact that he also committed adultery with that bitch," Lydia said. Crystie knew she had to go back, but she damn sure wished she could just disappear.

When Crystie walked back into the courtroom, all eyes were on her. She felt like the gazes were burning holes into her. She apologized to the judge for the interruption and took her seat next to her lawyer again. Quinton had a smirk on his face, which sent a flash of heat through Crystie's chest. *Die, you motherfucker,* Crystie thought.

The judge started the proceedings again, but Crystie was only half listening. She could no longer focus. Quinton presented pictures of the damage that had been done at his girlfriend's salon and told the judge that he had witnesses that said Crystie had done it. He produced surveillance video from the condo garage showing that Crystie had been outside and followed Darcy's car on numerous occasions. He produced a written statement from Darcy about the beat down Crystie had put on her and about Crystie showing up to her place of business threatening her.

Crystie just took it all. Slap after slap, she just sat there and let Quinton run her name into the ground. But then the gloves really came off.

"Your honor, my client is also asking for full custody of his two children, ages two- and three-years-old," Quinton's lawyer said. "It is my client's belief that Mrs. Bale is mentally unstable as we have witnessed by some of the items of proof my client brought to the court's attention today, and that he would be the best parent to care for the children."

The words seemed to explode in Crystie's ears and touched her someplace deep. "No! He cannot have my children!" Crystie screamed. "They are all I have, judge. Please, if you have any mercy in your heart. Pa-lease! He can keep all of his money! I will live in a shelter! But please don't take my kids from me! They're all I have left!"

Crystie's lawyer grabbed her by the arm and forced her to sit down. He was watching Crystie prove Quinton and his attorney right about her mental state with her seemingly erratic behavior. Crystie put her hands over her mouth in an attempt to suppress her sobs, but her whimpers could still be heard. Crystie could not believe Quinton was digging so deep to be so malicious. She knew he had no interest in caring for their children. It was only an attempt to make her suffer. Crystie couldn't for the life of her understand his need to be so cruel.

The judge asked to hear from Crystie's attorney, but his requests and arguments seemed like small pebbles compared to the huge boulders Quinton's lawyer had thrown. Crystie's attorney told the judge that Quinton had little or no real interaction with the kids. Crystie tried to read the judge's face, but she was unable to tell what the judge was going to do. She started to pray silently for her children as the judge gathered up all of Quinton's pictures, videos, and written proof. She also took some documents regarding the foreclosure and household bills Crystie was facing.

"I will review the information in chambers and I will return in one hour with my final decision in this matter," the judge said.

Crystie tried to plead with the judge with her eyes, but the judge never looked at her. With that, the judge dismissed them all for a lunch break.

Crystie put her head down on the table. She couldn't even move, much less eat. Lydia watched as Quinton slapped five with Mike and they laughed as they exited the courtroom together. Lydia chased after them.

"Quinton! Mike!" she yelled as she caught up to them. They turned to face her. "You both think you're smart, don't you? You think I couldn't figure out how you set up my cousin? You fucking purposely went there to sleep with her, didn't you, Mike? What did you do, Quinton? Did you call Mike as soon as you left to meet up with your bitch that day? Did you pay your gay best friend to go to your house and seduce your fuckin' wife so you could get out of a marriage?"

They both looked like deer caught in headlights. "Yeah, I'm on to both of you," Lydia said. "You don't think I know you both fucked each other in college? Hmph, yeah, Quinton, you're lucky I wanted to protect my cousin's feelings for you all of these years. It will be a cold fucking day in hell before you get those kids, Quinton. You don't even know anything about them—what they eat, when they sleep. All she ever did was love you. All she ever did was try to please you. Mark my words, you will get what is coming to you. Trust, revenge is a dish best served motherfucking cold."

Lydia then turned swiftly and went back into the courtroom to get Crystie. Lydia didn't know how much more Crystie could take. She knew hands down that if the judge gave Quinton custody of the girls, Crystie would lose it once and for all.

Crystie watched nervously as the judge sat down behind her tall desk. She balled up her toes inside her shoes and clenched her ass cheeks tightly. The judge shuffled a few papers and then started speaking. The first thing she said was that she was granting the divorce decree. It was final. Crystie's marriage to Quinton was officially over. Hearing the words gave Crystie an empty feeling inside her chest. She likened the feeling to a cross between severe hunger and severe emotional deprivation.

Next the judge granted Crystie alimony in the amount of two thousand dollars per month, but it was only until Crystie found gainful employment and could support herself. Crystie listened intently and quickly noticed that the judge hadn't said anything about child support. The judge ordered that Quinton vacate the condo and awarded it to Crystie to sell or do what she saw fit with it. Then the judge got to the topic Crystie had been dreading—the children, and who would win physical custody of them. Crystie's heart hammered painfully against her sternum as the judge's lips moved.

"In the matter of the Bale children, Tiana and Tamia Bale, ages three and two respectively, at this time I am granting temporary full custody to Mr. Bale until such time as Mrs. Bale has completed a full psychological evaluation. The matter of custody will be added to the family court docket and the children will be assigned a guardian ad litum. Mrs. Bale, you have until Monday of next week to produce the children at this courthouse. Mr. Bale will take custody of the children, you will complete the evaluation and whatever other recommendations the psychiatrist makes, and after that I'm sure a family court judge will return custody to you. That is, if you're deemed to be stable," the judge said.

Crystie felt like someone had buried her ass alive. "Noooo! Oh, God! No! Please don't do this to me! I can't take it! I have nothing else! Please don't take my kids away from me!" Crystie let out a blood curdling scream. Her scream sent chills into everyone in the room, even the judge. It was the kind of scream someone in severe pain releases.

Crystie thrashed and continued screaming while shaking her head and flailing her arms. Crystie's attorney tried to contain her, but Crystie was inconsolable. Lydia raced over, but Crystie continues to flail her arms wildly and scream.

"I can't lose them! Please! Please, judge, don't do this to me!" Crystie yelled.

"Sssh," Lydia comforted. Lydia was crying herself. There was nothing like a mother's love being shattered.

"Mrs. Bale, I'm sure you will get the children back when you get yourself together," the judge said, standing to leave. The judge wanted to get out of there as fast as she could. Crystie's screams of anguish had even threatened to make the judge shed a few tears.

"Fuck you! Fuck all of you! Nothing but death can keep me from them! Nothing but death! Quinton, you won't win! I will die first! Nothing but death!!" Crystie screeched as Lydia forced her down the center aisle of the room. Lydia didn't want her cousin to get arrested for making threats or cursing out the judge on top of everything that was already happening to her.

Lydia turned around one last time to see Quinton smiling and shaking his attorney's hand. She shot him an evil look and returned her focus to her cousin, who was now a shell of a person.

Crystie rocked back and forth in the car during the ride back to Lydia's house. Lydia didn't bother trying to speak to Crystie. She knew any attempt would be useless.

The mere thought of having her children for only three more days made Crystie want to die. A million thoughts danced in her head, one of which was eliminating the threat—Quinton.

When they arrived at Lydia's house, Crystie was out of the car before Lydia could fully pull up. Crystie banged on the door frantically as if somebody was chasing her. When the babysitter pulled back the door, Crystie almost knocked her down racing to find her kids. Both of the kids were sitting in front of the television watching Nick Jr.

"Hi, babies!" Crystie sang out through newly falling tears. She grabbed both of her girls, struggling with the weight of them. She squeezed them against her so tightly that they started to whine.

"Mommy!" Tiana complained, trying to break free of Crystie's death grip.

"Nobody is going to take you from me," Crystie said. "I won't let anything happen to either of you," Crystie whispered through her tears. Crystie didn't want to let them go. She held them like that for the next half hour, although they squirmed and complained. Lydia had to force Crystie to allow the children to get down and play.

Lydia begged Crystie to spend the night with the kids, but Crystie wouldn't hear of it. She told Lydia she just wanted to be home alone to spend the next few days with the kids before she had to turn them over to Quinton. Lydia was very worried about Crystie, but there was nothing she could do to convince Crystie to stay over.

Lydia watched as her cousin, who now resembled a soulless zombie, loaded her two babies into the car and pulled off.

She said a silent prayer that Crystie and the kids would be all right, and she promised herself that she would go check on Crystie first thing in the morning.

Ex-Wife Status

BY AMALEKA MCCALL

•••

CHAPTER 8
The Best Laid Plans

Crystie sat in front of one of Quinton's old laptops staring blankly at the computer screen. She typed in her search term: GUNS FOR SALE NEAR NASSAU COUNTY. Crystie hesitated. She knew handguns were illegal in the city, but in Long Island she figured that she would probably be able to purchase one from a personal owner, but she was still nervous. Shaking her head, Crystie deleted the words before she clicked on the search button. What was she thinking? What the hell would she do with a gun anyway? Crystie pinched the bridge of her nose, trying to relieve the banging tension headache she had been battling for days.

"Something has to give," she whispered. "There is just no way I can turn my kids over to Quinton and his bitch. There is just no way."

Crystie climbed the stairs in her house and looked at her sleeping babies. They were so innocent. They didn't deserve to be in the middle of her and Quinton's battles. Crystie still couldn't believe he would throw them into the mix by petitioning the court for full custody. She was still absolutely flabbergasted that Quinton wanted the girls to live with him full time

| 233 |

when he hadn't ever paid the kids any attention when he lived with them.

Quinton had never held either of the girls longer than ten minutes after they came home from the hospital. He never fed them or changed either of their diapers. He certainly never took them to a doctor's appointment or took care of them when they were sick. Quinton didn't know his own children's likes or dislikes. He had never called them by their nicknames—TeeTee and Mia. He didn't know how to comfort them when they were in distress, and more importantly, the kids didn't know him. Yes, they recognized him as the man Crystie referred to as their daddy. They even called him Daddy, and whenever he came around they ran to him, but other than that, Quinton hadn't been involved with them much.

Crystie knew that Quinton saw the kids as a hindrance to their marriage. She also believed that he was jealous of how much attention Crystie paid to the girls after they were born. Prior to their births it was all about Quinton, but after they came along he had to share her time and attention with the kids. Quinton didn't hide his feelings about it either. Crystie remembered one night when Quinton held her down in the bed, having forceful sex with her while she fought to get up so she could comfort Tiana, who was a newborn and screaming from the other bedroom. The memory made Crystie shudder now.

The thought of handing her kids over to Quinton made Crystie physically sick. She had thrown up three times that day alone. She only had one and a half more days with the kids, and Crystie didn't know what she'd do, but she did know giving them to her now officially ex-husband was not an option.

Crystie banged on Lydia's door early the next morning. Lydia swung open the door and looked at her cousin like she was crazy.

"What's the matter, Crystie?" Lydia asked, noticing how disheveled and frantic Crystie appeared. It was not like Crystie to be out with the kids so early. Lydia had an ominous feeling about the situation.

"I have to go someplace real quick. Can you keep an eye on the girls until I get back?" Crystie asked, her hair wild and her eyes wide.

"Yeah, but what's going on, Crystie? You're in your pajamas. Are you all right?" Lydia asked, looking Crystie up and down. Nothing about this visit and Crystie could be good.

"I'm fine. I just need to make a run," Crystie said hurriedly. She was shifting her weight from one foot to the other and moving as if she had to go to the bathroom.

Lydia had to think about the kids and their safety, although she knew something was wrong. "Bring them inside," Lydia said. She wasn't going to ask Crystie any more questions, because it was clear she was having some sort of an episode. Lydia badly wanted to shake Crystie by the shoulders and tell her to snap out of all this erratic behavior. It was just a divorce, which Lydia didn't think was the end of the world.

Lydia knew that she had always been the stronger person, even as children growing up. Crystie was always the nice one. She was quiet and people often walked all over her and bullied her, while people often referred to Lydia as the bitch, who would fuck up anyone who messed with her cousin Crystie. But some of the older women in their neighborhood used to say "the quiet ones are the ones you have to watch. They always end up being the worst ones." And that piece of advice came flooding back to Lydia now.

Crystie handed the kids to Lydia for safekeeping. She promised Lydia she'd be back soon. Crystie didn't want to miss her last minutes with the kids, but what she had to do was imperative. She had made up in her mind about what she needed to do.

She raced through the streets of Brooklyn until she finally made it to the Belt Parkway. Crystie drove over the Verrazano Bridge, through Staten Island, and straight to New Jersey. She finally pulled up to a gun store in Lakewood, New Jersey. After entering the Brick Armory, she stood in awe. A feeling of nervousness came over her and little beads of sweat lined her hairline. There were so many guns on the walls, in glass counter cases, and hanging up behind the counter. Crystie swallowed hard. She was starting to think that maybe she was out of her league.

Crystie whirled around a few times, contemplating leaving. Then she thought about her kids again. She thought about Darcy tucking them in at night while Crystie would be home crying herself to sleep. She thought about Quinton acting as if he was father of the year, bribing her kids with candy and shit she didn't want them to have. Once those thoughts surfaced, Crystie decided she was doing the right thing. She was in exactly the right place.

Crystie had already spoken to the salesman over the phone. With her hands shaking, she approached the counter. "Hi, I . . . um . . . called before. I spoke to Dave," Crystie stammered, her words coming out awkward and choppy.

The tall, white man behind the counter smiled at her. "Yes, Mrs. Bale, I have just what you need right here," he said, pointing to something inside the glass.

Crystie smiled back. She sat her purse on the counter so she could examine her new purchase. Finally she felt like her problems would come to an end soon.

Crystie tapped her foot impatiently as she sat outside Quinton's building. She had rented a compact Hyundai, a car neither Quinton nor Darcy would recognize. As Crystie waited for Quinton to come home, she thought about what she would say to him. She just wanted to talk, then maybe negotiate. She would ask him to drop his custody request, and then she might let him and Darcy live in peace.

But the more she thought about her plan, the more Crystie remembered how ignorant Quinton could be. Since negotiations might not work, Crystie had her newly purchased Glock .22 stashed between her thighs. She was gnawing on her nails in anticipation. She had played the scene over and over in her mind. She would scare the shit out of them both, and then she would force Quinton to listen to her and leave her and the kids alone for good. Yes, that was her plan.

The voices in her head were back and stronger than ever. All the years that Crystie had worked with therapists to put those voices to bed had been erased with the stress of the situation. When she'd gotten married and was happy, the voices had subsided, and for the most part were gone. Now they were back in full force, telling her *just shoot them, just kill them. You can't give your kids to them.* Crystie had tried her best not to listen, but they were overwhelming her now.

Crystie promised herself that whenever Quinton and Darcy pulled up, whether separate or together, she would jump out of the car and try to talk to them. If that shit didn't work, she was going to get rid of them and then go get her children and go on the run. The longer she waited, the more she heard the voices telling her to do bad things, destructive things. They were telling her to fuck negotiating.

Crystie waited three hours, but Darcy and Quinton never arrived. She pulled out her cell phone and scrolled through her address book. After retrieving the number to Darcy's salon, which she had gotten from the salon's sign, she dialed the number.

"Yes, may I speak with Darcy, please?" Crystie asked, disguising her voice to sound like she had an accent.

The receptionist for the salon told Crystie that Darcy was on her honeymoon and would be back tomorrow. The information might as well have been a knife in Crystie's chest. She really wanted them both dead now.

"That motherfucker couldn't even let the ink dry on the divorce papers. He expects me to turn my kids over in the morning so he can come back from his sweet little honeymoon and play house with my fucking kids? He will see what I turn over to his ass," Crystie growled as she moved the rental car away from Quinton's building and headed to Lydia's house to get her kids. Her plan had been derailed . . . for now.

"It's OK," Crystie said aloud as she drove. "Sometimes the best laid plans just need to be changed up a little bit. You'll regret the day you fucked me over, Quinton Bale. You will regret it." It wasn't over just yet.

•••

CHAPTER 9
Momma's babies...Papa's...well
never

I t was six o'clock on the morning that Crystie was scheduled to turn her children over to her ex-husband and his new bitch. Crystie hadn't slept a wink the entire night. Nothing had worked for her—sedatives, warm milk, nothing. Her mind had been defeating her lately and sleep just wouldn't come. She had the kids in the bed with her and lay next to them weeping off and on for hours. She would teeter between anger and sorrow and back again.

The night before Crystie had packed up their favorite toys and things they liked to eat just as her attorney had instructed her to do. But she knew it would all be for nothing. Crystie was suffering now with huge knots in her stomach on top of sleep deprivation. She kept picturing her kids screaming and crying when she handed them over and had to walk away from them at the courthouse. The thought alone threatened to make her hurl. She envisioned Quinton forcefully putting them into their car seats while they writhed and kicked in protest, their little faces blood red and covered in tears. Crystie could also see that bitch Darcy trying to console her crying babies. She just couldn't let that happen. She wouldn't let her babies suffer like that. It wasn't their fault that their father was a selfish, adulterous, cowardly asshole.

Crystie's mind was weighed down with these thoughts, and now the voices were back again, stronger than ever. The voices told her that the kids would be better off someplace else, rather than with Quinton. Crystie had thought about that too. She'd contemplated going on the run with her kids, but she knew that they would put out an Amber Alert and she would be found and put into jail. That wouldn't help the kids either. Besides, Crystie didn't have any money to be on the run with her babies.

Crystie swatted at her ears. She wanted the voices to stop. Now they were telling her that heaven was the only place that could protect her children from the evils of the world and from their father. She stared at the ceiling, thinking about this. She could meet her kids in heaven and they would live happily ever after. That was a definite possibility.

Crystie looked over at the kids. Tiana turned over in her sleep, startling Crystie. Crystie smiled at her sleeping daughter. She stroked the little girl's soft, curly hair. The texture of her daughter's hair reminded her of her husband. Then Crystie remembered again that she would be handing her kids over to him very soon. With her heart hammering, Crystie suddenly bolted upright in bed. A serious feeling of anxiety came over her.

"No! I won't let this happen," Crystie whispered to herself in a crazed voice. "He can't have them. He can't have them. They are mine . . . all I got."

She threw her legs over the side of the bed and stood. As she started pacing, she looked at the red numbers on the cable box. It was six twenty in the morning. *Already!* Crystie thought. Time was moving too fast. The numbers seemed to be taunting her, a reminder that in just a few hours Quinton would take away the rest of everything she had left.

Crystie walked the length of her bedroom as the unbearable feeling of anxiety got worse and worse. Her stomach seized and released over and over again, causing Crystie to sweat. She needed a bag to breathe into to help her, but in her mind there was no time for all of that. She had to prevent Quinton from getting the kids. Somehow, some way.

"I can't let them go. God forgive me," Crystie finally whispered. She rushed over to the bed and picked up her pillow. With tears streaming from her eyes like a waterfall, she moved slowly toward her eldest child. "I have to do this to protect you, my baby. God forgive me."

Crystie continued to cry. She was crying so hard that her body trembled fiercely. She closed her eyes and placed the pillow over her three-year-old daughter's beautiful, peaceful, sleeping face. The sobs came in waves now and Crystie's body shook. Closing her eyes tightly, she leaned on the pillow with all of her weight, pressing the feathered pillow onto the little girl's head, covering Tiana's face. Crystie's body continued to shake, but she didn't move. She continued to smother her child. Crystie thought she was doing the right thing, saving her child from living in hell with Quinton.

At first Tiana continued to sleep soundly. But the weight of Crystie's body and the pillow began suffocating her. As her little body fought for air, she was jolted out of sleep. Tiana started moaning. In response, Crystie pressed down harder.

"I can't let him take you, baby. I'm doing this for your own good," she mumbled through her tears.

Soon the little girl's legs began thrashing wildly like she was trying to peddle a bike, her heels digging into the mattress each time. Her muffled cries sent stabbing pains through Crystie's chest. Tiana's little body began to buck under her mother's weight as she fought for air.

"Shhhh, you're going to be with God. Mommy will come see you soon," Crystie said, pressing with all her strength.

Tiana's body continued to move for longer than Crystie expected. She thought it would be easier. She never wanted her child to suffer. A sudden pang of remorse and regret came over Crystie, but it was too late. Finally the little girl's legs went still, then her arms stopped moving, and then her chest went still. A cold chill came over Crystie and she immediately regretted what she'd done. She was deathly afraid now as she looked down at her daughter's still form.

Frantic and overcome with fear, Crystie had to finish what she'd started. There was no stopping now. She took the same pillow and put it over her two-year-old's head. Unbeknownst to Crystie, Tamia awoke when Tiana started thrashing. So before Crystie could secure the pillow over her baby girl's head, the baby started to scream.

"Help me, God! Forgive me. Forgive me," Crystie chanted, but she didn't stop what she was doing. She pressed the pillow over the screaming baby's face and mouth. Crystie felt the baby squirming and thrashing under the pillow, and Crystie felt her heart breaking into pieces at the same time. It seemed to take much longer the second time. But soon baby Tamia was dead as well, and the voices in Crystie's head told her she had done the right thing.

Crystie positioned the kids next to one another as if they were asleep. Then she got on her knees and started praying. Crystie prayed for her soul and the souls of her kids. When she was done, she raced into her closet and retrieved the new gun she had purchased. She examined the black steel. She felt powerful as she held it. Crystie wasn't finished with the mission she had started. This time she would end this ordeal once and for all.

Quinton had turned Crystie into this monster, and now she was going to show him just what she could do, just how much of a monster she really was. In Crystie's mind, her kids were in a better place, and now she had to finish. She had suffered enough embarrassment and humiliation to last a lifetime. And with the kids gone, she no longer had anything else to live for.

When Crystie arrived at the condo, she didn't wait outside. Instead she boldly entered the lobby and rang the door buzzer for her old apartment.

"Who is it?" Darcy sang through the intercom.

"Fed Ex," Crystie said in a gruff voice, trying to sound like a man.

"We're not expecting anything," Darcy said suspiciously.

Crystie twisted her lips and silently mouthed the word *bitch*. Just as she was trying to come up with another method of getting past the lobby door, someone came out. As soon as the door swung open, Crystie rushed through it. She smiled, because now she was in.

Crystie reached into her coat pocket and touched the weapon. She wanted to make sure it was still there. This was it. Quinton had fucked with the wrong person, and there was no more Mrs. Nice Wife. Besides, she was ex-wife status now anyway, so what did she care.

When the elevator stopped on the fifth floor, Crystie felt a flitter of excitement in her stomach. She wasn't afraid at all. This was part of what she needed to do. Crystie crept slowly toward the door. She listened for a few minutes, and she could hear that both Quinton and Darcy were home. She smiled wickedly. Crystie pressed the small bell that sat at the side of the door and stepped aside so they couldn't see her through the peephole.

"Quinton, I think this is the Fed Ex person that rang the downstairs buzzer," Crystie heard Darcy call out. "No, I didn't order anything, nor am I expecting anything, unless it's a package from your lawyer," Darcy said.

Of course you're not expecting anything, Crystie thought. *Especially what I have, you bitch.*

| 243 |

Quinton snatched open the door and Crystie rushed him. He didn't even have time to react. She barreled into him like a battering ram, sending him stumbling backward.

"What the fu—!" Quinton started to yell, but his words were cut off when the cold steel of Crystie's Glock was pushed into his face.

"Now, motherfucker! It's time for my revenge for everything you ever did to me," Crystie growled.

"Oh, my God!" Darcy belted out when she saw that Crystie had a gun.

"Shut the fuck up and get over there," Crystie growled, directing Darcy and Quinton to sit down in front of the fireplace.

"What are you doing, Crystie? Where are the kids?" Quinton asked. He had never felt his heart beat so fast in his entire life.

"Don't ask about my kids! You don't love those kids, and you'll never have them!" Crystie gritted through clenched teeth. She adjusted her grip on the gun, which caused Quinton and Darcy to flinch.

Crystie started laughing at seeing their fear. She wanted them to feel just like she had felt over the past couple of months.

"What are you going to do to us?" Darcy asked as she gripped Quinton.

"You'll see," Crystie said calmly. "Quinton, you drove me to this. What I know now is that you never loved me. You never cared about me, oh, no. Quinton only cared about himself. Why would you take everything from me? After all I've done for you? Why would you drag my name through the mud and flaunt your bitch at our church? And then, the biggest one yet, you tried to take my kids from me? Those kids are the only thing you have ever done that was good. They are all I had, you bastard!" Crystie barked, waving the gun in their faces.

"Crystie, we can talk about this. There is no need for violence," Quinton said, trying to stay calm. His voice was cracking, a sure sign that he was fucked up and nervous as hell. He was trying his best to calm Crystie, but little did he know that the more calmly he tried to speak, the angrier it made Crystie. That calm voice reminded her of the way he had been in court.

"Shut the fuck up! Your calm voice and smug fucking attitude. You did all of this! You're a selfish piece of shit—always was and always will be. Yes, you drove me over the edge after everything I did for you, for us. Look at me. Look at how I look compared to your little skinny bitch there. You turn around and leave me with no money to even feed my kids!" Crystie yelled.

Crystie placed the gun against Darcy's temple. Darcy started to cry uncontrollably. She held on to Quinton's arm as her body was trembled.

"Awww, look at your little wife. She's scared, Quinton. Why don't you comfort her?" Crystie taunted, moving the gun from Darcy's temple to Quinton's forehead.

"Shhh," Quinton instructed Darcy. She muffled her cries and they came out more like small whimpers.

"Did Quinton ever tell you all of the things I did for him, Darcy? All of the nights I stayed up writing his research papers? All of the days I worked like a dog and handed all of my money over to him? I bet he never told you any of that. Oh, yeah, what about the nights I listened to him cry like a little faggot over the abuse he suffered as a kid?" Crystie asked Darcy, placing the tip of the gun by her ear and moving it through her long, silky hair. Darcy moved her head, trying to get away from Crystie.

"I knew he didn't tell you any of that shit! Why would he tell you that I gave him every bit of myself—my heart, my soul, my mind, my body, and now my kids!" Crystie screamed, a large vein pulsing in her neck.

Quinton could tell that his ex-wife was not all together. He immediately started to worry about the kids.

"Crystie, where are the kids?" Quinton asked, his voice taking on a frantic tone.

Crystie started laughing. "Ohhh, now you wanna know about your fucking kids? When you left them and barely visited them, you weren't worried about them. You weren't worried about them when you decided to fucking leave for this little stupid bitch you got here. Where are the kids? How fucking dare you! Shut the fuck up and don't ask about my kids!" Crystie rambled through clenched teeth.

The thought of the kids sent a wave of nausea through Crystie. She had had enough. It was time for her to end this bullshit once and for all. Crystie extended the gun in front of her and trained it on Quinton and Darcy.

"Oh, God!" Darcy screeched, ducking her head and closing her eyes tightly. Quinton closed his eyes as well. His nose flared in and out rapidly.

"Say you're sorry, Quinton. I want to hear you say that you're sorry for everything you've done to me," Crystie said through her tears. She was on yet another emotional flip flop. "Say it, Quinton! Say you're sorry to her so we can live," Darcy cried out.

"Stay out of this, bitch! You ended my marriage! You stole my husband! Soon you're gonna be ex-wife status too, bitch!" Crystie screamed. Snot and tears now covered her face.

Crystie placed her pointer finger on the trigger guard and pulled back. The gun erupted in her hand and Crystie jumped. She watched as Darcy's body flew back and slumped to the floor. Blood ran out of a hole in Darcy's head. It almost made Crystie vomit, but she was too numb to react.

Now she turned her full attention to her ex-husband. Darcy had just been a casualty of their war, but he was Crystie's real target. He had been the one to leave her with nothing to live for.

"Crystie! Don't do this!" Quinton pleaded. She looked at him wickedly and aimed her gun at him. Facing the barrel of the gun, Quinton pissed his pants.

"Well she's out of the picture now. I guess she's really your ex-wife now too, Quinton," Crystie said, her voice sounding unstable and deranged.

"I will always love y—" Quinton started to say.

Bang! Crystie didn't give him a chance to let what she considered a big lie leave his lips. His words were cut short after the shot rang out. Quinton's body fell to the side and sprawled on the floor. She felt a powerful reverberation from the gunshots, and then she just stood there, staring. She wasn't going to let him tell her another lie. It was over. It was all finally over.

Crystie placed the gun to her head several times and tried to pull the trigger, but she couldn't. She knew she should've run from the condo, but she couldn't do that either. She didn't know what had paralyzed her, but she was completely stuck. Finally she heard police sirens wailing in the distance.

After the police investigated the scene and handcuffed Crystie, she was pushed into the backseat of a squad car. At that moment she finally remembered her children.

"My kids! Someone needs to go get my kids!" Crystie screamed.

"Where are your kids?" a female officer asked as she prepared to pull off.

"They are in a better place. They're dead," Crystie said in a low whisper.

The female officer's eyes grew wide as she looked at Crystie through the rearview mirror. "What did you say?" the officer asked for clarification.

"They are dead. I sent them to a better place so he wouldn't get them. They are dead," Crystie repeated with no emotion behind her words.

The female officer began screaming into her radio. Crystie knew it wouldn't be long before they found the kids' bodies.

The police rammed the door off of Crystie's Long Island home as if they thought there was a chance they might find the kids in there alive. When the police pounded into the house, they immediately began trying to locate the kids. Some ran into the kitchen, some into the basement, and more went upstairs to check all of the bedrooms. Finally the words they were all dreading came.

"Up here! Two DOA!" one of the officers screamed out, his voice already cracking. The officer was a grown man, but when his fellow officers found him, he was standing next to Crystie's bed sobbing like a baby. All of the other officers had almost the same reaction as they stared at the two tiny bodies, lying on the bed, dead. The kids had already started turning blue and rigor mortis had set in.

"What fucking kind of piece of shit animal would do this to their own kids?" one officer asked angrily.

"It had to be somebody who just snapped, man. If this mother really killed her kids, she just snapped," another officer answered.

Ex-Wife Status

BY AMALEKA MCCALL

•••

CHAPTER 10
The Deal Breaker

"**I**n breaking news today, police say a Long Island woman committed several heinous acts of murder. Police say they found the woman at the scene of a double murder of her ex-husband and his new wife. Police also say that they found the woman's children dead in the Long Island home that the woman once shared with her ex-husband. A police spokesperson said that this was the worst act of domestic violence this city has seen in decades. It appears that the woman just snapped."

Lydia spit her coffee all over her kitchen table when she heard the news reporter's words. She knew right away that the woman referred to in the story was Crystie.

"No! No!" Lydia started screaming. Her husband came racing into the kitchen to see what had happened. Lydia was on her knees screaming. "It's all my fault! Crystie snapped and I knew it was going to happen. I should have saved them! I should have helped them!"

Lydia cried and her husband held her tightly as she sobbed for the kids and Crystie. Lydia told her husband that she wanted to claim the kids' bodies. She wanted them to have a proper and beautiful home going service.

Crystie sat in a small solitary cell in the mental health ward at Rikers Island. She was on suicide watch and she was also being protected from other female inmates who had heard that she had killed her kids. Crystie knew she would be spending the rest of her life in prison, but she was too psychotic to care.

She stripped off her sheets and began pulling them apart with her teeth and hands. After a few unsuccessful attempts, the sheet material finally ripped. Crystie waded up the sheet and tied it around her neck. She tied one end of the sheet to the small grate that covered the top of the steel door that locked her in. When the sheet was secured, Crystie threw herself onto the floor. The tight tie around her neck and the weight of her body pulling it down began to strangle her. Crystie's tongue hung from her mouth and her eyes began to roll back into her head. She started to drift away. She could feel her soul leaving her body and finally she stopped moving. It was finally over— completely over.

COMING SOON

KIKI SWINSON
PRESENTS

CHEAPER
to
KEEP HER

PART 2 THE SAGA CONTINUES

A NOVEL
UNIQUE